of Anna J. Evans

"A wonderful read full of sexual heat and a potent tale."
—Coffee Time Romance

"Evans pens a tale that is hot, scary, and sweet all at the same time. The protagonists . . . will keep you turning the pages long into the night, and the happy ending is emotional enough to please any romance fan." —*Romantic Times* (4½ stars)

"Anna J. Evans weaves a tale full of passion, intrigue, betrayal, and friendship that will leave readers in awe of the raw power behind the words." —Romance Junkies

"Enough sexual heat to create an avalanche." —Fallen Angel Reviews

"Arousing, amorous . . . pulled me right into their sexual encounters. . . . Ms. Evans's storytelling ability was amazing, without a single flaw." —The Romance Studio

"A powerful story about the deep and undeniable connection between soul mates. . . . The love scenes were so primal and raw that you're going to want to keep a spare pair of dry panties, a bucket of ice, and extra batteries nearby." —TwoLips Reviews

"Extraordinary. . . . I didn't put this down until it was read all the way through." —Romance Divas

ALSO BY ANNA J. EVANS

Shadow Marked

DEMON MARKED

A Demon Bound Novel

ANNA J. EVANS

A SIGNET ECLIPSE BOOK

SIGNET ECLIPSE
Published by New American Library,
a division of Penguin Group (USA) Inc.,
375 Hudson Street, New York, New York 10014, USA
Penguin Group (Canada), 90 Eglinton Avenue East, Suite 700, Toronto,
Ontario M4P 2Y3, Canada (a division of Pearson Penguin Canada Inc.)
Penguin Books Ltd., 80 Strand, London WC2R 0RL, England
Penguin Ireland, 25 St. Stephen's Green, Dublin 2,
Ireland (a division of Penguin Books Ltd.)
Penguin Group (Australia), 250 Camberwell Road, Camberwell,
Victoria 3124, Australia (a division of Pearson Australia Group Pty. Ltd.)
Penguin Books India Pvt. Ltd., 11 Community Centre,
Panchsheel Park, New Delhi - 110 017, India
Penguin Group (NZ), 67 Apollo Drive, Rosedale, North Shore 0632,
New Zealand (a division of Pearson New Zealand Ltd.)
Penguin Books (South Africa) (Pty.) Ltd., 24 Sturdee Avenue,
Rosebank, Johannesburg 2196, South Africa

Penguin Books Ltd., Registered Offices:
80 Strand, London WC2R 0RL, England

First published by Signet Eclipse, an imprint of New American Library,
a division of Penguin Group (USA) Inc.

First Printing, January 2011
1   3   5   7   9   10   8   6   4   2

Copyright © Stacey Iglesias Fedele, 2011
All rights reserved

SIGNET ECLIPSE and logo are trademarks of Penguin Group (USA) Inc.

Library of Congress Cataloging-in-Publication Data:

Evans, Anna J.
Demon marked: a demon bound novel/Anna J. Evans.
p. cm.
ISBN 978-0-451-23210-6
1. Demons—Fiction. 2. Lawyers—Fiction. 3. Gangs—Fiction. I. Title.
PS3605.V363S53 2010
813'.6—dc22   2010034843

Set in Albertina

Printed in the United States of America

To Kerry, who was absolutely right

ACKNOWLEDGMENTS

Thank you to the production team at Signet Eclipse, to my agent, Caren, and to my amazing readers. Thank you, readers, for every e-mail and every book you pick up off the shelf. I appreciate you so much. Also a big thank-you to my family, my husband, my writer and nonwriter friends, and my children for love and support. I am lucky to have you all.

New York's Demon Habitat

 Demon Patrol Locations

1. The 14th Street Barricade 2. Southie Docks, demon-infested waters
3. Shaded area—the Demon Habitat, tours offered daily
4. The Demon's Breath Pub 5. South Methodist Hospital
6. Yang's Curiosity Shop 7. The History Project Museum

DEMON
MARKED

CHAPTER ONE

*E*mma Quinn took a pull on her beer and scanned the crowded bar—Death Ministry gang members, some frat boys from Columbia looking for danger they couldn't handle, and a couple of prostitutes trying to masquerade as party girls. The real party girls never wore dresses or heels. They stuck with jeans and sensible shoes, even in the soupy humidity of August in New York. When you lived on the wrong side of the barricade, you never knew when you might need to make a run for your life. Heels weren't suited for a jog through the rubble of the demon ruins.

No, the real party girls had left hours ago, the frat boys were well on their way to being too drunk to stand—let alone make their way to one of the all-night diners where they could get a coffee and sober up while waiting for the barricade to open at five a.m.—and the gang members . . . well, they just stank of trouble.

Death Ministry thugs had never come into the bar before. They usually preferred to haunt the abandoned docks near what had once been East River Park, plotting their drug runs, planning who to kill, and taking care of whatever other assorted business Very Bad Guys had on their nightly to-do list. But tonight . . . they were here shooting tequila—and interested looks in the prostitutes' direction.

It was three a.m. at the Demon's Breath Pub, and all was not well.

But it never was at this time of night; Emma had learned that much in her first few weeks as manager.

Most of the tourists had left hours ago—trundled across the barricade that ran along Fourteenth Street in their tour buses—and demon-infested New York City had dropped its civilized veneer. Gone were the shiny-faced men and women offering guided tours and the food trailers selling demon-inspired snacks—ice cream cones painted gold to look like Hamma demon claws, funnel cakes dusted with silver sugar to mimic the Squat demon nests.

In their place were hard men and women tough enough to party in the urban jungle, addicts looking for their fix of demon drugs, and nocturnal predators waiting for humans foolish enough to wander too close to the ruins. The demons—ancient monsters descended from dinosaurs—were amazingly well adapted to the habitat they'd created when they'd surged from caves deep in the earth during the earthquakes of the previous century.

They lurked in wait for easy prey, killed, ate, and disappeared back into the rubble. The bounty hunters and gang members who earned their livings killing and harvesting demon parts were their only predators—aside from one another. The demon ecosystem was as well balanced as any other on earth. Large demons fed on smaller ones, and smaller ones fed on rats and mice. New York City hadn't had a vermin problem for years.

It was something Emma had been grateful for during the months she'd spent locked in her sister's psycho ex-boyfriend's basement. It was cold and dark down there, but at least there hadn't been any rats.

Always looking on the fucking bright side, Quinn.

Emma grimaced and downed the rest of her beer. She *did* look on the bright side, in her own jaded fashion. Growing up where she had, the *way* she had, she'd been forced to create her own happiness. Even Father Paul had only so much time, so much energy, and most of it was used up by the time he got back to the halfway house at the end of the day. He'd saved her life, but Father Paul was too busy to worry about her contentment.

Her long-lost sister and brother had been able to lean on each other, but Emma had only ever had herself. Even now—months after she had helped save her sister, Sam, from her ex-boyfriend and the nasty aura demons he'd been trying to summon onto the earthly plane—she still hadn't learned to depend on anyone else. Even her new family. Sam and her husband, Jace, were good people, but they were just so . . . *grossly* in love—and lust—with each other.

Emma didn't do love. Or lust. She'd never been able to afford the luxury of either.

"Dude, do you think we should call demon patrol? Or . . . somebody?" Ginger, the bartender on duty, asked, pouring a shot of whiskey as she closed out one of the frat boys' tabs.

Ginger cast a pointed look toward the corner of the room, where several Death Ministry members—easily identified by the scars marking their faces, one long slash for each life they'd taken in the name of gang business—sat sharing a bottle of tequila.

"Nope." Emma placed her empty beer glass in the dishwasher under the bar. "Demon patrol doesn't deal with gang stuff."

"What about the police?"

"They haven't done anything illegal." She shrugged and started up the machine, holding it closed as hot water blasted the glasses. It wasn't staying shut on its own anymore, the dishwasher just one of the things that was falling apart around the pub since her brother's "disappearance" five months before.

Since her brother's *death*. But most people didn't know Stephen Quinn was dead. No one but Emma, Sam, Jace, and a handful of Italian mobsters—Jace's family—knew the truth, and they meant to keep it that way. The last thing Emma needed was police sniffing around, wondering why the former owner of the Demon's Breath was still missing in action.

"They're just drinking," she said.

"So far. But who knows what they'll do after they've had a few." Ginger slammed back the whiskey shot and took a deep breath. "Why couldn't they come in when Jace was here?"

"Don't worry. We'll be fine." Emma watched Ginger pour herself another shot without saying a word.

According to rules, Ginger wasn't supposed to be drinking while she was bartending, but Emma wasn't going to tell. Hell, *she* wasn't supposed to be drinking, either. She was still a year away from the legal drinking age of twenty-one, but no one questioned her right to imbibe.

Emma didn't look underage. Despite her shoulder-length blond bob and soft brown eyes, she looked hard, edgy, and far older than her years. Sam said it was because she was too skinny for a woman who was five-eight. Emma knew it was because she was too messed up for a girl who was still a teenager.

But then, when you spent the first couple of years of your life in a hospital after nearly being *killed* by your own parents, you sort of got a head start on the messed-up thing. Emma, Sam, and Stephen had all been scarred by what their parents had done when they were kids—using them as human sacrifices for their cult's aura-demon summoning ritual—but Emma wondered whether she wasn't the most twisted of the three.

The aura demons—invisible demons most people believed were an urban legend—had been banished from the earth last March, but their mark on the Quinn family remained. Sam, though legally blind, had prophetic dreams, as well as moments when her eyes changed colors and she was literally able to *see* men and women who were on the verge of major psychic shifts in their lives. It was creepy to watch Sam's brown eyes turn blue, but nothing compared to Emma's own demon mark.

Sam's mark hadn't mutated something at the very heart of her. It didn't drive her to steal in the name of survival. It didn't make her feel aged and rotten on the inside—a wine gone bad that no one would ever want to drink.

"I'm going to have another shot. You want one?" Ginger asked.

Emma's stomach cramped. No, a shot wasn't a good idea. It was time for her to get something real to eat, something more than beer and stale pretzels. "No, I'm good. But you go ahead." She couldn't care less if Ginger was trashed on the job.

In fact, it worked in her favor if her roommate and coworker was too smashed to pay much attention to Emma as she prepped for closing at three thirty. It would make it easier for Emma to sneak away and find something to sustain her. Or maybe she wouldn't have to go out to find food. . . . Maybe she had something suitable right in the bar.

Emma's eyes drifted back to the Death Ministry thugs. There were five of them, each one scarier than the last. Still, they were paying customers, customers who looked like they were running low on tequila.

"Check on the frat boys again, will you? I think they need another pitcher," Emma said, waiting until Ginger turned away before grabbing a bottle of Jose Cuervo and slipping out from behind the bar.

She let a little wiggle creep into her walk as she crossed to the darkened corner. Her low-heeled biker boots thumped on the bare floorboards, catching the rhythm of whatever angsty, techno-pop tune the frat boys had selected from the jukebox. She'd never been dancing at a club, but she imagined this was the kind of crap they played at the places where young men and women went to grind against complete strangers for a few hours every Friday and Saturday night.

It was painful listening, and for the hundredth time Emma was glad she had no urge to grind against another person . . . at least not in a public place, and not for the reasons the average twenty-year-old girl would press her body up against someone else's in the dark.

"Looked like you guys were running low." Emma plunked the fresh tequila bottle in the middle of the Death Ministry table.

A shiver raced along her skin as five pairs of flat, cruel eyes tracked up her body—taking in her tight black jeans and black tank top on the way up to her face—but it wasn't fear that made the blond hairs on her arms stand on end. It was excitement . . . anticipation. . . . Oh, yeah, these men were bad. Plenty bad for her purposes.

She'd bet one of their lives on it.

"We didn't order another bottle." The man who spoke had bright blue eyes and seemed a little younger than the rest, but his face was still heavily lined with kill scars.

He'd taken a dozen lives, if those ruined cheeks were anything to judge by. Surely not all of those people had deserved a grisly death. Odds were at least a few had been innocents. The Death Ministry was notorious for taking out an addict's entire family when drug tabs weren't paid in a timely manner—using moms and dads and sisters and brothers to get the message across that unpaid debt to the DM was a bad idea. It was one of the major reasons for the occasional violent clash between the gang and the Conti family. The Contis didn't make a habit of killing innocent people. They also didn't like losing money. For every demon killed or mutilated by the Death Ministry in the name of acquiring more drugs to sell, the Contis had one less demon body to turn in to the city. The demon-control agencies wanted their specimens taken alive or not at all.

"Yeah, I know," Emma said, cocking her head in Blue Eyes' direction. "Consider it a gesture of good faith. This bottle is on the house, provided you guys don't make trouble while you're here tonight."

"Make trouble? What kind of trouble would we make, blondie?" guy number one asked.

"Vanish, *chica*. Leave the bottle." The speaker was a brown-skinned man with a Mohawk and a low opinion of women. He didn't bother to look at her when he spoke but kept his dark eyes trained on the tiny dance floor, where one of the prostitutes writhed to the pounding beat.

Most of the other men had shifted their eyes elsewhere as well— unimpressed by the skinny blonde with the crooked nose and mud brown eyes—except for the young guy. The blue-eyed dude with the crew cut and a sprinkling of acne across his wide forehead was still looking—and he would do just fine. More than fine.

God, Emma could already feel how good it would be, how much stronger she'd be afterward.

Her heart raced as if she'd downed a triple shot of espresso instead of a couple of light beers, pounding so hard her ribs ached. Her pulse thudded unhealthily in her ears. It had been too long. She should have taken care of this sooner, before she needed it so badly. But she always tried to put it off, to find a way to keep from committing the same, necessary sin.

That was the thing about *necessary* sin. . . . It was just so . . . *necessary*.

"Exactly." Emma stared at her victim through lowered lashes. "I'm sure you boys aren't anything to worry about. I'm just going to take out the trash. Be good while I'm gone. Or . . . not."

Emma turned slowly, maintaining eye contact with Blue Eyes until the last second before sauntering away. On her way back across the room, she did one last sweep of the bar, making sure Ginger was occupied and none of the other patrons were paying attention as she slipped through the thick plastic strips separating the pub from the storage room. All eyes were elsewhere. She was clear. No one would notice the thug slipping out behind her and think about playing hero.

Hurrying across the cracked brown tile, Emma headed for the

silver door and the back alley beyond, certain the man was behind her. He didn't seem to be the sharpest knife in the case, but he was smart enough to read the interest in a woman's eyes and horny enough to go for a chick who barely filled out an A cup.

Or maybe he was simply frugal—preferring to get his pussy for free instead of paying for it like his buddies were intending to do. Not everyone cared to spend their hard-earned money on prostitutes.

Emma could sympathize. Money had always been tight around the halfway house growing up. Father Paul worked as a chaplain for a hospital, and collecting weird kids was an expensive habit. There were nights when everyone went hungry for *traditional* sorts of food. No one ever had their supernatural needs unmet, however; Father Paul made sure of that. He considered it a holy calling to provide for the strange children in his care, to teach them how to manage their inhuman powers, to control their baser cravings, to feed their unnatural hungers with the appropriate sort of food.

Food. Damn, she was hungry. The dark craving that had been her companion since the day her parents offered her as a sacrifice surged through her body, making her fingertips itch and burn.

"Come and get it," Emma whispered under her breath as she slipped into the shadows behind the bar.

The alley was wide and clear except for two small Dumpsters and an oversized ashtray—the city made sure the streets were kept tidy to prevent infestation by demons who made their nests in tight, crowded places—but it was still dark. It wasn't a place where a woman should walk alone. There were predators in Southie who didn't need teeth or claws, who used fists and knives and guns to dominate, steal, and kill.

She wondered what kind of weapon Blue Eyes was packing—the trademark DM knife or something with a little more firepower. Either way, it wouldn't matter, not as long as she got him close enough to touch before he whipped anything out.

Anything other than his dick, of course. Emma didn't mind when men whipped out that particular "weapon." A man with his dick in his hand was a man with his head in the clouds. Or maybe someplace less wholesome than the clouds, someplace darker, more dangerous . . .

The door creaked open, and Blue Eyes stepped out of the bar, his movements confident but careful. He was a man used to watching his back, accustomed to keeping one eye peeled for possible threats. But she was one "threat" he would never see coming. They never did, not one person in all the time she'd been stealing from the wicked.

"Over here," she said, her voice trembling a bit. The man turned toward her, looking even scarier in the shadows. "What's up?"

"You said you were taking out the trash. Figured I had something that needed to be thrown away." He held up the nearly empty tequila bottle, and his features twisted into what Emma supposed was meant to be a smile.

"That was thoughtful of you."

"That's me. Thoughtful." He closed the distance between them in four long steps and reached out, cupping her breast in his hand and squeezing, making his intentions abundantly clear.

Guess he wasn't much for verbal foreplay. Good. She wasn't, either.

"So you want to do this here?" she asked, running one hand up into his greasy hair as he pulled her close, willing her fingertips to find the pressure points on the skull that made her job so much easier. She had to make sure he was one of the bad guys. It was what Father Paul had insisted upon, and she'd never gone against his teachings. She'd never wanted to. She might be a killer, but she wasn't a monster.

"Fuck yeah. Here's good." He laughed and tipped the tequila bottle back, emptying it before throwing it against the bricks behind them.

"Good, I—" Emma groaned as he slammed his mouth down on hers, his tongue probing between her lips, sending secondhand tequila rushing into her throat. It was swallow or gag, but Emma regretted her decision to drink as soon as the tequila hit her stomach.

Her belly clenched and cramped, and the dark craving grew even stronger, sizzling along her nerve endings, making her fingers feel like they would catch fire at any moment. The telltale blue light erupted from her hands before she could control it. She'd waited too long. She couldn't remember feeling this weak, this needy, even in the months she'd been Ezra's captive. He'd known what she was and helped her survive, bringing her suitable "snacks" every few days.

Thankfully, the thug's eyes were closed, but he'd notice the pale blue glow sooner or later. She had to hurry.

Forcing her attention away from the thick tongue that moved sluggishly in her mouth and the meaty fingers squeezing first her breasts and then her ass, Emma concentrated on the hands pressed against Blue Eyes' greasy head, sending her intention out through her fingertips.

Almost immediately, images flashed on her mental screen— Blue Eyes' rat hole of an apartment near the ruins, the interior of a nearly empty fridge, a pile of dirty laundry he'd dug through to find his shirt for the evening. The mundane flooded in first, as it always did, but Emma swam deeper, sending her mind into the man she touched, the need within searching for what it craved.

She found it seconds later—the pale face of a little girl with a split lip, bleeding from where one of Blue Eyes' fists had connected with her face, the gutted corpse of a man he'd shoved out of a boat into demon-infested waters, the mascara-stained cheeks of a woman who screamed as his hand fisted in her hair.

Emma had seen enough. More than enough.

Silently, she reversed the flow of her energy, no longer diving into her victim, but swimming to the surface, pulling his evil along with her. The sin-filled memories flowed into her fingers, up her hands, surging through her arms and into her chest, where her heart slammed against her ribs, her body working to disperse the energy to her demon-altered cells.

The aura demons fed on the pain and suffering of humans; Emma fed on evil. It was a slight difference but an important one. When her parents had given her blood to the demons, the very essence of her had been changed, mutated. A part of her became more demon than human. In many ways, she was like the monsters that had nearly killed her. She craved human life force and had to steal the vitality of others to survive. But she stole only from those who deserved what she did to them, those whose karmic balance was firmly tipped into the realm of evil. The choice allowed her to sleep at night, and as an added bonus . . .

Evil was damned tasty.

Emma moaned as she pulled harder on the man's soul, sucking out all the bad mojo he'd created with every horrible thing he'd ever done. She didn't know how her body fed on the nastiness flowing into her fingers, but it did. *God*, it did. She hadn't felt this good in weeks, since the last time she'd lured a very bad man into a very dark alley.

Faster and faster the energy flowed, until the blue glow in her hands burned so bright that Emma could see it behind her closed eyes.

Blue Eyes pulled his mouth away from hers, removing the repugnant tongue Emma had hardly noticed was still moving against hers. Once the feeding began, the awareness of everything else faded away. "What? What the . . ." The man's voice cracked, and he swayed on his feet.

"Don't stop. You feel so, so good." Emma smiled up into his face, not at all troubled by what she saw there.

The blue light from her hands lit up Blue Eyes' head like a jack-o'-lantern, revealing a second face lurking beneath the skin and bone. It was the face of his soul, the hidden visage only she could see. She watched as the face shriveled before her eyes, wrinkles became tears in the spirit flesh, rotten places that would fester long after she removed her hands.

No one else would ever witness the transformation—she herself would see nothing but a healthy young man as soon as the blue light faded—but the damage had been done. She'd sucked away his vital energy, gobbled up his life force, and there would be a price to pay. He'd die from what she'd done, sooner or later, simply fall over dead from a heart attack or stroke that no one would ever understand.

And no one would be able to connect it to her . . . assuming she stopped before it was too late.

With more effort than she would have liked, Emma pulled her

hands away from Blue Eyes' head. Immediately the blue light disappeared and the soul face vanished. Once again, he looked like what he had been—a healthy young monster at the beginning of a lifetime career of evil.

But now that lifetime was going to be a whole hell of a lot shorter.

"I feel . . . sick. . . ." The man's hands fell to his sides.

"Bummer." Emma looped his arm around her shoulders when he swayed again. "Must be the tequila."

"Yeah. Fuck. Just give me a second . . . and I'll be ready to go. . . ." He groaned and clutched at his stomach. Emma had just enough time to jump back before he bent double and emptied his stomach on her favorite pair of black boots.

"Great," she whispered beneath her breath, hand flying to press against her nose. Ugh. The smell was noxious, like rotten eggs mixed with pizza and a tequila-and-stomach-acid cocktail. It was all she could do not to gag. "I'll go get your . . ."

Gang buddies? Fellow killers? BFFs?

Blue Eyes heaved again. Emma flinched and danced back a few steps.

"I'll get somebody," she said, turning toward the door. Or maybe she wouldn't. The man was a monster, and she'd just taken the majority of his life away. It seemed hypocritical to fetch someone to hold his hair while he barfed. Not to mention the fact that he had a crew cut.

Yeah. He could sleep in his own vomit for all she cared. She'd just have to make sure he was gone . . . before they closed up. . . . Maybe she could . . .

Her head spun, and black flecks teased the edges of her vision, but Emma didn't think much of it until she tried to reach for the silver door handle and found that her arm wouldn't move.

Just. Wouldn't. Move.

Her legs followed the disturbing trend seconds later, her knees buckling, sending her pitching toward the pavement. Her bony shoulder hit first, followed by her temple. Pain bloomed inside her head, like something from her sister Sam's flower shop.

"Ginger . . ." Emma heard her own voice from a distance, as if the sound were drifting through water. Then she was pulled under the waves, too, swept away from the conscious world.

CHAPTER TWO

$S$and doesn't always stay inside the sandbox, and demons don't always stay within the rubble of the actual ruins.

The entire barricaded area of south Manhattan—Southie, as the locals called it—was a high-risk area. If you lived inside the ten-foot-high, heavily fortified barrier, it paid to be on your guard. Attacks in residential areas were rare, but they happened, especially late at night. It was dumb to wander around in dark, abandoned places.

It was even dumber to *pass out cold* in dark, abandoned places.

Emma woke up with a start, thrashing her arms, sending the cat-sized gray demons crouched around her body scurrying away into the darkness. She shuddered, skin crawling as she swiped at the sticky trails the demons' tongues had left on her exposed arms.

Ugh. Gross. So gross. But it could have been so much worse. Squat demons were repulsive—hairless beasties that looked like a cross between a naked mole rat and a pug dog—but at least they were largely harmless to humans. One of the larger demon species would have killed and eaten her. Hell, the Squats might have started to nibble—though they preferred to dine on rodents—if she'd stayed out much longer.

Or if they hadn't already filled their bellies. Blue Eyes lay on his side a few feet away—unconscious, as she'd been a second ago—but his puke puddle was gone.

Blech.

It was no wonder her gang thug had passed out—considering the amount of tequila he'd chugged combined with the drain she'd put on him—but what the hell had happened to her? Why had she fainted? And why was it so dark?

Emma looked up, just barely able to make out the silhouette of the unlit spotlight that usually illuminated the back door against the night sky. It must have blown while she was passed out.

Great, now she was going to have to drag a ladder back here and replace it before closing. She certainly didn't want any of the Squats coming back and trying to nest in the Dumpsters. No matter how crappy she felt, she had to make sure the demon-deterring light was burning before she headed for home.

Mouth dry and head aching, Emma pushed to her feet, casting one last look at the Death Ministry dude. He was still out, but the Squats were gone. He'd be safe enough while she went inside and grabbed a new lightbulb. She'd have Ginger clue his buddies in to the fact that he was passed out drunk in the back alley and let them decide whether to mess with Blue Eyes or not.

Emma reached for the door—grateful that her arms and legs seemed to be working again—but the handle didn't budge. Frowning, she pushed down harder, leveraging her weight against it. Still nothing.

"What the hell?" Emma kicked the door. Ginger must have locked the door early.

Ever since Stephen had "disappeared," Ginger had been more anxious about living in demon-infested New York, so anxious that she'd talked about getting a second job and trying to move to midtown. She'd encouraged Emma to come with her even though they'd been roomies for only a few months, but Emma wanted to stay in Southie.

She was sure there were bad guys outside the barricade, but they might not be as easy to find or to lure into dark, secluded areas where there was no one to observe when her hands started to glow. Being a freak with an aura demon's hunger had its challenges, and it was easier to get what she needed on the wrong side of the tracks.

Emma kicked the door again—once, twice, three times—then called out for Ginger. "Hey! Come open the door! I'm out back!" She waited for a beat, then kicked the door again. Where the hell was Ginger? Maybe she couldn't hear her over the music. . . .

Wait a second. There wasn't any music. Emma pressed her ear to the door, straining to hear inside the bar. The metal was thick, but she could usually hear the beat of whatever song was playing and the rumble of voices through the door. But now . . . nothing. It was eerily quiet.

Had Ginger closed up already? What time was it?

"Shit," Emma whispered, patting her pockets. She didn't have the keys with her, and her purse was still locked in the safe beneath the bar. The bar keys, her house key, the stupid earbud Sam had given her to use instead of her tragically outdated cell phone—they were all locked inside the Demon's Breath.

Unless Ginger was still here, waiting for her out front. She'd have to run around a long city block to find out, which would be no big deal except . . .

"Hey, you," Emma said, crossing back to the man still passed out on the ground. "You need to wake up."

Blue Eyes lay as still as a stone, so blasted he wasn't within the reach of the human voice. She was going to have to try more aggressive measures.

"Come on, wake up." She toed his wide back with her boot, then nudged him a little harder but barely produced a ripple in his muscled flesh. The guy was enormous. There was no way she'd be able to drag him around to the main street.

Shit! Despite the voice in her head screaming she should leave the murdering, child-beating asshole to be eaten, she knelt down beside him and grabbed his arm.

She might have sucked his life force, but she couldn't let him be demon food, no matter how many horrible things he'd done. The death she'd helped speed his way would be fairly merciful; being eaten alive by demons would not. She didn't go in for torture . . . even for evil bastards like this one.

"Dude, you need to—" Her words ended in a gasp as she pulled hard on Blue Eyes' arm and he rolled heavily over onto his back. For a second she thought he was awake, before she realized that those striking, cruel eyes weren't blinking, but staring sightlessly into the night.

Emma bit her lip and forced back the wave of nausea that threatened as she realized what she'd done. She'd killed him. She must have taken too much. She'd waited too long, let the craving grow too strong, and she'd taken too much of the man's life. Despite the fact that he was a criminal and that she'd known her actions would bring about his death sooner or later, the moment of understanding still hit her hard. Very hard.

It had been a long, long time since she'd looked into the face of one of her victims and seen the emptiness of a soulless corpse. Not since those first few kills, when she'd been so young and lacked control. Since then, Father Paul had kept her informed of which of their carefully chosen targets had passed, and occasionally she heard about a death secondhand—read an obituary or watched a death reported on the news—but she'd been spared having the consequences of her twisted hunger shoved in her face.

It was horrific, bringing home the *wrongness* of what she was in a nightmarish way.

"Okay . . . okay . . ." Trembling, Emma rose, swiping her hands back and forth against her jeans as if she could brush away the lingering taint of death.

But she couldn't. The man was *dead*, and there was a damn good chance she would be connected to his murder. No one had seen her leave the bar, but what about Blue Eyes? He might have told his kill buddies that he was going out back to bang the pub manager, for all she knew. Even if he hadn't, she'd talked to the Death Ministry members just before going outside. She was the only person who'd dared approach them all night. No matter how much tequila they'd had, one of them was going to remember the stupid blond girl who'd warned them to behave.

Come tomorrow morning, or whenever this body was found, she could have four very scary men on her trail. They might never guess that she'd killed the man, but they would suspect she knew something about how old Blue Eyes had bit it. It didn't matter that an autopsy would prove this man had died of a heart attack; there might not *be* an autopsy. There would be a Death Ministry–style investigation; she'd be questioned and killed if she didn't provide answers that satisfied.

Hell, she might be killed anyway. They might kill her just for fun.

The thought made Emma shiver. She turned in a slow circle, searching the darkness for some clue as to what she should do, some way to banish the unfamiliar feeling sliding its cold fingers up her spine. She'd never feared the bigger, nastier people in the world—having a "gift" for sucking the life out of the bad guys made a girl cocky—but now she was starting to fear. Big-time. She might be able to handle one or two members of the Death Ministry, but what if there were more? There were ways to wield the dark craving as a weapon, but she'd never dared try any of the chants she'd read about in the spell book she'd stolen from Father Paul.

The spell book. *Shit!* She'd left it in her purse as well.

She'd been working on translating the spells in the demon grimoire for months, and the hours between four and six were usually slow on Tuesdays. She'd thought she'd have time to work on the translation at the bar. She hadn't, and the book had stayed in her purse all night, tucked in with the other valuables.

It was probably locked away right now—safe and sound—but realizing she couldn't get her hands on it made her even more anxious. The book had taught her almost everything she knew about aura demons and the ways ancient people had controlled them. Without it, she couldn't have saved her sister's life five months ago or had hope that she might someday rule the hunger that drove her—there were spells designed to help those altered by the demons gain more control over their marks—but still . . . the demon grimoire was . . . scary.

But not as scary as a dead body at her feet and not so much as a dollar to her name to call for help.

Not that she had anyone to call. Sam and Jace were on the West Coast on their honeymoon, and Ginger would be useless in a situation like this . . . even if Emma trusted her enough to explain how she'd killed this man. But she didn't trust Ginger that much. The fewer people who knew about her curse, the better.

Which left . . . no one to turn to . . . except . . .

"The mob," Emma whispered aloud. Uncle Francis knew she "wasn't quite right." He didn't know the true extent of her mark, but he knew she'd been damaged by the aura demons. He'd been there when Emma's brother had turned into some kind of humanoid monster—the consequence of his own demon mark—and Uncle Francis's bounty hunters had helped dispose of the bodies after the craziness that went down last spring.

The Italian side of Jace's family ran Conti Bounty, the biggest bounty-hunting operation in New York City and a convenient cover for Uncle Francis's illegal activities. The Contis dabbled in a bit of everything typically mob—from extortion to arms dealing to construction—but they drew the line at demon drugs. They left the peddling of demon highs to the Death Ministry, as long as the DM kept their harvest respectable. In the past few months, the gang had killed more demons than usual, leading to increased tension between the two groups. Relations were strained as Uncle Francis tried to work out an agreement before an all-out street war erupted.

The Contis wouldn't be happy to hear she'd killed a DM member. This was the kind of thing that halted negotiations and ended in bloodshed, even the deaths of innocent people.

Emma's trembling hands flew to her face, fingers rubbing at the tops of her eyes as if she could scrub away this nightmare, erase her own stupidity. But Blue Eyes was still there when she dropped her arms to her sides. This wasn't going to go away, and she wasn't equipped to handle a murder cover-up on her own. She was going to have to make that call to the mob, but maybe she didn't have to go straight to the top. . . . Maybe she could find someone a little lower on the totem pole to help her out, someone who might be convinced to keep her mistake to himself.

Andre was far from her favorite Conti, but he *was* a lawyer, a *mob* lawyer. Who better to help her figure out how to avoid the long arm of the law and the swift retribution of New York's deadliest gang?

But first things first. Something had to be done about . . . the body.

Swallowing hard, Emma bent down and wedged her hands beneath Blue Eyes' arms, struggling not to think about how cold he felt, or that she'd had this corpse's tongue in her mouth earlier in the evening. He was a wretched excuse for a man. It was better for everyone that he was dead—everyone but her.

With a minimum of grunting and groaning, she maneuvered the body over to the twin Dumpsters and shoved it into the shadows between. It was a lousy hiding place but the only one available. There was no way she could drag more than two hundred pounds of deadweight much farther. She was just going to have to pray that no one found Blue Eyes before she found a way to get rid of him. The recycling and garbage truck didn't come until Friday, and in the meantime, most people would be too afraid to wander around in a dark alley.

The Death Ministry wouldn't blink. You're just lucky they haven't come back to look for their missing coworker already.

The scaremongering inner voice was right. She had to hurry.

Emma ran down the alley, boots thudding softly on the pavement. It took only a few moments to reach the end of the block, but her heart was racing by the time she emerged onto the sidewalk and circled back around to the front of the row of buildings. She felt so thready inside . . . weak and loose . . . as if the systems in her body were slowly disconnecting.

She shouldn't feel this way so soon after a feed. Usually, she was high on life for days afterward. But then, she usually didn't pass out or kill people immediately, either.

Emma slowed to a walk, though there was no reason to worry about attracting attention. There wasn't a soul on the street. Even the prostitutes who lingered under the streetlights until the last party boy vacated the bars and clubs on the west side of Southie were strangely absent. The utter lack of movement made the avenue seem wider, ominous.

Even before she reached the Demon's Breath, Emma knew she'd find the windows dark and the red CLOSED sign—the devil's tail curling out from the D—glowing above the door. It had to be late, *really* late. She must have been out for nearly an hour.

She crossed her thin arms, fingers digging into the bare flesh, suddenly cold despite the warm summer night. She had to figure out what had gone wrong with Blue Eyes and make sure she never did whatever it was again. She couldn't afford to lose consciousness when she fed, and she certainly couldn't afford to collect any more dead bodies.

Emma supposed she should be grateful that Ginger hadn't thought to look for her out back before she'd closed up and headed for home—if she had, she would have called the cops, and Emma would have had a *lot* of explaining to do—but she was still angry that her roommate hadn't made any effort to track her down. Emma made a point of letting people know she could take care of herself, but still, it—

Oh no. The door—it wasn't locked.

And apparently, the alarm system wasn't activated, either. No blaring siren cut through the night when Emma pushed on the door. The crackle of neon was the only sound as she stepped inside the musty, sour-smelling bar and searched the shadows for some sign of life.

The pub was deserted, and everything seemed to be fine—all the demon artifacts that made the Demon's Breath a tourist attraction still hung in their places on the walls, and the bottles sat in orderly lines behind the bar. But still . . . this wasn't right; something bad had to have happened. All critical thoughts of her roomie faded in a wave of panic. Ginger was a little flighty and had a tendency to drink her daily caloric intake, but she wasn't irresponsible. She never forgot to lock up or arm the alarm.

Emma crept across the room, slipping behind the bar, feeling strangely like an intruder in her own place of business. She'd expected to find some clue as to what had gone wrong during closing, but the glasses were washed and stacked and all the well drinks capped and put away. Ginger had even remembered to put the plastic pour spigots to soak in the sink. The register was locked, and the safe . . .

The safe was open. Wide open.

Emma hurried to the end of the bar, crouching down to peer inside the small, square-foot space. It was empty. *Shit!*

The safe was tiny, just big enough to hold whatever valuables the staff brought with them on a given night. The cash taken in by the Demon's Breath was deposited directly into a vault deep underground after each transaction and emptied weekly by a pair of armed guards in a secured truck, a common practice for businesses on this side of the barricade. Most criminals would know there was nothing worth stealing inside the safe. Any thief with half a brain would know the demon artifacts on the wall were worth way more than a couple of purses.

Which meant Ginger had probably taken Emma's purse home with her, leaving Emma with no phone, no keys, no cash, and no spell book.

For a second, the anxiety at being separated from the book returned with a vengeance. Father Paul had been right—the book wasn't safe in just anyone's hands. It was a powerful tool and should be locked away in a museum, ensuring that no one could ever use it for evil again.

But then . . . Ezra had proven how "safe" museums kept dangerous artifacts. Any teacher or historian with the proper clearance could get his or her hands on occult relics. The fact that the average citizen believed invisible demons with supernatural powers were a bunch of horseshit and that the dinosaur-like demons infesting major cities were the only monsters to fear worked in the bad people's favor.

The book had been safest with Father Paul . . . at least until she'd stolen it and proved once and for all that kids like her couldn't be trusted. Now it was her cross to bear. At least she had enough restraint to keep from casting any of the spells before she understood what she'd be doing if she chanted the ancient words.

Of course, she could have locked the book away in a safety-deposit box somewhere and truly kept it safe from everyone, even herself. But she hadn't. And she wouldn't. She might be strong enough to resist temptation, but she wasn't strong enough to resist the urge to play with it a little, to dance along the edge of giving in. She wondered whether Ginger would feel the pull of the grimoire, the urge to open it and paw through its contents and discover its secrets. Or was Emma drawn to the book only because she carried the mark of the aura demons? She couldn't be sure . . . but the dark craving was always stronger when she held the grimoire in her hands.

That—more than any of her strong principles—was the true reason she'd never dared to work any of the book's spells. Anything that made her unnatural hunger worse couldn't be good news.

"No good news tonight," Emma muttered to herself as she dug the slim Southie phone book from the end of the bar and switched the phone on the wall to voice-activated mode. "Ginger," she ordered in a sharp voice.

"Dialing," a feminine-sounding robotic voice announced. Seconds later Ginger's phone was ringing—once . . . twice . . . three times—and then Emma was sent to voice mail.

"Hey, it's Ginger! I'm probably out and can't hear my phone ringing over the music. So leave me a message. If you sound sexy, maybe I'll tell you where the party's at. Hollah!" Ginger's message ended in a giggle, a very *drunk* giggle.

"It's Emma. I need to talk to you. Call me . . . or at least leave my key with Gary at the liquor store so I can get into the apartment. Later," Emma said, barely managing to keep her tone civil.

Ginger was probably out partying with the stupid frat boys she'd been waiting on half the night. With the barricade closed and only a handful of bars open this late, there was a good chance Emma would be able to find her roomie if she went looking, but she couldn't waste the time.

There would be opportunities to rip Ginger a new one for taking her purse and leaving the bar door unlocked later. Right now, she had a ticking time bomb wedged between her Dumpsters. She needed to wake up Andre and see whether she could sweet-talk the womanizing bastard into meeting her. The clock on the wall read four fifteen, so it would be only another forty-five minutes until the barricade opened.

Hastily, she flipped through the Southie phone book, looking for Sam's familiar scrawl. Andre lived in Manhattan proper, but she thought she remembered seeing his number scribbled somewhere in the book, where Sam had jotted it down for her in case she ever needed it.

For her first few months on the job, Emma had felt like a kid with an overprotective parent. Sam was always hovering, trying to make her home-cooked meals, giving her endless lists of people to call if she encountered trouble in the forty-five minutes it took Sam and Jace to grab some dinner. Emma had secretly been relieved when Sam and Jace had announced their intention to take a month-long honeymoon on the West Coast. *Finally*, she would have some space to breathe. She'd been looking forward to it. She'd never dreamed she'd actually be wishing her control-freak big sis was close enough to come running when she called.

She flipped faster through the book but couldn't find the number she searched for.

"Andre," she ordered aloud, taking a chance that Sam or Jace might have programmed his number into the bar's phone.

"Dialing," the robotic voice announced again, making Emma release the breath she hadn't realized she'd been holding.

A stroke of luck . . . the first she'd had this entire horrible night. Now, if only Andre wasn't too out of it to answer his phone. Andre wasn't a big drinker—she'd never seen him have more than a couple of glasses of red wine when she tagged along with Sam and Jace to the Conti Bounty meetings at the family restaurant every Thursday night—but he had other *hobbies* that kept him up late.

Blond hobbies, brunette hobbies, white hobbies, African-American hobbies—Andre had a healthy appreciation for a wide variety of women. As long as they were model thin, with legs that went on for miles, and pretty enough to earn a living pouting at a camera. He brought a different girl with him every Thursday, leaving her for Sam and Emma to entertain when he went into the back room for the private, criminal portion of the evening.

So far, Emma hadn't been impressed with any of his arm candy, and even less impressed with Andre himself. Shallow, pretty boys who spent ridiculous amounts of money on designer suits and ten-thousand-dollar watches made her ill.

Still, when Andre's sleep-scratchy voice picked up on the fourth ring, her relief was so strong that she would have leapt into his arms and hugged the bastard if he'd been standing in front of her. She couldn't remember the last time she'd been so grateful to hear someone's voice.

"Andre, it's Emma," she said, her voice shaking more than she would have liked. "Sam's sister. I—"

"I know." He sounded sharper, all fuzziness banished from his tone. "What's wrong? Are you okay?"

"Uh . . . no." The understatement of the year. "I . . . I've run into some trouble."

"Where are you?"

"I'm at the bar."

"I'll be there in ten, fifteen minutes."

Emma shook her head, shocked speechless for a moment by the realization that he didn't even want to know what was wrong. He hadn't hesitated, hadn't yelled at her for waking him up late; he'd simply heard that she was in trouble, and that had been enough. It was . . . surprising. . . .

"But the barricade is closed until—"

"I can get through." Of course he could; he was the nephew of the most powerful mobster in the city, a man who owned half the guards working the barricade. "Just sit tight and—"

"No. We shouldn't meet here." Emma was suddenly hyperaware of the dead body just outside the back door. She didn't want Andre coming here. It was too close to the scene of her crime. It wouldn't be right to implicate him in that without his prior knowledge, and this confession wasn't the kind of thing done over the phone. "I'll meet you at the coffee shop just off Broadway, near the barricade."

"Fine. Fifteen minutes."

"Okay. And . . . thanks, Andre."

A moment of silence, and then Andre sighed. "Just be careful on your way over there. Jace will kill me if you get hurt when I'm supposed to be looking out for you." And then he hung up before Emma could say another word.

Probably for the best. Telling him she didn't need anyone looking out for her would be dumb. Ninety percent of the time, the words would be true, but tonight . . . well, she needed all the help she could get. Even if it came from a chickenshit, asshole lawyer.

CHAPTER THREE

*S*outh of the barricade, Andre Conti's Canali suit stood out like a perfectly shaped thumb in a hand full of sore fingers.

Just the fact that he'd brushed his teeth before jumping in the car that had spirited him through a sleepy Manhattan would have attracted attention, but the suit . . . It was definitely overkill.

Heads turned, and bleary, red-eyed men and women stared as he slipped into the coffee shop. The small, cramped room smelled of burned beans and fried eggs with a top note of sweat—compliments of the drunk people who had spent most of their night partying before stumbling into Hair on Your Chest just before dawn to wait for the barricade to open. The tile was dirty and cracked, the white walls smeared with streaks of brown, and not even the large, framed photographs of the ruins just after the demon emergence were able to distract from the absolute filth.

It figured Emma would want to meet in a place like this.

She was the complete opposite of her sister. Sam ran a flower shop, dressed in flowing, filmy skirts, and surrounded herself with soft, fresh-smelling things—except for her husband, Jace, of course. Emma ran a bar, wore black unisex jeans and T-shirts, and gravitated toward the roughest crowd she could find.

Andre spotted her right away, huddled in a corner booth over a cup of coffee, her dirty blond hair hanging limply around her narrow face. She was thin but muscular, with well-defined arms that made her look like she could kick a little ass if she had to.

Which she did, occasionally, working at the Demon's Breath. Andre would have said it was a dumb call to give a teenage kid responsibility for managing a rowdy bar, but Emma usually handled herself. She was tough, hard . . . acidic, like the oily coffee in the cup she clutched so tightly her fingertips were nearly white.

"Your nails are filthy," Andre said; the words came out of his mouth before he could think better of them. But then, her nails *were* filthy, and it wasn't quite five in the morning. He couldn't be expected to achieve lawyer levels of diplomacy this early.

Emma looked up, her brown eyes soft and vulnerable for a moment before the familiar toughness seeped in. "Yeah . . . well, that's the least of my problems," she said, letting her gaze roam over his suit as he sat down. "You're looking pretty. As usual."

"Thanks. Due in court later this morning." Andre smiled, deliberately ignoring the derision in her tone.

Emma didn't care for him, and that was fine. He didn't really care for her, either, but his cousin Jace had asked him to take "excellent" care of his wife's little sister while he was away, and that's what he intended to do. Even if she was a little . . . rough around the edges for his taste.

He might take hygiene to obsessive-compulsive-disorder extremes, but she didn't take it nearly far enough. She was usually clean, but the girl neglected all the little touches that made a pretty woman beautiful. An eyebrow wax, makeup, highlights, and some intense exfoliation could have made Emma the type men dropped their briefcases and turned to stare at. As things stood, she was more the type some beefy biker would throw over his shoulder and drag back to his seedy apartment.

Which made Andre wonder . . .

Did her "trouble" involve a man? If it did, if some Southie piece of shit had messed with his cousin's wife's sister, he was going to have to call Uncle Francis. He didn't dirty his hands with that sort of thing anymore, but he couldn't deny that he'd want a man who hurt one of the women in his family castrated or worse.

Realizing that Emma might have been hurt, remembering how small and frightened she'd sounded on the phone, made him feel like an ass. She looked okay—aside from the filthy hands—but he knew better than most people that some scars couldn't be seen by the naked eye.

"So . . . what's up? Are you okay?" He deliberately softened his tone. He and Emma might be total opposites and suffer from a case of mutual antipathy, but they were family now. He owed her protection and civility if nothing else. "You aren't hurt, are you?"

"No, I'm not hurt. I'm just a disgusting girl with filthy fingernails," she said, her sarcasm offering assurance her words didn't. Emma's smart mouth was clearly in working order; she couldn't have been hurt too badly. "I don't see how you can stand to sit across from me."

Andre inclined his head, giving her the point she was obviously looking for. "Sorry. I'm an asshole."

"You *are* an asshole . . . but I appreciate you coming." She paused, eyes darting back to her coffee. The cup was completely full. It didn't look like she'd taken a sip. "I didn't know who else to call."

Andre sighed. He really *was* a jerk. At thirty-one, he was more than a decade older than Emma and—despite working in the bounty-hunting business with his cousin Jace during his undergrad years—Andre hadn't experienced one-third the violence she had endured in her life.

Jace had never told him the entire story, but Andre gleaned from their conversations that Emma had nearly died when she was a baby in the same cult ritual that had left Sam blind. He knew that she'd had a very rough childhood in a halfway house upstate. And that was *before* she'd spent nine months locked in a basement, the prisoner of some psycho who thought she could help him pacify a bunch of invisible demons.

She'd been through all that without losing her mind and had even retained her sense of humor—a dry, cynical one, but a sense of humor nonetheless. So she had a tendency to bait him and get on his last nerve. So what? He should be above responding in kind. He should know better than to pick fights with a messed-up kid. He was an adult.

Allegedly . . .

"You did the right thing." He reached across the table, encircling her slim wrist in his hand and giving a gentle squeeze. "I'm always here, anytime you need me."

She looked up, eyes narrowed, as if searching for the punch line in a bad joke.

"I'm serious," he said, thumb rubbing back and forth against the bare skin at her wrist. She felt so much softer than he'd imagined she would, her narrow bones delicate and fragile in his hand. "You're family. Anytime you're in trouble, you can call me. And I promise not to be an asshole next time."

"I don't know if that's possible." Emma pulled away from his touch, crossing her arms at her chest, brown eyes rolling toward the ceiling. "For you, anyway."

Andre laughed and motioned to the waitress staring at him from behind the greasy counter that he didn't want to order. He'd rather lick his own shoe than willingly put anything made or washed in this establishment in his mouth.

"Well, I'll at least try. How's that?"

"Thanks." She smiled, a tight twist of her lips that quickly faded. "But I don't really care if you're nice . . . as long as you get the job done."

"What kind of job?"

"I . . . I found a body . . . behind the bar."

"You what?" he asked, looking around, making sure no one was listening to their conversation. But they were seated a good distance from the other patrons, and Emma's voice was a soft, husky whisper that didn't travel.

"I found a body, a dead body. Behind the bar." Her hands returned to her coffee cup, clutching it like it was the last thing she had left to hold on to. "I stuffed it between the Dumpsters."

"What?" The stupidity of touching a corpse was . . . epic. He had to fight to keep his voice calm and even. "Why didn't you call the police?"

"I couldn't. The guy was Death Ministry."

"And?" It was all he could do not to grab her by her scrawny shoulders and shake some sense into her. Relations between the Death Ministry and the Contis were at an all-time terrible. The last thing they needed was someone close to the family implicated in a gang-member death. "That's even more reason to call the—"

"No, I . . . just . . . I couldn't." Her voice was infected with a healthy dose of pure fear. "I'm not sure how he died."

"You're not sure how he died? What do you mean you're not sure how he died?" he asked, already knowing he wasn't going to like her answer. He'd heard that tone before, usually right before people told him—

"I think . . . I'm worried that . . . I think maybe I did it. That I killed him."

Right before people told him that they were in some kind of deep legal shit they expected him to dig them out of.

Damn it. He'd gone back to school to get his master's in taxation law for *exactly* this reason. He was sick of dealing with the criminal element—his family included. He might cook the books and bribe a judge or two when the occasion called for it, but he didn't mess with murder and mayhem anymore.

Not even for blood relatives, let alone a cousin-in-law by marriage.

"I'm sorry." Andre flicked an imaginary piece of dirt from his sleeve. "I can't help you. I—"

"Please." She grabbed his hand when he tried to stand, her strong fingers threading through his in a way that was surprisingly intimate.

How long had it been since he'd held hands with a woman? Months, maybe? Even longer, perhaps? He'd had a couple of women in his bed this week alone, but he hadn't held hands with a single one. As a tried-and-convicted womanizer, Andre knew better than to give a female any evidence that he might be looking for more than fun of the horizontal variety.

Or the vertical variety.

He'd had Terry in the shower last night, pressed up against the slick wall, driving inside her until they both screamed, their well-pleasured voices echoing off the tile. Just thinking about it made things stir low in his body, and that all-too-familiar hunger sparked inside him.

He was going to have to figure something out for tonight. He couldn't call Yasmin or Hannah again—they'd been over last week, and he didn't like to issue invitations two weeks in a row—but most of his other go-to girls were out of town. But . . . it *was* Wednesday. The sex addicts support group met on the Upper East Side tonight. If things at the office were quiet, he could make it up to the meeting by six o'clock. The group leader frowned on addicts facilitating each other's dependency, but what Amir didn't know wouldn't hurt him.

And what did he really expect? That he'd get a bunch of sex addicts together in a room talking about their driving urge to screw and *not* have them hooking up as soon as they hit the streets? It was ridiculous. He expected far too much of people who would do just about anything to get laid.

"Please. Don't go. I don't know who else . . . I don't have anyone else," Emma said, tightening her grip on his hand. For the first time, he noticed the flecks of gold in her deep brown eyes and the insanely thick lashes that framed them. She really did have a lot of potential.

But not that kind of potential.

Andre took a deep breath and eased back into his seat, pulling his hand from Emma's. She was a kid and family and possibly a murderer; he shouldn't be considering her potential for anything—aside from landing herself and the Contis in a huge mess of trouble.

"Okay." Andre leaned close and whispered his next words. "But how do you 'think' you killed someone? Either you killed him or you didn't."

"Maybe in your world," she said, the tension in her expression enough to make Andre's jaw ache. "But for some of us, life is a little more complicated."

"For some of who?"

"For people . . ." She swallowed, clearly not thrilled to be saying whatever she was preparing to say. "For people who have been marked by aura demons. Sometimes we're different. Things aren't so black and white."

Andre dropped his face into his hands, sending up a silent prayer for patience.

Great. She was going *there*, to the crazy head space where she and Sam had dragged half the men in his uncle's operation. Conti Bounty now employed a dozen hunters who believed in invisible demons. They swore they'd been attacked by aura demons the night they'd helped save Sam and Jace at the museum last spring and couldn't be convinced that there was any other explanation for what they'd experienced.

Andre suspected some sort of nerve gas, but no one seemed interested in his realistic, *plausible* theories. Even Uncle Francis—a man who didn't believe in anything he couldn't see, including God and germs—had taken to wearing a demon-protection pendant from the New Age store beneath his white dress shirts.

It was ridiculous. There was no such thing as invisible demons, especially invisible demons that could turn grown men into monsters or make a blind girl see. Uncle Francis swore he'd seen Sam and Emma's big brother, Stephen, transform into some kind of demon-man hybrid, and Jace insisted that Sam's eyes changed colors and she was able to see people on the verge of major change in their lives, but Andre had a hell of a time believing the stories. Any rational person would.

Demons were animals hunted for money or killed for the mind-melting effects of their various parts. They were flesh and bone, not myth and shadow. And they weren't one-fifth as dangerous as the human monsters roaming New York. People killed thousands of other people in the city each year. The demons took down maybe a couple hundred, even in the years when harsh winters killed off many of the smaller demons the larger depended upon for food. Demons weren't anything to be afraid of, as long as you stayed smart and sober and out of their territory.

People, on the other hand . . .

"So, you're saying the invisible demons made you kill this man?" He really didn't want to think Emma was a killer, but people had been making up stories to explain away the horrible things they'd done for centuries.

"No, I'm not saying that at all." She abandoned her coffee cup to grab a handful of napkins from the dispenser and promptly began tearing them into shreds. She would be a horrible witness. Her every action screamed "guilty conscience." "I . . . I don't even know if I killed him."

"Once again, I'll ask: How can you not—"

"He and I were talking in the alley behind the bar."

"Talking? Why were you talking to a Death Ministry—"

"Okay, fine." Emma rolled her eyes, and her napkin shredding grew a bit more frantic. "We weren't talking. He was the kind of guy I . . . Let's just say he met my needs."

"Oh. Okay." Andre stared dumbly at Emma's hands for a second, shocked and the tiniest bit . . . aroused by her words.

The shocked part was easy to understand—he'd come to think of Emma as a kid, like her sister and his cousin did. The aroused part was just . . . wrong. Sex addict or no sex addict, he shouldn't be turned on by the thought of Emma dragging some thug into an alley for a quickie.

But he was. God help him.

"And right after we'd finished . . . talking, he started throwing up," she continued, meeting his eyes, obviously having no clue she'd made him start looking at her full, soft lips in a way he never had before. "I was going inside to find someone to help him, but I passed out before I could reach the door."

"What?" Perverted thoughts fled in the wake of concern. Once more Emma went from potential sex object to troubled kid. Silently, Andre vowed to keep her in the latter category, where she belonged. "How much were you drinking? You're nineteen, for Christ's—"

"I'm twenty, almost twenty-one."

"That's still not—"

"And I only had a couple of beers. It takes a lot more than that to get me wasted," she said, sounding like the petulant near teen she was. "I don't know why I passed out; I just . . . did. And when I came to an hour later and tried to wake the guy up, I couldn't. He was dead."

Andre breathed a little easier. If what she'd told him was true, she had no reason to worry . . . aside from the fact that the guy had died outside her place of business. "So he probably choked on his own vomit. Or maybe he overdosed on alcohol or a mix of alcohol and whatever else he might have been on. You didn't kill him; you were—"

"We weren't just talking, Andre."

"Yeah. I gathered that, Emma." Andre tried to ignore the odd thrill of intimacy inspired by saying her name. "I'm a big boy. I know how those things work."

"I'm sure you do," she said, meeting his gaze with those intense eyes of hers. "But you don't know how *I* work."

No, but I'd sure be interested in learning.

Andre silently vowed to attend the meeting uptown for reasons other than scoring a partner for the night. He obviously needed a meeting badly if he was having inappropriate thoughts about a girl like Emma at five o'clock in the goddamned morning.

"The aura demons . . . they did things to me when I was a baby," she continued, blissfully unaware of his thoughts. "They changed me. I'm not . . . I'm not a normal girl."

"Not a normal girl? You look pretty normal to me, except for the lack of fashion sense and—"

"This isn't funny," she said, loudly enough to make a couple of heads turn. She bit her lip, visibly forcing herself to regain control before continuing in a whisper. "I really think I killed that man."

"I get that, Emma. What I don't get is why."

"The aura demons feed on the pain and suffering of humans," she explained. "When my parents offered me as a sacrifice when I was little, the demons made me like them. I need the energy of other people to—"

"Emma, I'm sorry." He had to stop this crazy talk before it went any further. "But I don't believe in invisible demons. And I really don't believe you're some kind of life-sucking vampire—"

"How can you not believe in aura demons? Jace and Sam and your uncle—"

"My family and I are different in a lot of ways," Andre said, digging out his wallet.

It was time to leave some money for Emma's coffee and go call Uncle Francis to take care of the body behind the bar. Emma clearly hadn't killed the man. She was insane, but she wasn't a killer. Still, she'd touched the corpse, so this had to be taken care of right away. The police would check for fingerprints, and Emma didn't deserve to go to jail.

And the Contis didn't need a dead Death Ministry thug to be found behind a place of business where they had close affiliations—no matter what had killed the guy. It would be better for everyone if this body was never found.

"I love my family," Andre continued, throwing a twenty on the table. "But that doesn't mean I don't think they're crazy."

"So you think *I'm* crazy?"

"Maybe *confused* is a better word."

"I'm not confused." Her hands fisted in the napkins she had ruined, her anger apparent to anyone who cared to look. "I spent two years in a children's hospital when I was a baby. I almost died *three* times before I learned how to get what I needed from the people around me. I have to—"

"Okay, fine. You eat people. Can we go now?"

"I don't *eat* people; I—"

"Then how does it work?" Andre asked, the part of him that had minored in psychology strangely intrigued. "How do you do this life-sucking thing you have to do?"

"I . . . I start off by touching the person. . . ."

"Okay." He kept his face in the neutral position, an expression he'd mastered in his early years of practicing law.

"And then I sort of reach into their mind, their memories, looking for all the bad things they've done," she said. "When I find the bad stuff, I pull it out."

"With your hands, or with—"

"No. Psychically. I *psychically* pull the bad deeds, the bad karma—whatever you want to call it—out of them and into me."

"All right."

She sighed and drove her long, thin fingers through her hair. "You still don't believe me."

"No, I don't."

"Well, you should," she said, shaking her head in disgust at his lack of imagination. "My hands fucking glow while I'm feeding on people. I'm not making this shit up. Why would I?"

"So why don't you show me?"

"What?" She seemed as shocked as Andre felt.

He had no idea why he'd thrown out the challenge. Did he want to prove to Emma that she wasn't the freak she thought she was, or did he just want to know what it felt like to have her hands on him? He couldn't answer the question, which should have made him get up and leave. But it didn't. He stayed, meeting her eyes, watching her lips part in surprise as she struggled to understand what he was asking.

"Show me the glowing hands," he said. "Suck my bad deeds."

Wow. *That* had come out sounding filthy. Thankfully, Emma didn't seem to notice.

"Are you nuts? Haven't you been listening to a thing I've said? I might have *killed* a man tonight because I took too much from him, and you—"

"Then just suck a little bit."

Still filthy sounding, absolutely filthy. And what's worse, Andre sort of liked it. He had to fight the grin teasing at the corners of his mouth, knowing Emma would probably strangle him if she caught him laughing at her.

"It will still hurt you. That's why I only take from bad people, dumb-ass," she said, her casual name-calling increasing his urge to laugh at her. Her toughness was strangely . . . cute, though he knew telling her that would be a good way to end up on her shit list. "I usually stop before I kill anyone, but what I do still shortens people's lives. I know that for a fact. They all die of heart attacks a few months, or maybe a few years, later. I've been doing this long enough to—"

"Then just take a teeny, tiny bit," Andre said. "I don't mind giving you a year or two in the name of separating fact from fiction."

She shook her head, the genuine concern in her eyes sending a sliver of doubt into Andre's assurance that she was nuts. She might be crazy, but she was so sure of herself . . . *positive* that she hurt people. How could she have become so sure of something without some sort of evidence?

The part of him that missed the danger of being a bounty hunter, that still craved the high of pushing life's boundaries, thrilled at the possibility that he was playing with something truly dangerous.

"You don't know what you're saying," she said. "You still think I'm crazy."

"I do. I really do. I think you're a crazy little girl with dirty fingernails," Andre said, throwing the words down on the table between them, an open challenge. "Now . . . don't you want to suck my life force? Just a little?"

"No, I don't."

"Okay, then how about this . . . ?" The noble part of him screamed for him to shut his mouth, but the ignoble part of him won out. It usually did. "I won't help you get rid of the body unless you show me what you can do."

"The dead guy's friends saw him go outside with me," she said. "This isn't a game. They'll think I know something about his death. I'll have the Death Ministry all over me. They could kill me, and they'll know that I have connections to the Contis; they'll know—"

"Then I guess there's a lot riding on you proving yourself to me, isn't there?" he asked, hating himself for pushing her but unable to stop this ball now that it was rolling. He was just so curious about her. . . .

"Fine," she said, forcing the word out through gritted teeth. "But not in here." Emma stood and headed toward the door. Andre followed, doing his best not to notice the way her ass filled out her jeans, and failing miserably.

Finally, he gave up on nobility and let his eyes roam over Emma's subtle but undeniably sexy curves. Sometime in the past half hour, she had transformed from a scruffy girl to an attractive young woman in his eyes, and there was no way he *couldn't* notice her in a sexual way. That didn't mean he was going to treat her any differently, however. She was still family and a great deal younger than he was, not to mention his cousin's kid sister by marriage. Sleeping with Emma would be a very dumb idea, even if she was interested in a purely physical relationship.

Which she certainly wasn't. She still thought he was an annoying jerk of a pansy-ass lawyer.

Her disdain was clear in her swift, irritated stride, in the way her ass twitched from side to side as if even her bottom were frustrated with his stupidity. When she finally stopped—stepping into the deep shadows of a recessed doorway a half block from the coffee shop—her eyes flashed, and her slim body practically vibrated with anger. It was enough to make him pause, uncertain whether to follow her into the shadows. The rational part of him knew there was nothing to fear, but another part of him warned that a predator lurked nearby, ready to take what it needed from him, the weaker, more vulnerable creature.

"Well, come on, Andre. No second thoughts now." Emma reached for him, burying her fingers in his hair, pulling him close, until his forehead rested on hers and her peppermint-gum-scented breath teased at his nose.

His arms went around her instinctively, and apprehension fled in a wave of desire. She was all muscle with only the slightest bit of softness, but she felt good pressed up against him. More than good. She felt . . . perfect, better than any woman in years, better than anyone he'd ever had.

Except for one other.

Andre regretted the thought immediately, as the memories descended like carrion-eating birds, picking away at all the time and emotional distance he'd put between himself and thoughts of her. *Katie.* The only woman he'd ever loved, the one it had nearly killed him to lose.

CHAPTER FOUR

A ndre was warm and solid against her, his arms comforting and disquieting at the same time.

Even as she dove deep into his mind—searching through the day-to-day images, hunting for memories that would make him a man worth stealing from—she couldn't help but notice how close his face was to hers, how his breath whispered across her lips. She fit perfectly against him, each curve finding a strong hollow, as if she was made to fill in all his missing pieces.

Shivers of awareness sizzled across her skin, making her ache in a way that was entirely new and a little . . . terrifying. She'd felt ghosts of this feeling before—with the one boy at the group home who she'd called her "boyfriend" for a few months—but never anything so strong. Nothing that made her nipples grow tight and sensitive against her shirt or made that quiet place between her legs wake up and celebrate the fact that a *very* good-looking man was very close.

This was what other people must feel when they rubbed against an attractive member of the opposite sex; *this* was the reason people hunted desirable partners to grind against in those darkened clubs. This was desire; this was . . . lust.

She was lusting after *Andre*.

The realization was nauseating. The man was contemptible in every way—from his excessive spending to his compulsive tidiness to his careless use of women to his smug assuredness that there was nothing in the great wide world that he might not completely understand. Even the way he smelled—of strong soap and heady cologne—had always made her cringe.

But for some reason, he smelled different now. What had made her head ache now made it spin, the spicy scent calling to a hunger entirely separate from the dark craving that surged to the surface as soon as her fingertips found the pressure points just above Andre's neck.

This hunger was base, instinctive, the hunger of a woman for a man.

Oh yeah, this was lust—no two ways about it—and it was . . . overwhelming. Her heart beat faster, and her hands yearned to roam across every inch of Andre, to intimately learn the body hiding beneath his designer suit. The lure of that undiscovered flesh was so strong that it took several long minutes for her mind to get past the unfamiliar need coursing through her veins and focus on the business at hand.

Andre's memories were practically slapping her in the face by the time she homed in on the source of the pain flowing in through her fingertips.

She saw a woman, a beautiful woman, but different from all the other beautiful women Andre had taken to his bed. This one was special. Emma watched Andre brush the woman's bright red hair behind her ear, saw the way she laughed, the way she smiled with tears in her eyes when Andre slipped a ring on her left ring finger.

A fiancée. Jace had never mentioned that Andre had been engaged. It made Emma wonder what had—

Before the question in her mind could fully form, Emma had her answer. The memories flew at her, faster and faster. The redhead, huddled in a corner, sick and wasted from demon drugs, Andre screaming at her, the woman crying, begging him to stay. But he doesn't, he can't, he can't keep watching her ruin herself. She's crawling across the floor on her belly when he slams out of the small apartment, leaving her there . . . leaving her there to die.

He never saw her again. She died, but it wasn't his fault. It was the drugs, the demon high she couldn't quit chasing once she'd had her first taste. Still, Andre blamed himself. For days, months, years . . . The grief Emma sensed in his memories was overwhelming. Even as he flirted and teased and seduced, the pain was there, the loss a wound that would never, ever heal.

Emma slid her trembling hands down to Andre's shoulders, severing her connection to his memories. She'd found nothing there worth taking. Bribing judges and aiding tax evasion were hardly punishable sins in her book, nothing compared to killing people; that was for damned sure.

And the pain that was so fresh in his memories . . . it had gotten to her . . . made her see Andre in a way she'd never dreamed she could, made her want to help him, to comfort him, to connect with the man who had lost someone he loved so deeply. That love intrigued her. She'd seen a lot of hate in the memories she'd sifted through over the years, but not much love, and nothing so . . . intense.

"Emma, I—"

His whisper ended in a moan as Emma pressed her lips to his, grateful that she'd taken the time to wash the taste of the Death Ministry thug out of her mouth before she left the pub. She wouldn't have wanted another man to color the flavor of this kiss. This perfect kiss.

Andre's lips moved against hers, taking the comfort she offered, devouring her with a naked hunger that drew an answering moan from Emma's throat. His arms tightened at her waist, pulling her closer. She wrapped her arms around his neck and held on tight, clinging to him as their tongues met with sweet, seductive strokes that made her ache all over.

This was so completely different from the invasion of Blue Eyes' kiss, from any kiss she'd ever known. This was a communion, a mutual exploration, a challenge neither of them was backing away from. With every passing second, Andre's kiss made her hotter, higher, bolder, until her hands were roaming down his broad back and up under his suit jacket, wanting to get closer to his warmth.

Her fingers clawed into the thick muscles of his shoulders, wishing the soft cotton of his shirt would vanish, wishing that she could be skin to skin with this man who made her body respond in a way no one ever had. There was no fear, no anxiety, only need, more than she knew what to do with. Not even the dark craving could compete with the desire flooding her every cell. The demon-created hunger faded into the background, a thread of smoke dwarfed by the fire that had sparked to life inside her.

She'd never understood, but now . . . she got it. She finally got it, and she wanted it, wanted *him*.

When Andre's hands cupped twin handfuls of her ass and pulled her close, pressing her against where he was obviously aroused, she didn't pull away. Instead, she tilted her hips forward, grinding against him. *Damn.* It was . . . unbelievable. He felt so good. So very, very good.

She was going to have to take back every critical thing she'd ever thought about the girls who made their dance partners into stripper poles at the Demon's Breath. She wanted to do a lot more than *dance* with Andre, and she didn't care if it happened right here. Right now.

Growing bolder, Emma smoothed her hands down to his waist, then around to the close of his belt.

"Wait." Andre broke off the kiss with a suddenness that left Emma gasping. He grabbed her fingers and removed them from his belt, then transferred his hands to her shoulders. "We shouldn't do this," he said, though his breath was coming as fast as hers and the look in his eyes left little doubt that he wanted to pick up where they'd left off. She'd seen that look in men's eyes plenty of times before, though she'd never been as pleased by it as she was at this moment.

"No, we shouldn't." Emma smiled. "But we could."

"You're nineteen."

"I'm twenty."

"I'm still eleven years older."

Emma laughed, a sharp, bitter sound. "If that's your only concern, you can relax. I'm not a child. I'm not anywhere close to being a child. I never have been."

She stared into his dark eyes, willing him to see that she was telling the truth. She'd never known what it was like to trust anyone or anything—even herself. It had shaped her, aged her well beyond her two decades. There was no need for him to consider her some kid in need of protection from his big, bad self.

When it came right down to it, she was way bigger and badder than he'd ever be.

"I know you've had . . . a difficult time."

"That's one way to put it."

"But I still have a lot more experience." Andre's hands slid down her arms, sending shivers across her skin. She still wanted him so much, so much that it hurt to watch his face harden with the resolve to put a stop to what they'd barely started.

"I doubt it," she said. She'd seen things, lived through things, *done* things that Andre couldn't even fathom. He was an infant in the world of pain and suffering and supernatural terror. So he'd slept with dozens of women and she hadn't slept with . . . anyone. So what?

Sex was just sex. It was like eating. It fed a basic human drive—the need to reproduce and replenish the species. Just because Andre had screwed around with more than his fair share of women didn't make him worthy of her respect, or better than her, or above her in any way. His excuse was ridiculous and thin and maybe just a flat-out lie.

Maybe he didn't want to sleep with her because he thought she was an ugly, gangly girl with nearly nonexistent breasts, stringy hair, and dirty fingernails. Maybe she repulsed him. Maybe he'd kissed her only because he would kiss just about anything female that rubbed up against him.

She'd seen other hidden truths in Andre's memories. She'd seen the way he'd changed after his fiancée's death, watched his womanizing morph into a flat-out addiction that, in many ways, ruled his life. A part of Andre was always thinking about where to score his next fix, wondering where he'd find the next willing, suitable partner, worrying that he'd eventually resort to hiring prostitutes.

Knowing he was a certified man-slut with a monkey on his back should have turned Emma off, but it didn't. She knew what it felt like to need something she didn't want to need, to prowl the streets looking for someone suitable to scratch the itch that made her skin feel too small and the hunger too large. She knew how scary it was to worry that someday the hunger would rule her completely.

For her, that day might be closer than she had suspected.

A man was dead, and she'd blacked out for an hour after feeding on his energy. What did that mean? And why did she still feel so . . . *off*? She hadn't been able to take a single sip of her coffee back at the diner. Just the smell of it had made her stomach heave and pitch. And now that the rush of kissing Andre was behind her, she felt sick again. And dizzy. And . . . wrong.

"It's been a long night. I need to go home," Emma said, pulling away from Andre's lingering touch.

"So we aren't going to finish this?" Andre actually blushed when she glanced up at him in surprise. "I mean the life-force-sucking thing. I didn't see any blue light. Did you—"

"That's because I didn't do it." She crossed her arms. "I couldn't find anything in your memories that made you worth stealing from."

"You saw my memories? Like . . . inside my mind?"

"I did. You're not such a bad guy, after all," Emma said, though it was obvious Andre didn't believe in her power any more than he had ten minutes ago. "So there's not going to be any blue light. I guess that means there's not going to be any help."

Andre adjusted his collar, looking embarrassed. "No, of course I'll help. I'll make a few phone calls, and the body will be gone within the hour."

"Are you going to call your uncle? Is he going to be angry that I—"

"Don't worry about my uncle. I'll take care of it. No one's going to be angry with you." His warm hands came down on her shoulders once more, but this time the touch was purely friendly. "Trust me."

Emma nodded, ignoring the sparks of awareness even his casual touch inspired. "I do."

Andre smiled, that sarcastic twist of his lips she'd seen a hundred times before but never found half as sexy as she did now. "Because you read my mind?"

"Yes." Frowning, she shrugged his hands off her shoulders.

"Okay, okay." Andre held up his hands in mock surrender, his face a study in amused disbelief. "If you say you did . . . you did. I wouldn't think reading my mind would make anyone trust me, but—"

"I don't care about the illegal shit," Emma said. "I always figured you cooked the books for the Conti family, and what do I care if you have a judge or two in your pocket?"

"Oh, come on, is that the best you've got?" The bastard actually had the balls to laugh, like this was all some kind of joke. "You're going to have to give me more than that if you expect me to—"

"I was prepared to give you more." Emma stepped closer, until her lips were only a few inches from Andre's. He was close to six feet, but in her heeled boots their faces were nearly level. The slightest movement on either of their parts would bring them back into intimate contact. The sizzle of attraction arced between them once more. She could tell he felt it, too, see it in the way his smile faded and his breath picked up speed. But was that because he was attracted to *her* or because he'd do anything with a pussy?

She didn't know, and it bothered her more than it should have.

"Emma, please," Andre said, his voice not much more than a whisper. "You're a beautiful girl, but—"

"But I'm not Katie. I get it."

Andre's breath rushed out as if she'd punched him in the chest, and his self-assured facade crumbled before her eyes. For a split second she imagined she saw Andre as he'd appeared as a younger man, before events had conspired to make him an arrogant ass. He looked so hurt, vulnerable, almost frightened.

A part of her felt awful for putting such a stricken expression on his face, but the rest of her was too angry to care. She could handle the smug chuckles and the insinuations that she was crazy, but the condescending rejection had pushed her to the edge. He could take his "beautiful girl" comments and shove them.

"Thanks for helping me. I'll call you later to make sure everything worked out," Emma said, shouldering her way past Andre and back out onto the street.

The city air glowed pale pink and orange, and the sounds of cars and buses lining up to get through the barricade rumbled toward her from Broadway. It must be after five o'clock. Ginger had to be back at their apartment by now. Emma knew she could have asked Andre to call for her, but there was no way she was turning around. Instead, she lengthened her stride, hurrying toward the street corner.

She half expected him to come after her, but he didn't. He let her go, which made her feel even sicker than she had a few minutes ago. But then, what else was new? Being around Andre always made her a little ill. She shouldn't have expected this encounter to be any different, especially not because of some stupid kiss.

Andre watched Emma's narrow form hustle down the street and turn the corner, presumably heading back to the west Southie apartment she shared with one of Sam's friends. He knew he should go after her, follow her, and make sure she got home safely—she'd said she'd passed out earlier and might not be in top form—but he couldn't seem to make his feet move. He didn't want to look at Emma again, not until he'd had some time to pull himself back together.

And call Jace in Seattle and *rip* him a new asshole. He didn't care if his cousin was on his honeymoon. He deserved every harsh word Andre intended to hurl at him.

How dare he tell Emma about Katie? Even if Jace had told Sam and Sam had told Emma, it was still unacceptable. Katie was Andre's own private business, his own private misery, not to be shared with anyone. She'd been dead for eight years, and no one in the Conti family had mentioned her name since the funeral.

Even his mom and dad pretended he'd never been engaged. His parents hadn't said a word when Andre started bringing other women to the family restaurant only a few weeks after Katie was put in the ground. They simply cleared a place at the table and ran back to the kitchen to make an extra salad, because they knew better than to do anything to pick at the empty, aching hole Katie had left inside him.

But Jace had spilled his guts for some stupid reason. Maybe Katie had come up in reference to Jace's own addiction—he'd still used demon drugs for almost two years after she'd overdosed, a fact that had nearly destroyed the cousins' friendship—but that didn't offer much comfort. Jace was one of the few people Andre felt he could count on. Jace should have known better than to open his big mouth.

Maybe he does. Maybe he didn't tell Emma. Maybe she really did read your mind.

"And maybe she killed a man with her life-sucking magic hands," Andre whispered under his breath as he flipped his earbud into the "on" position and ordered it to call Michael—one of Conti Bounty's most formidable bounty hunters and another of Andre's many cousins. Michael was Uncle Francis's younger son and one of the most dependable men Andre knew.

Especially when it came to attending to *sensitive* situations.

His cousin answered on the third ring, growling into the phone in typical Conti fashion. If it weren't for Andre, the entire lot of them would be an uncivilized tribe of sweaty men with guns. "This better be important. It's five o'clock in the morning."

"Good morning to you too, Mikey," Andre said, forcing the usual banter.

"Don't call me Mikey, dickweed."

"You kiss your mother with that mouth?"

"I kiss *your* mother with this mouth."

"Don't bring Mary into this, Mikey." Andre started down the street toward the barricade, the hint of a smile on his face. "Unless you want me to tell her to take the pesto gnocchi off the menu for Thursday."

Mikey sighed. "Jesus, Andre. What are you calling me for? Seriously, I was out late and—"

"And you're going to be up early, so start getting dressed. I need the laundry for the restaurant picked up. The usual guy canceled."

"Okay, I'm up, I'm up," Michael said, nothing in his voice giving away that he was on his way to pick up a dead body, but Andre knew he'd understood the code phrase.

The very idea that he'd really call Michael to "pick up the laundry" was ludicrous. The Contis owned a chain of laundry services, the better to "launder" some of the profits from the family's extracurricular activities.

"Oh, and on your way, could you stop by the Demon's Breath? I think they left a few things out back that they need washed up." Andre would usually e-mail the location of a corpse to Mikey in code, but he figured his cousin would get the message.

And if the police were listening in on the phone call, they wouldn't be suspicious. It was common knowledge that the Demon's Breath was now considered a Conti business, though Samantha Quinn was the owner on paper.

"No problem." Michael's voice was muffled for a second. He was probably pulling on clothes without bothering to shower after his long night. Speed was paramount. The body had been behind the pub for more than an hour. It was time to make sure this mess was taken care of before any Death Ministry came sniffing around and complicated an otherwise easily handled situation.

Mikey was a pro. He'd collect the corpse, transport it to one of his secret dumping places near the river, and make certain the entire thing was consumed whole by one of the water-dwelling demons. Andre had heard rumors that Mikey had some sort of spice rub he worked into dead skin to make the flesh irresistible to the amphibious demons haunting the waters near the old East River Park. He'd never asked whether the rumor was true. Some things were just too much for a sensitive lawyer's stomach to handle.

"The bar's right down the street from my place," Michael continued. "I'll call Little Francis and—"

"No, don't worry about calling Little F," Andre said, keeping the words casual. "I'm headed over to the office later today; I'll let him know you'll be in late. But I won't tell him about the laundry thing; wouldn't want him to think he can get you to do all his errands, too."

Uncle Francis had been out of town on business for two weeks, and in his absence Conti Bounty had been under the thumb of Little Francis, his uncle's oldest son and a man who needed a hobby in a bad way. Little F was a decent guy, but he had a tendency to micromanage, a habit that crawled up the asses of most of the Conti Bounty hunters, especially his little brother, Mikey.

"Sounds good to me. I hate errands," Michael said, making Andre breathe a little easier. "Call you later."

"Later." Andre tapped his earbud, ending the call.

He'd taken a risk hinting that Mikey should keep this from his brother, but he didn't want Little Francis losing his cool and calling his dad in a panic. His father was close to finalizing an agreement with the DM leaders—setting a number of demons they could kill per month and arranging to supply them with stun guns that couldn't be used to kill innocent people. He would *definitely* lose his cool if he realized they had a dead Death Ministry member on their hands and someone in their organization implicated in the murder. It killed Little F to see Conti Bounty profits sag as more demons fell prey to the Death Ministry and the growing demand for demon highs. He'd want to know who had dirtied their hands and put the agreement at risk, and Andre wasn't ready to tell him that Emma Quinn was the lady in question.

What Little Francis didn't know wouldn't hurt anyone. Andre would explain the situation to Uncle Francis himself . . . when the time was right. Maybe two or three months down the road, once the entire situation had resolved itself and any accompanying angst had blown over.

It wouldn't be the first time he'd kept his uncle in the dark. Uncle Francis was the big boss, but he was also on several heart medications. His family conspired to keep stress away from his door unless it was absolutely necessary, and Andre wasn't convinced this situation was that critical.

Emma hadn't killed this guy—no matter what she thought—and there would have been no reason for them to get involved if the thug hadn't made the poor decision to die on Conti turf. Even if Emma *hadn't* touched him, it would have looked strange for a DM member to be found dead behind the Demon's Breath. She wasn't to blame. She'd just been in the wrong place at the wrong time.

This from the man who was telling her how stupid she was half an hour ago? How quickly you change your tune once things get physical.

Andre ignored his smart-ass thoughts and hurried across Broadway, threading his way through the cars idling in a line that stretched as far as the eye could see in every direction, filling the area below Union Square with exhaust fumes. His own car and driver sat in the employee parking structure, the one with the special access ramp that dumped the fortunate back into Manhattan on Park Avenue South without waiting in the horrendous line or paying the ten-dollar toll.

Thank god. He'd never been more grateful for his uncle's connections. The sun wasn't even fully up and it was already hot and sticky enough to make his light cotton dress shirt stick and cling. It was a miserable morning to sit in traffic and sweat, so he'd head back uptown, get a coffee and some eggs at a clean, cool, patisserie instead of some Southie rat hole, and—

His earbud pulsed, then announced a call from Michael Conti, interrupting his fantasies of air-conditioning and coffee that came with its own little pot of warmed cream.

"What's up, Mikey?" Andre asked.

"Nothing much. Just wanted to let you know there wasn't any laundry outside the Demon's Breath." Mikey sounded completely at ease, but Andre sensed the urgency in his words.

"What do you mean? You're already there?"

"I told you I lived close, dude. I got here a couple of minutes ago and—"

"Shit." Andre stopped dead in the street, ignoring the cabbie who honked and screamed for him to get out of the way. The barricade had opened just a couple of minutes ago. This asshole wouldn't be going anywhere for a good thirty minutes. "You checked out back? By the Dumpsters?"

"I checked out back, out front, everywhere," Mikey said. "Unless you want me to climb up and take a look on the roof, then—"

"No. It's fine." It wasn't fine at all. It was bad news. *Very* bad news. Andre spun on his heel and hurried back to where he'd last seen Emma.

"Are you sure? I can get up to the roof if I need to. I—"

"Hold on, Mikey. I'm going to try the Demon's Breath manager on my other line," Andre said. "Hold, line one. Line two, Emma Quinn."

Emma's bud rang three, four times and then went to voice mail. *Shit again.* She'd called him from the pub earlier in the evening. She must not have her earbud with her. "Emma, it's Andre. I need you to call me ASAP. Stop whatever you're doing and call me." Andre ended the call and broke into a jog, weaving through the increasingly crowded sidewalk, searching for any sign of Emma.

He wasn't sure where she lived, but he could find out. He'd call her sister. It was two in the morning in Seattle, but knowing Sam and Jace, they'd probably been out hunting demons until at least midnight. Hopefully Sam would have her bud on.

"Line one," Andre said. "Mikey, I've got to go."

"I'm still here. I can—"

"Don't worry about it. Head into work. I'll call you later." Andre ended the call with a firm tap on his bud and broke into a flat-out run, all thoughts of keeping cool vanishing in a wave of concern. What if the Death Ministry members had found their dead comrade? What if the gang had already decided to track down the girl they'd seen him talking to last night at the bar? Emma could be in very real danger.

"Samantha Quinn," Andre ordered. He hated to bother his cousin-in-law on her honeymoon, but he had no other choice. Sam would know how to find her sister, and he *had* to find Emma . . . before anyone else did.

CHAPTER FIVE

*E*mma knew something was wrong as soon as she reached the top of the stairs.

The long, narrow hall leading to her apartment was a dark, cramped passage without a single window. The only illumination came from a pair of bare bulbs hanging at the beginning and end of the hallway. It was usually so dark she could barely see to fish her key from her purse and fit it into the lock.

This morning, however, a bright shaft of light pierced the gloom from the second apartment on the right. The door to Emma and Ginger's shared living space stood open, illuminating the flat, gray plaster on the opposite side of the hall, revealing the faint striped pattern of ancient wallpaper that had been painted over at least a dozen times.

Emma's hand instinctively reached for her purse, searching for her special "hair spray."

She didn't worry about styling her hair—products were useless against its stubborn straightness—but she did worry about protecting herself on the Southie streets. A lot of women carried Mace in their purses. Emma took things a step further and had purchased a six-pack of miniflamethrowers from the secret back room at Yang's Curiosity Shop.

Any bad guy who tried to mess with her would soon find his face on fire.

A girl couldn't always depend on her life-sucking hands. Emma still followed Father Paul's advice and did her best not to show the world at large what she could do. She fed in private, and criminals often attacked in public. Ginger had been mugged three times in the past five years, all three times in broad daylight on a crowded Southie street.

If her roomie had been hanging with Emma, however, Emma was pretty damned sure the men who'd robbed Ginger wouldn't have gotten away with her purse. Just like whoever had broken into their apartment wasn't going to get away with any of their meager belongings. She might not have her purse or her special hair spray, but she still had the dark craving. It had probably gotten her into this mess. Now it might just have to get her out of it.

Slowly, she crept down the hall, ears straining for any sounds coming from the apartment. There was no point in turning and running down the stairs. If the Death Ministry had found the body and come looking for her, she would be better off dealing with them now.

They wouldn't have found anything to connect her to Blue Eyes in her apartment. Hopefully, she could convince them she'd had nothing to do with his death, that she'd passed out and could have died in that alley if she'd had the misfortune to collapse in a puddle of her own vomit the way their friend had. Maybe they would believe her. Maybe she wouldn't need to take matters into her own hands....

By the time she reached the door, her heart was beating in her throat. She couldn't remember being this afraid since the night the aura demons were banished last spring.

But then . . . this wasn't just her life on the line. If the Death Ministry had found the corpse at the Demon's Breath, then Sam and Jace and Ginger and everyone she cared about would be in danger. Emma might not feel comfortable getting too close to her new friends and family, but the thought of someone hurting them made her crazy. She'd do anything to keep them safe.

Sam was so good, *too* good to spend her time with a kid sister who was basically a serial killer. And Ginger was just a sweet party girl. She'd never done anything to deserve the kind of pain and suffering the Death Ministry could dish out. But what if Emma was too late? What if whoever had broken into the apartment had already hurt Ginger?

If they had, she would kill them. No matter how many of them there were.

Emma's jaw clenched and her hands shook as she risked a quick glance into the apartment. "What the hell?" Muscles relaxing slightly, she eased inside, surveying the destruction.

The combination living room and kitchenette was wrecked— pots and pans flung from the cupboards, dishes smashed on the bare wooden floor, and the ancient sofa gutted, its yellow stuffing erupting from the blue flowered upholstery. The bookshelf in the corner was overturned, and ripped pages fluttered across the room, carried by the breeze from the open window.

ANNA J. EVANS

Ginger's and Emma's cramped bedrooms hadn't fared much better. Clothes exploded from the doors to the left and right, spilling out into the main room—a great puddle of black from Emma's and a riot of color from Ginger's.

"Ginger? Are you here?" Emma asked, even though she knew no one would answer. It was too quiet. Whoever had done this was already gone and hadn't left anyone behind to hang out in the mess they'd made.

Hopefully, Ginger hadn't come home yet. If Emma could get her on the phone—

"Shit," Emma cursed, running her dirty hands through her hair. No Ginger meant no purse and *no phone*.

She was going to have to ask one of their neighbors to borrow a bud, which was going to be a *lot* of fun. If Ginger's tales were to be believed, the dude at the end of the hall was some kind of hoarding freak who had six cats and a collection of ten thousand old *Playboy* magazines stacked to his ceiling. Emma had never seen any sign of the man aside from the occasional bag of dirty kitty litter pitched out his back window and didn't want to see more of him anytime soon.

The single moms in apartments two and four would be a better choice if they would answer their doors, but they probably wouldn't. Parents guarding children on this side of the barricade couldn't afford to take any chances, even on a relatively harmless-looking woman like Emma. She might appear young and innocent, but for all they knew she could be a demon drug junkie willing to kill and steal in the name of her next high. She could be—

Wait a second. . . . "They didn't take anything." Emma turned in a slow circle, surveying the room once more.

The television still sat silent and dust covered on its rickety wooden stand. The Internet uplink box was cracked in half, but all its various wires and chips were still inside. If this were a simple robbery, the thieves would have taken the lightweight flat screen and the box. She and Ginger didn't have much else worth stealing except their purses and earbuds, but some of Ginger's clothes would have fetched something on the street.

Emma picked her way through the clutter, peeking into Ginger's empty room. The mattress was ripped apart and Ginger's ceramic Day of the Dead figurines smashed to pieces, but her leather coat and vast collection of boots—some of them demon skin and worth nearly a grand new—seemed intact. Whoever had wrecked their apartment had been looking for something other than things to fleece for drug money.

Which meant the Death Ministry must have found the body and come looking for Emma. She couldn't think of any other reason that this had happened. Ginger certainly didn't have any enemies . . . or at least she hadn't until Emma screwed up and put both of their lives in danger.

Emma cursed again and leaned heavily against the doorframe as her stomach clenched and a wave of sickness rolled from her aching midsection up to her throat and back down again. The nausea was getting worse, as was the dizziness that had lingered at the edges of her brain since she woke up in the alley a couple of hours before.

Something had gone wrong tonight, not just for the man she killed, but for her as well. She'd never felt this ill after a feeding. Hell, she rarely felt ill, period. Whatever the aura demons had done to her when she was a baby, it had made her damned near invulnerable to disease. Once she'd learned how to meet her supernatural needs, she'd walked out of the children's hospital on her own two feet and hadn't needed anything more serious than a painkiller since. Father Paul had said her health was a blessing from god.

Father Paul . . . It had been more than a year since she'd stolen the book from his library and ran away in the middle of the night. He probably thought she was dead by now. No matter how standoffish she'd been with most people, she'd never been able to go more than a few days without talking to the father. He was the closest thing she'd had to a parent, the only person she'd ever truly believed she could count on.

He would help her if she called. He would use his knowledge of the supernatural to try to figure out why this feeding had left her so dizzy and ill. He wouldn't even be angry that she'd killed a man.

For all his kindness, Father Paul had a taste for the blood of those who preyed on the innocent. Her first victim had been a priest the father had discovered was molesting young boys in his parish. Father Paul had dressed her up as a little boy, stuffing her long, blond hair under a ball cap. Emma had been only three and a half, but she could still remember the way the other priest's eyes had gleamed when he looked at her, remember the wickedness in his touch when he pulled her onto his lap.

The man hadn't survived thirty seconds. She'd killed him, taking too much, too fast. Luckily, the priest was old and had a history of heart problems, so no questions had been asked and no autopsy performed.

Emma and Father Paul hadn't been so lucky on their second kill—a teenage boy from a neighboring town who was convicted of killing his two younger sisters, but then set free on a technicality. Emma had killed him as well, and the coroner had been unable to pinpoint a reason for the heart attack. The police suspected foul play, and Father Paul was questioned since he'd been spotted talking to the boy only a few hours before his death.

After that, they'd had to be more careful. Father Paul had made Emma practice using the blue light on some of the comatose patients at the hospital where he worked until she could control how much she stole, until they could make sure her theft didn't result in the immediate death of her victims. But Emma could still remember those first few kills: the two evil men and the one sweet woman she'd never meant to hurt. Not one of them had made her feel so ill. To the contrary, she'd felt energized, powerful, high on the stolen life force.

The fainting, the nausea, the dizziness that made her head spin and her knees feel so weak that she slid down the doorframe to sit on the clothes-strewn floor, were all wrong. *So* wrong. If she could just get to a phone . . . she could call Father Paul, and he would try to figure out what had happened. He would drop everything to come help her.

But even as her heart raced and her skin broke out in a cold sweat, Emma knew she wouldn't call the priest—even if someone walked into the room and stuck a bud in her ear right now. She'd stolen from him, betrayed him, and turned her back on everything he'd done for her. He was the only person she knew who might have some clue what was going on with her crazy, demon-warped body, but she couldn't call him. She didn't deserve his help.

You don't deserve anyone's help.

With a soft groan, Emma lay down and curled up on the floor, hands clutching at her aching, roiling stomach.

It was true. She didn't deserve anyone's help. She'd stolen from someone who loved her to bribe a complete stranger who'd promised to help her find her "real" family. Ezra had led her to Stephen and Sam, all right, but the spell book she'd given him had killed her brother and nearly killed her sister as well before she'd even had the chance to meet them.

If Ezra hadn't shown her pictures of Sam and Stephen, she wouldn't have known what they looked like, would never have been able to trail them through Southie in an attempt to save their lives and redeem herself for having put them in danger in the first place. She'd saved Sam, but Stephen was dead. Now, for all she knew, Ginger could be dead, too. And maybe Andre would be next if he was caught sniffing around the Demon's Breath looking for the body. Emma should have known better than to try to be close to anyone, to dare to live among people she cared about. She was poisonous, a freak who ended up bringing misery to every life she touched.

Emma felt the tears hot on her cheeks before she even realized she was crying.

She swiped at the wetness, shocked at how warm the tears felt compared to the cold sweat on the back of her hand . . . the very gold, *glittery* sweat on the back of her hand.

Oh . . . crap. She was sweating gold. Gold! The sickness made sense now.

The good news was that she could rest easy knowing she hadn't killed Blue Eyes, after all. He must have overdosed on Hamma claws—the only demon drug she knew of that made users sweat shiny gold glitter—and would have died if she'd never laid a hand on him. If it hadn't been so dark in the alley, she probably would have seen the telltale shimmer all over his acne-speckled face.

The bad news was that he must have slipped ground-up claws into his tequila, the *same* tequila he'd forced down her throat when they'd kissed. For a hard-core addict, drinking ground-up claws would produce a hell of a high, but for someone who'd never touched demon drugs, it would just make them as sick as a fucking dog.

Casual users sniffed tiny amounts of claw dust; they didn't ingest it. Emma had never touched the stuff, but allegedly the high from snorting the claws was mild and enjoyable, with few side effects other than increased wakefulness and "sparking"—breaking out in sparkly sweat. A lot of celebrities used Hamma for exactly that reason. Nothing looked better with a California tan than a little gold sparkle.

Emma probably looked great—like a grungy supermodel on her way to a party; she just *felt* like she was going to die. And maybe she was. Some people were deathly allergic to Hamma claws. One sniff and they were gone.

Shit. She had to get to a phone . . . had to call someone. . . . Maybe Ginger was okay and would answer her bud. If so, she might know what to do in the case of a possible overdose. She'd earned her good-time girl reputation and had to have had some experience dealing with friends who'd partied too hard.

"Oh . . . god." Emma moaned as she pushed herself into a seated position. Her stomach echoed her displeasure with a violent contraction. The room spun, but Emma managed to totter to her feet and take a few unsteady steps toward the door before she fell to her hands and knees once more. She hissed and hurried to snatch her right hand off the floor, but it was too late. Tiny shards of shattered glass stuck in her fingers, bringing bright red blood to the surface to mingle with the gold glitter of her toxic sweat.

Ugh. She felt about two years old, so unsteady and out of control of her own body. Even if she managed to stand up, she wouldn't be standing for long. There was no way she was going to make it to the door, let alone down the hall to knock on one of her neighbors' doors. She was screwed, *completely* screwed—

"Emma? Emma, are you there?"

Even with her pulse pounding in her ears, Emma recognized Andre's voice immediately. "In here!" she screamed, ignoring the way her heart leapt even as her stomach did another swan dive into her guts. She was excited to hear Andre's voice because she'd be excited to see *anyone* right now. Even Death Ministry members would have been welcome.

Okay . . . so maybe not Death Ministry members, but just about anyone else.

"Emma, are you—" Andre's voice broke off in a sharp exhalation as he hurried to her side. Emma fought the urge to lean into the arms he wrapped around her and failed. He felt so good, even better than he had earlier in the morning. With a sigh, she let him pull her into a seated position and halfway onto his lap. "What the hell happened? Are you . . . You're not okay."

"No. How did you—"

"Your sister told me where you lived."

"Oh no, did—"

"Don't worry, I didn't tell her what was happening. No need to ruin her honeymoon, unless there's no other choice."

"Thank you." Emma swallowed hard and lifted her eyes to meet Andre's, determined not to barf on the man who'd saved her ass twice in the past two hours. "I came home and found the apartment like this. But whoever wrecked it didn't steal anything. I think it must have been the Death Ministry. I can't think of anyone else who—"

"The body was gone," Andre said, confirming her fears. "The guy I sent over to pick it up said there was nothing behind the bar."

"Oh god." Emma fought another wave of nausea. "They must have found him; they must have—"

"We don't know that. It could have been the police."

"The police wouldn't have remembered I talked to the guy last night and come over to trash my apartment."

"No, they wouldn't," Andre agreed. "But I think we have bigger things to worry about right now. How much did you take?"

"What?"

"How much did you take?" he asked, slowly, clearly, as if talking to someone with very little brain. "A couple hundred milligrams?"

"I didn't take anything. I—"

"You're sparking, Emma." Andre's lip curled as he glanced down at his suit, now smeared with gold shimmer in the places where her bare skin had brushed against him. "You're covered in Hamma dust."

"I know, but I didn't take it. I think the guy I was with last night spiked the tequila we were drinking," Emma said, needing to prove to Andre that she wasn't a demon drug user. After what had happened to his fiancée . . . Well, he obviously didn't need any more drug-related drama. "That must be the reason I passed out. I—"

"I think we both know you wouldn't be sparking now from something you drank several hours ago."

"No, I don't *know*." Emma tried to contain her irritation and failed. Andre didn't know her from Adam, but she still resented being called a liar for a second time this morning. She might kill people, but she didn't lie . . . at least not to anyone except the investigating authorities. "I don't take drugs."

"Right." Andre laughed, a humorless sound that made Emma shiver. "Come on, get up."

"Wait, I don't think—"

"You've got to get up. It's not safe here, and we have to get you to a doctor."

"No doctors," Emma said, panic setting in. "If they test my blood, they'll report me to the police and—"

"That's why we're going to a Conti doctor, someone who knows how to keep his mouth shut."

"But I don't—" Emma sucked in a breath on a gasp as Andre hauled her to her feet, swinging her arm over his shoulders as his other arm went about her waist.

The room spun so fast that colors blurred, smearing before her eyes. Her brain joined her stomach in a heaving pitch, and Emma knew she would have fallen back to the floor if Andre hadn't scooped her into his arms. Her entire body tensed but just as quickly relaxed as she realized Andre was more than capable of keeping her aloft. He had some serious muscles under that suit, the product of all those early mornings in the gym that made Jace poke fun at him for being a vain bastard.

He might maintain the body to please his endless stream of women, but Emma couldn't deny that his strong, capable arms felt nice . . . better than nice.

Had a man *ever* held her like this? She couldn't remember, but a part of her wished Andre was holding her for reasons other than the fact that she was too messed up to stand.

"Do you need anything from the apartment?"

"No, I—"

"Good," Andre said, whirling toward the door. "We're out of here."

"Oh . . . okay . . ." She looped her trembling arms around Andre's shoulders and fought the urge to be sick with everything in her, focusing on the way he held her—so tight and close and safe—instead of the revolt being staged in her digestive system.

Why did people take this toxic crap? Surely something that made her feel so wretched couldn't really make anyone feel good. Could it?

"Little Francis," Andre said, ordering his bud to call his cousin.

"And call Ginger, too—my roommate," Emma said, biting back a whimper as Andre bounced down the steps, shaking up her insides until she almost lost control of her stomach. "I need to make sure she's safe and that she doesn't come home. At least not alone."

Andre grunted. "Hey, cousin," Andre said as Little Francis answered his bud. "I've got a situation. I need Dr. Finch to meet me at your office."

He paused, listening to his cousin as he pushed the door to her building open with one foot and strode out into the morning light. Emma winced and turned her face into his chest. The light made the spinning in her head worse, made her brain feel like it was going to turn to liquid and come streaming out of her ears.

"Ten minutes ago would be best. It's Hamma claws, so we'll probably need the antivenom. Also see if you can track down Emma Quinn's roommate. Some girl named Ginger—"

"Ginger Spatz." Emma forced the words out through her buzzing lips. Her entire face was starting to go numb, making her worry she might truly be overdosing. What if they didn't make it to the doctor in time? What if she died and left everyone she cared about to believe she'd been using drugs? She didn't want to go out like that, couldn't stand the thought that she'd disappoint Sam so profoundly.

"Ginger Spatz," Andre repeated to Little Francis. "If you get in touch with her, tell her to head uptown to one of our safe houses and I'll be in contact soon. Her apartment was trashed, and we have reason to believe the people who broke in might still be hanging around."

Andre bent down suddenly, making Emma gasp until she realized he was sliding her into the backseat of one of Conti Bounty's many luxury cars. She smelled the well-tended leather of the seats even before she felt the cool, smooth brush of it against her skin. She lay down, pressing her cheek against the cold, and tried to form the words to tell Andre that—assuming she survived—she'd pay for any damage her glittery skin did to his car. And his suit . . . and anything else she'd messed up . . .

But her lips had gone from numb to frozen. All she could do was moan low in her throat and cling to the hand Andre slipped into hers as the driver pulled out into traffic, speeding toward the waterfront offices of Conti Bounty.

CHAPTER SIX

*A*ndre watched Dr. Finch wipe the last of the glitter from Emma's skin with a damp cloth and struggled not to think about how many times he'd done the exact same thing. He'd lost count of the times he'd sponged Katie down after an especially nasty spark had left her weak and boneless on the bed in their apartment.

The Hollywood glitterati—movie stars famous for sparking in public—got only the best Hamma. The rest of the world's addicts had to take their chances with claws gathered and ground by people who had no idea how to process them safely.

One in every dozen or so batches of Hamma claws was steeped in lye too long, transforming the chemical compound in a way that caused shakes, sweating, vomiting, and occasionally a deadly heart attack or stroke in those unlucky enough to ingest it.

In the end, that's what had killed Katie—a bad bunch of claws had been too much for her emaciated, wasted body to handle. What had started off as a way to stay awake a few extra hours to get in a little more study time before the bar exam had taken her life and destroyed her dreams. *Their* dreams.

They were planning to get married the summer after the bar and move upstate somewhere to practice together. They were going to get out of the city, away from the demons and the Conti family and start fresh, just the two of them.

Instead, Andre had attended her funeral one week and taken his bar the next, determined to hang on to something in the wake of Katie's sudden death. In the years since, he thought he'd put the worst of the grief and sadness and bitter disappointment behind him. But watching Emma twist and moan on the narrow couch outside Little Francis's office as the antivenom worked its way through her system brought back every feeling he'd ever buried—like zombies bursting out of the ground looking for a pound of human flesh.

Emma didn't look a thing like Katie—a curvy redhead with bright blue eyes—but something about Emma reminded him of the only woman he'd ever loved. She fascinated him, just as Katie had.

Maybe it was the way Emma walked like she was ready to take on the world that drew him, making him wonder if she might be the kind of woman who could give as good as she got—in bed and out. Maybe it was the fragility he sensed beneath that tough exterior that made him long to protect her, to stand between her and danger and let her know that she didn't have to be alone. Maybe it was simply how good she'd felt in his arms that compelled him to stay by her side. Carrying her out of her wrecked apartment had awakened feelings he hadn't known he was still capable of. Protective feelings . . .

As well as a mess of anger and hurt. He was *hurt* that she'd lied to him, which was absolutely ridiculous. He and Emma were nothing to each other and probably never would be. He had no reason to expect her honesty, and even if he did, there was always the chance that she *wasn't* lying. She could simply be so strung out on claws that she'd convinced herself she had magical life-sucking powers and the ability to take out Death Ministry members three times her size with her killer—

Emma screamed, her back arching as another jolt of pain ripped through her body.

"I'll be right back," Andre mumbled under his breath. The antivenom was really doing a number on her, worse than anything he'd ever seen. He couldn't stand helplessly by and watch her suffer anymore. He had to *do* something.

He turned and slipped through the heavy door leading into Little Francis's office. Crazy or not, Emma hadn't trashed her own apartment. She hadn't had time to wreck the place so thoroughly. Someone else had been there and been determined to find something. But what?

Even if Emma had hidden a body behind the pub that had later been picked up by fellow gang members, the Death Ministry wouldn't have trashed her apartment and left. If they were looking for answers, they would have stayed and cut them out of Emma's body—piece by piece.

So it must have been someone else. But who? And why?

"How's Miss Emma?" Little Francis asked around a mouthful of cashews. Andre's cousin—an exact replica of Uncle Francis minus twenty-odd years, right down to the curly black hair and barrel chest—had a passion for cashews that was probably unnatural and definitely unhealthy.

"She's going to be okay." Andre silently willed the words to be true as he gestured toward the bowl of nuts on Francis's desk, changing the subject. "You know how much fat is in those, right?"

"Yeah. I heard, gym rat." Francis smiled. "Real men don't care about fat. Real men don't even know what foods have fat in them and which don't."

"Real men are ignorant. Good to know," Andre said, unable to resist the dig. He and Francis had been digging on each other since Andre joined the family business as an apprentice bounty hunter when he was sixteen.

It was how they showed their cousinly love . . . and made sure the other knew the competition for future alpha dog was still ongoing, despite the fact that Little Francis's father was the commander in chief. Andre would never want to run the family—women and practicing law kept him plenty busy—but he was among the increasing number of Contis who thought Jace would be a better replacement for Francis when the time came, even if he *was* technically a Lu. Jace had roamed the Southie streets for nearly a decade. He was skilled at dealing with thugs and was the smart choice to lead the Contis in this new era of gang-mob cooperation. If they didn't learn to work together and keep the bounty numbers high and the death toll of innocents down, the police and the National Guard would be swarming all over Southie the way they had in the early days of the emergence.

And that would be bad business for everyone.

Little Francis had picked up on the shifting winds of favor, but you'd never guess it bothered him. He was an expert at keeping his emotions close to the chest, at least whenever Andre was around to observe them.

"Real men aren't ignorant; they just keep their heads full of things that matter. Like running their businesses and knowing who's doing what in their territories." Little Francis paused and reached for another handful of cashews. "So why don't you tell me what you know about Emma? How's she involved with the Death Ministry?"

"What?" Andre asked, feigning ignorance even as he cursed Mikey for opening his big mouth. Why did today have to be the *one* time Michael felt compelled to give his older brother the complete scoop? "I don't know her that well, but I seriously doubt Emma's involved with a gang. Pretty girls like her get their drugs from other places, small-time dealers."

"Yeah. So I heard."

Andre ambled over to the window, watching the hot summer sun glint on the peaceful waters of the river, taking his time before responding to the unspoken question in Francis's tone. "And I'm sure Jace made it clear to her that the Contis and friends of the Contis stay out of Death Ministry business as long as they stay out of ours."

"Probably," Little Francis agreed, though when Andre turned back to look at him, he didn't seem any more certain than he had a second ago. "I bet he made it clear the Contis don't care for demon drugs, either, but it don't look like that lesson took."

Andre shrugged. "I guess it's like eating too many nuts, Francis. People don't always make healthy choices, no matter what people tell them."

"You're a smart-ass, Andre."

"No, Francis, I'm just smarter than you," Andre said with an easy smile.

Francis scowled, actually looking pissed for a second before his expression cleared. "Well, cousin, if you're so smart, why don't you tell me why a bunch of Death Ministry stopped by our training warehouse near the old park this morning looking for the blonde who works at the Demon's Breath?"

"Looking for Emma?" *Shit.* Maybe the Death Ministry were the ones who'd trashed her apartment. And maybe Michael hadn't talked to his brother, after all. This was why it paid to play dumb and never assume the person questioning you had all the facts. "You're kidding."

"Nope. Not kidding." Francis abandoned his cashews, wiping his greasy hands on his dark jeans. "I don't kid about assholes with knives threatening my employees."

"Of course not. Was anyone hurt?"

"Not this time, but they promised to come back and leave a few bodies behind if some guy named Greg didn't show up soon." Francis rose from his chair, crossing to the liquor cabinet in the corner. "This could ruin that peace treaty we've been cooking up. If they go after our people, we'll have no choice but to retaliate."

Andre couldn't help but notice that he looked tired. The stress of running the family business in his father's absence was taking its toll. With the Conti history of heart disease, he should be getting more sleep and staying away from the cashews and the alcohol. Especially at six o'clock in the morning.

"You want something?" Francis asked as he poured himself whiskey on the rocks.

"It's breakfast time, Francis. I think I'll pass."

"It's happy hour when you've been up since two o'clock yesterday, smart-ass. If you hadn't called with your list of demands, I would be at home in bed right now, so don't give me any shit."

"Wouldn't think of it," Andre said, waiting until Francis took a sip of his drink before steering them back on topic. "So the Death Ministry lost track of some guy named Greg. What does that have to do with Emma?"

"Seemed Greg went missing last night, right after he stepped outside the Demon's Breath to have a few words with her."

"That's crazy." Andre shook his head in confusion, trusting his ability to pull off a lie with the best of them.

He *was* a lawyer. He usually made it a habit not to lie to family, but today he would make an exception. He didn't want Little Francis finding out Greg was dead, not missing. Not until he had a chance to talk to Emma and get her side of the story. The real story this time, not some drug-inspired hallucination.

"So they think she had something to do with his disappearance?"

"They do," Francis confirmed. "And they want to talk to her. Real bad."

His cousin's words made his blood rush in a way it hadn't in years. That part of him that had once been a card-carrying, gun-toting bounty hunter itched to have a weapon. If the Death Ministry was after Emma, he might have to be prepared to kill to keep her safe. Strangely, he knew he would, without a second thought. Sometime in the past few hours, Emma had become more than a casual acquaintance or a family obligation. He felt compelled to help her. Not just out of this mess, but with the demon drugs, too.

No matter how many times he'd taken Katie to the doctor or begged her to check herself into rehab, he hadn't been able to save her. But things with Emma could be different. . . . She was stronger than Katie; she had it inside her to kick the drugs if she had a little help, even just one person who believed she could do it. Andre hadn't expected to be anyone's "one" anytime soon, but despite the sister who loved her, this girl obviously felt very alone. She needed him, and the good man buried deep inside him couldn't turn his back on her.

"I don't have to tell you that this could start a street war between the Contis and the Death Ministry if it isn't handled properly." Francis collapsed back into his chair with a sigh. "We need to smooth this over, get the Death Ministry to agree to our terms, and get back to making some serious money. Miss Emma needs to tell us everything she knows or thinks she knows about this Greg guy."

"I'll question her myself," Andre said. "But first I'll need to get her to a safe house as soon as she's ready to travel. I want her out of Southie."

Francis nodded. "Already got a room reserved at the place near Columbus Circle, right next door to her friend."

"You got in touch with Ginger?"

"Douglas, my new assistant, got her on the phone about twenty minutes ago. She's going to meet Antonia and Kelly at the diner down the street from the safe house. They'll get her settled in within the hour. Hopefully."

"Why *hopefully*?"

Francis downed the last of his drink before answering. "I'm not sure this chick is going to show up. She might end up passed out in the street somewhere before she gets there. Douglas said she sounded wasted. He couldn't understand half of what she was saying."

Andre sighed. "Great."

Now he had two messed-up young women on his hands. Not that Ginger was really his responsibility, but she was someone

Emma cared about, and so he felt ... obligated. Just like he'd felt obligated to help Katie's sad-sack group of druggie friends every time they ended up on the wrong side of a bar fight or carted down to the city lockup to sweat out their spark.

It would be stupid to get sucked into that kind of situation again, no matter what his gut said about Emma being tough enough to kick the Hamma habit. Katie's death should have taught him that addicts couldn't be saved. He should turn around, walk out of this office, and keep walking until he was back on the right side of the barricade. Let Little Francis handle Emma.

But he wasn't going to do that. There was a part of him that still believed that people like Emma, like himself, could turn their lives around. He had to keep believing that, or all those nights he'd sat through twelve-step meetings and prayed to get his own compulsions under control would be for nothing. He had to have hope. For himself, and now for Emma.

Besides, he didn't want Francis anywhere near her. He didn't want his cousin handling her. He didn't want anything male "handling" Emma except himself.

"I'm going to check with Dr. Finch and see how much longer he'll need to monitor Emma's progress with the antivenom." Andre ambled toward the door, casually throwing his next words over his shoulder. "You want to catch a ride uptown with me when I'm done?"

"Nah, I'm going to stay at my new place."

"New place? Where?"

"I got an apartment on the Southie side," Francis said. "Figured it was time for me to come back where I belong. The head of the family has always lived in Southie. It's tradition."

"Right," Andre said, ignoring the implication in Francis's words. There would come a day when Andre would have to tell Francis to his face which way he'd be voting, but today wasn't that day. He had other priorities. "Then I'll stay here and wait. I've already had to cancel my court date, so—"

"I bet she'll be here another few hours. Dr. Finch doesn't mess around with his private clients. He likes to make sure they're good to go before he leaves," Francis said. "You've got time to head uptown and attend to some business. Why don't you go check and make sure Antonia and Kelly don't need any help with this Ginger girl."

It was as close to an order as anything Francis had ever said to him, and it made Andre inexplicably angry, despite the fact that he'd done his share of ordering this morning. "I do the lawyering, Francis. That's why I went to college."

"Of course. You're the big-shot smart guy, Andre; everybody here knows that." There was enough sarcasm in his tone to make Andre's jaw clench. "But if Ginger is sparking like the one out there, Antonia and Kelly might not be able to handle her. You might need to bring her back here to see the doc, too."

"Don't you have someone who—"

"A bad batch of claws isn't something to mess around with." Francis shook his head. "But I don't need to tell you that, right?"

"No, you don't." Andre fought the urge to cross the room and punch the look of concern off his cousin's face. Real or not . . . the fact that Francis had the balls to bring up Katie made him crazy. "I'll go by Columbus Circle and be back in a few hours. Will you be here when I get back?"

"You bet. I wouldn't leave Emma alone, even with Dr. Finch. I don't trust men with pretty young girls," Francis said. "Especially family. You consider Emma family, right?"

"Of course."

Francis smiled. "I figured you must. That's probably why she called you when she was in trouble, because she knew she could trust you."

"What can I say? I'm a trustworthy guy." Andre tried to infuse the words with his usual lighthearted tone and failed. He didn't like where this conversation was going or the predatory look in his cousin's eyes.

"Yeah. I'd say so." Francis leaned forward in his chair. "And I could trust you to tell me if there was anything going on between you and Miss Quinn? Couldn't I?"

Andre stared hard at Francis, considering his next words carefully. There was a chance his cousin knew more than he was letting on, that Michael had indeed spilled the beans about the body he was supposed to pick up that morning. But if that was the case, Andre couldn't believe that Francis wouldn't have said something sooner. Surely his cousin would have been demanding answers about the missing corpse from the moment Andre walked in the room.

So he had to assume Francis meant something else entirely, something that made Andre's hands itch once again for that weapon he'd been craving a few minutes ago. "There's nothing sexual between us, if that's what you mean."

"And no intentions on your part?"

"Why do you want to know?"

Francis smiled again. "Why wouldn't I want to know? You know me. I've always had a thing for blondes. I just wanted to make sure I wasn't going to be getting your seconds. With as many women as you 'date,' that can be a challenge."

"Don't touch her, Francis." Andre barely kept his tone civil.

"I wouldn't think of it . . . until she's recovered. After that, I think that will be her call. She's a big girl."

"She's twenty years old."

"Last time I checked, eighteen was legal."

Andre literally bit his tongue. He had no reason to feel so possessive of Emma. One kiss didn't mean anything. It didn't matter that it had been the most intense kiss in recent memory, or that holding Emma as he carried her out of her apartment building had awakened all his sleeping protective instincts.

"Okay. Fine. Just promise me something, okay?" Andre managed a deferential tone that actually sounded sincere. "Leave her alone until I get back. I want to make sure she's up to answering questions before I ask her about the Death Ministry stuff."

"No problem." Francis sat back in his chair and reached for another handful of cashews. "See, we can get along great when we cooperate."

Andre forced a tight smile before he turned and strode from the office. Outside, Emma was still sacked out on the couch, but she was at least lying still on her side. Dr. Finch was getting coffee at the station a few yards away, looking calmer than he had since the tiny, white-haired old man had arrived. The good doctor had sold his practice several years ago to become one of the two docs on twenty-four-hour call to the Conti family. He was a man who was used to pulling out bullets and sewing up knife wounds, but he'd still paled when he saw Emma. By the time they reached Conti Bounty's offices, she'd barely been breathing.

If they hadn't gotten the antivenom when they had . . .

Andre squatted down by Emma's face, wondering whether she

was really seeing him through her slitted eyes, and whether she would be able to understand the words he leaned forward to whisper in her ear. He prayed to all the saints his mother loved that she could. Because if she started talking to Little Francis while he was gone, they were both going to be in a shitload of trouble.

CHAPTER SEVEN

For a second Emma thought Andre was going to kiss her on the cheek. Despite the fact that she was sure she looked and smelled as horrible as she felt, the idea was oddly thrilling.

But then his lips drew close to her ear, and she felt like a fool for even thinking about stupid, impractical things like kisses. "Don't talk to Francis. The Death Ministry was looking for you at the training facility this morning. They were asking about some guy named Greg who's been missing since last night."

Oh shit. The DM hadn't found the body. Someone else must have taken it. Now she was a person of interest to a deadly gang and might very well be on her way to jail if the police had found the corpse. Her fingerprints were all over Greg.

Greg. How sad was it that she hadn't even known the guy's first name? But then, she preferred to know as little as possible about her victims; it made it easier to concentrate on the information she pulled from their minds if her focus wasn't cluttered with her own impressions.

"So don't talk to anyone until I get back and we can figure this out," he said. "Do you hear me? Don't talk to anyone but me."

Andre had never been her favorite person, but he'd proven today that he was someone she could depend on. Little Francis, on the other hand, had always made her uncomfortable. He seemed like a decent guy but was way too *friendly*. Every time she'd been seated by LF at Conti family dinners, she'd felt coated in smarm by the time the main course was served, and she always made excuses to escape to the stockroom when he stopped by the bar.

Any other man would have gotten a clue and given up, but not Little Francis. He seemed positive she'd eventually throw herself at his feet—or his groin, if he had his preference. His opinion of himself was even higher than that of the average Conti man, which was reason enough for her not to tell him jack, even if Andre had thought fessing up to the boss's son was a good idea.

Emma tried to tell Andre she understood but could manage only a small nod. She was still so weak.

"I want to check on a few things before we talk to anyone else about the . . . missing person." Andre leaned back, studying her face, fear and anger mingling in his expression. "I'll be back in a few hours. Do what the doctor tells you to in the meantime."

Emma swallowed hard but still couldn't seem to get any words to come out.

Probably for the best. Andre certainly didn't want to hear that it wasn't the antivenom that had brought her back from the brink but a hearty dose of Dr. Finch's life force.

She'd laid her hands on the doc as soon as Andre had disappeared into Francis's office. Andre had said he wanted proof of what she could do, but she wasn't about to let him know she'd snacked on the Conti family doctor, just in case Dr. Finch decided to drop dead sometime in the next few hours. She was convinced Blue Eyes' death was drug related and had nothing to do with her feeding, but she was still in deep shit.

Any more and she'd be up to her neck in it.

Luckily for her, Dr. Finch was too distracted by her moaning and clutching at his head to notice the pale blue light coming from her fingers. Even more luckily for her, the doc wasn't the sweet old man he appeared to be. She'd been in so much pain, from both the venom and the antivenom, that she hadn't been able to see his memories as clearly as most, but she'd seen enough to know his fat bank account was earned dealing death as often as healing the sick.

He'd done something very, very bad . . . something involving illegal organ harvesting . . . or . . . *something.* . . . The images had been blurred, hazy. She couldn't say for certain what he'd done, but Doc Finch had been wicked enough to suit her purposes, evil enough that she knew she'd have to talk to Sam and Jace about the man as soon as they got back from their honeymoon.

Sam, at least, would believe that Emma had seen inside the doctor's mind. Her sister would know who to talk to in order to make sure the Contis replaced Finch ASAP. For all their illegal activity, the Contis were decent people and didn't make it their business to profit from others' pain. They wouldn't knowingly employ a man like the doctor.

Still, Emma was glad Finch had been in the wrong place at the right time. Without the energy she'd taken from him, she was fairly certain she *would* be dead.

The mix of venom and antivenom on top of the ever-present dark craving had nearly overwhelmed her. It had become almost too much for her to physically bear—she'd felt that truth in the way the demonic craving writhed and screamed inside of her as soon as the antivenom hit her bloodstream. Her only recourse had been to do something to make the craving stronger than the mix of drugs that threatened to destroy it.

As much as she'd love the chance at a life without the need that haunted her, Emma knew the death of the darkness would be her death as well. She and her demon mark were inseparable. Even the spell book made no mention of destroying the part of her that had been transformed by the aura demons, only managing it.

"Ginger . . ." Emma croaked, praying her roomie—and her purse and spell book—had been located.

"She's fine," Andre said. "I'm going to meet her now and help her get settled in a safe house. You'll be staying there, too, until we get everything sorted out."

At any other time, his calm assurance that she would be doing what he told her would have made Emma livid, but at the moment it was strangely comforting. *Ugh.* She was definitely going to have to make sure she never ingested or injected anything unnatural ever again. Her physical weakness was bleeding over into the emotional arena. At this rate she'd be asking Andre whether she could stitch up his socks and clean his kitchen floors.

Or maybe just offering up your ancient virginity.

Even in her present state, the idea was *way* more exciting than it should have been. She'd never seriously considered sleeping with a man, let alone a man with a sex addiction whose partners probably numbered in the hundreds. It was crazy. She was losing her mind from the demon drugs.

Yes. That had to be it. It certainly had nothing to do with the way Andre's full lips had felt against her own, or the heat in his eyes when she'd reached for his belt earlier in the morning.

"Ginger has . . . my purse. . . ." Emma swallowed again, willing the last of the numbness away from her tongue and the lustful thoughts from her mind. "Could you get it . . . for me?"

Andre rolled his eyes. "Sure, why not. I'm everyone's fucking errand boy today." He stood and adjusted the already immaculate seam in his pants. "Be good while I'm gone, and remember what I told you."

"Got it, boss," Emma said, her smart-ass tone making Andre's scowl grow even darker.

"Great. And maybe you should spend some time thinking about what a dangerous, stupid thing you did today," he said, casting a pointed look at Dr. Finch as he wandered back into their general vicinity.

"It's true, Miss Quinn," Dr. Finch said. "I was very concerned."

I just bet you were, concerned about how a dead girl would mess up your afternoon golf game.

"Tell her that she could have died," Andre said.

"You could have died. He's right."

"But I didn't. Now you can . . . go play golf," Emma said, not missing the flash of recognition in the doctor's eyes. Bastard.

Andre cursed beneath his breath before squatting back down beside her and talking in a hushed whisper. "Listen, you can be an asshole to the people who are trying to help you if you want, but remember this is your fault. Think about that the next time you're putting that shit into your body."

Even though she'd been thinking the exact same thing, Andre's words still made her eyes sting as he turned and walked away. She got it that he'd lost someone he cared about to demon drugs and had no clue Finch was a bad man, but that didn't give him the right to treat her like a dumb kid. She'd been telling him the truth—she was cursed with a demon mark, but she didn't touch demon drugs. Stupidly, it hurt that he wouldn't even consider that she was an honest person.

"Is there anything I can get for you, Miss Quinn?" Dr. Finch asked, the picture of the sweet, helpful old doctor.

"No, thanks. I'm just going to rest."

"Would you like me to prepare a cot in the staff break room? Or I could—"

"I'll just . . . stay here."

"That's probably best." He nodded, evidently pleased that she wouldn't be a high-maintenance patient. "Be sure to drink some of the water on the table when you feel up to it. Water helps flush the system of the antivenom."

Emma shifted, taking in the glass of ice water on the table near her head. "Will do." She closed her eyes, hoping the doctor would take the hint that she was done with conversation. She heard the doc shuffle away down the hall a few seconds later and relaxed into the soft, comfy couch with a sigh.

All she needed was a power nap, and then she'd be ready to go. She had to help Andre find out what was going on with the missing body. They had to figure out who had found the corpse she'd

ANNA J. EVANS

shoved between the Dumpsters—the police or someone more dangerous. There were other gangs roaming the ruins, though none as feared or powerful as the Death Ministry. At least not yet.

If the Demons' Army or one of the other smaller gangs could help incite a street war between the Contis and the Death Ministry, however, they might be able to seize control of the Southie drug trade away from their rivals. The Death Ministry had controlled the waters near old East River Park for years and earned riches by running demon drugs out to the man-made pleasure islands off the coast of New York in international waters. This wouldn't be the first time another gang had tried to get a piece of the DM's action, but it might be the first successful attempt.

Andre might find her theory a little far-fetched, but she knew another gang member was the most likely candidate for body thief. The gangs roamed the dark alleys and twisted corridors of the ruins. The police certainly had no reason to be patrolling behind the Demon's Breath in the early hours of the morning. And even if the Squat demons had returned and fed on the body, they would have at least left bones behind.

Emma turned the problem over and over in her mind until the seams of her sanity began to shred and unravel. No matter how weak she still felt, she couldn't just lie here and take a nap; she had to get up and *do* something; she had to—

"Mikey! Michael, you here?" Little Francis yelled the words from the door to his office, obviously unconcerned with waking the sleeping girl on his couch. Emma kept her face still and her eyes closed, determined not to say a word to Francis if she could help it.

Andre was right; they would be better off if they had more information before they went to the boss's son. Once her involvement in this mess was confirmed, LF would have to call his dad, and she'd feel more prepared for the wrath of Uncle Francis if she and Andre could find out what had happened to the body.

"Douglas," Francis yelled. Footsteps sounded from down the hall, the scurrying of an obedient minion hurrying to do his master's bidding. "Get me Mikey, or get Mikey on the phone. We've got a situation. The girl showed up at the meeting place but ran off before we could get her into the safe house."

Oh no. *Ginger*. It had to be. How many other girls were the Contis checking into a safe house this morning? What the hell was wrong with her? Why had she run?

"I want Mikey uptown coordinating the search," Little Francis said. The fact that he was willing to send one of his best hunters and a team of his men to look for her friend changed Emma's opinion of him. At least a little bit. He might be sleazy, but he was a sweeter sleaze than she'd realized.

"Yes, sir," a young man Emma assumed to be Douglas said. "Do you want the team already in place to keep looking or—"

"Of course I want them to keep looking, Douglas. Use your fucking brain."

Geez. Francis was really passionate about finding Ginger. Or maybe he always talked to his assistant like he was demon waste stuck on his shoe. What did Emma know?

Nothing. She knew a whole lot of nothing, a state of being she meant to remedy as soon as possible.

Emma waited until she heard Douglas's footsteps hurry away down the hall and Francis's door close before slitting her eyes. Good. Francis had indeed returned to his lair. She lifted her head, searching the long hall that led to the main entrance of Conti Bounty. She was alone, except for the doctor lingering near the coffee station and Douglas, who would be manning the front desk.

Still, she might as well have had a team of armed bounty hunters between her and the door. The doctor and Douglas weren't going to let her walk out of here. She was going to have to get a little more . . . creative.

Her eyes drifted along the wall, searching for a window. She'd done her share of sneaking out—and back in—through windows in her time at the halfway house, but never through one that opened out on demon-infested waters. The East River was pretty to look at, but she didn't want to go swimming in it anytime soon, especially not when her arms and legs still felt like taffy twisted one too many times.

That left her only one option.

Emma hefted herself into a seated position with a sigh, pushed to her feet, and tottered down the hall toward Dr. Finch. She felt fairly steady but played up the sway in her step as she closed the distance between her and the doc.

"Dr. Finch, I was wondering if—"

"Miss Quinn, you shouldn't be up," the doctor said, looking annoyed when she reached out and took his arm. He'd clearly had enough of her touch when she'd mauled his head earlier in the morning.

"I know. I just can't sleep." Emma blinked her eyes, hoping she didn't look as horrible as she suspected or her plan might be made to fail. "I feel so . . . dirty. I was wondering if there was somewhere I could take a shower."

Dr. Finch hesitated. "I'm not sure. The bounty hunters have a locker room, but I think it's only for the men."

"Oh, well . . . maybe I could shower there?" Emma leaned closer to the doctor, until the curve of her breast nearly touched his arm. "You could watch, make sure no one came in and that I didn't fall down or anything. I mean, you're a doctor, so it would be okay for you to see me naked, right?"

Finally, the familiar glimmer of lust crept into the doc's pale blue eyes. He nodded and hurried to set down his coffee. "Of course. That would be fine. Come with me—I'll show you the way to the locker room."

Emma smiled and took the arm he offered, leaning on him as he led her past Douglas's desk. Thankfully, the young man was busy on the phone and didn't seem to think anything of the doctor leading his charge down the hall. Perfect. Now all she had to find was a way to ditch the doc and—

The women's restroom. It was on the right side of the building and would allow her to escape onto the street instead of into the river. Now if only she'd get lucky and the lav had a window.

"I need to use the bathroom before I shower," Emma said, untangling her arm from the doctor's, shaking off his warm, papery hands. "I'll be right back."

She slipped away into the bathroom before he could say a word, sending up a silent shout of victory as she spied the window on the opposite side of the room. The lock twisted easily. The window itself took a little shoving—the wood swollen from the summer heat—but it finally gave with a small groan. Emma popped the screen out with a few well-placed punches and was easing out of the window on her belly seconds later.

All told, she'd been in the bathroom less than two minutes. She hoped that meant she had at least another five or ten before the doctor came looking for her and realized she was gone.

She hated to sneak out on the Contis, but she couldn't just lie on the couch. She had never been good at letting other people take care of her business. She needed to start figuring her way out of this mess, but first she had to get that shower. The doctor had wiped away some of the spark, but her skin still glittered in the bright morning light. She couldn't afford to attract that kind of attention, especially since she couldn't be sure the police weren't already looking for her.

Her apartment was out of the question, but Sam and Jace's place wasn't too far away. Surely the Death Ministry hadn't been able to find out where her family lived so easily . . . though it certainly hadn't taken long for them to find her and Ginger's place.

Emma sighed and hurried through the maze of streets, picking her way around the ruins toward the west side of Southie. Safe or not, she was going to have to take a chance on Sam's place. She had no money, no earbud to call anyone, and very few options. Besides, if she was going to break and enter, she preferred it be someplace where she was fairly sure the occupants weren't going to press charges for the damage.

CHAPTER EIGHT

*T*hirty minutes later, a freshly showered Emma stepped out of Sam's apartment building wearing a borrowed pair of jeans—with a hundred borrowed dollars tucked in the front pocket—and a short-sleeved white button-up shirt. The shirt was more feminine than anything she'd worn in years, and the jeans about three inches too short, but she'd stuffed them inside her boots, added one of Jace's thick black belts, and pulled together an outfit that was nice and plain and hopefully wouldn't attract attention.

Outside, the summer day was picking up steam, but the wind still felt cool as it blew through her damp hair.

God, it was hard to believe it was barely eight in the morning. She felt like she'd lived three days in the past few hours. Still, she wasn't sleepy. Once the last of the sluggishness left her limbs, she'd felt energized, sharp, the way she usually felt after a feeding.

That sharpness had convinced her that she had to go back to

her apartment and take another look around. Her gut was telling her she'd missed something in her first, messed-up stagger through the wreckage. It still seemed odd that nothing of value had been taken. She would have thought that even the Death Ministry would take the television. The men at the top of the gang were rich thugs, but the younger men, like Greg, lived in slums inside the ruins until they'd gained sufficient status in the organization. Surely a guy like that wouldn't pass up a free television. But then, the police wouldn't trash her place without a warrant, so who else could it be?

The only thing she could think of was that Ginger was on someone's shit list. But whose? Maybe an old boyfriend? Or the wife of one of the married men she occasionally messed around with at the bar?

Unfortunately, Emma had no way of finding out anything from Ginger. Ginger still wasn't answering her bud. She'd tried to reach her roommate twice on the wall phone at Sam's.

She'd also sent Andre a message from Sam's home computer, letting him know where she was headed.

Like it or not, she and Andre were in this together. He'd made that call when he urged her to keep Little Francis out of the loop. Besides, she couldn't deny that she wanted to see him again, wanted to try to convince him that she hadn't been lying about the drugs.

Looked like she'd get the chance sooner than she'd expected.

Half a block away, a tall, handsome man in a ridiculously expensive suit lounged outside Good Stuff market, looking as out of place on this side of the barricade as ever. She should have realized that Andre was smart enough to figure out which direction she'd be coming from and head her off at the pass, but still . . . it was surprising to see him leaning against the brick near the market's recycling machine, looking as pulled together as he had a few hours ago, despite the chaotic events of the morning.

Emma cocked her head, taking him in as she closed the distance between them. Damn, but the way he wore fancy clothes was almost enough to make her reconsider her definition of wasteful spending. Was it really wasteful to drop a few grand on a garment that made a man look like *that*?

"Good morning. Glad to see you got the dust off your suit," Emma said.

"You're crazy, you know that?"

"Good to see you, too."

"I'm serious. What were you thinking?" Andre's tone left little doubt how very angry he was, despite the fact that his eyes were hidden behind dark sunglasses.

Too bad it didn't get in the way of the energy that leapt between them, a spark of sexual recognition that made her acutely aware of how her borrowed jeans clung to her body. She wondered whether Andre would notice, whether he'd check out her ass the way he had when they'd left the diner.

"I see you found that shower you were looking for. You look . . . clean."

Emma smiled. Looked as if he *had* noticed. "Thanks. You look pretty, too."

Andre grunted and fell into step beside her, his shoulder brushing against hers as they threaded their way through the early morning shoppers. "Little Francis was getting ready to send a search party until I told him I'd heard from you."

"You didn't tell him we were—"

"I told him you were meeting me uptown. He assumes you're in a cab waiting to get through the barricade, so we should have a few hours," Andre said. "Not that I think it's a good idea for you to go back to your apartment."

"But you think it's a good idea for someone to go back and check things out."

"I do, but—"

"And I'm the best someone for the job. I'm the only one who will know if something's missing." Aside from Ginger, of course. *Ugh.* Ginger. Why did today have to be the day she went completely off the deep end? "So I guess you heard Ginger ran away from the people trying to take her into the safe house?"

"I did," Andre said. "Between the two of you, I think you've made Little Francis suspicious that you're keeping secrets."

"I have no idea why she ran," Emma said, willing Andre to believe her. "We don't have any secrets. At least not any shared secrets."

"Still, this is going to make telling him about your connection to the missing body a hell of a lot more complicated." Andre sighed, a weary sound that reminded her that not everyone had supernatural energy to draw upon. He'd been up since four in the morning and had carried a hundred-and-twenty-pound woman down two flights of rickety stairs. He was probably starting to feel this day in a major way. "I should have just told him everything when we—"

"No, I think you were right," Emma said, strangely tempted to smooth her hand along the tense line of Andre's shoulders.

She never wanted to touch people. Ever. Her first impulse was to keep her hands to herself, especially with people she cared about. The mark had made her wary of offering physical comfort, but she couldn't deny she wanted to reach out to Andre, to feel the strength hidden beneath his clothes, to press herself against him the way she had this morning.

That kiss . . . It had occupied far too much space in her troubled mind. But she hadn't been able to keep from remembering the way his lips moved against hers, the taste of him, the smell of him. A part of her had wished she could linger in Sam's shower, take her time moving the soap over her own body, imagining her hands were Andre's hands.

Emma cleared her throat and moved a few inches away as they walked, ignoring the way her body began to ache just thinking about the places she wanted Andre's hands.

She had to pull herself together. She didn't have time to ogle some bossy, womanizing lawyer or think about how insanely attractive she'd started to find him. Good guy or not, Andre was still the same man he'd been before.

And he wasn't interested; he'd made that clear. He didn't want to get naked with her. He wanted to check her into the nearest loony bin, or a demon drug rehab, or maybe a demon drug rehab for loonies . . . if they had such a thing.

The thought banished the last of the tingles sizzling along her skin. She had to remember this was business, life-and-death business if it turned into a street war between the Contis and the Death Ministry. She debated telling Andre her theory but decided it was best to wait until she had some sort of evidence. Obviously Andre wasn't going to believe anything just because it came out of her mouth.

"I think it's best if we try to get more information first," she said. "The fewer people in on the secret, the safer the secret." At least that's what her years with Father Paul had taught her. For the second time in less than a few hours, she longed to call the father, to hear whatever words of wisdom and criticism he cared to speak.

"True, but his younger brother is the one I contacted to do the collection this morning." Andre turned right, heading back toward her apartment. "Mikey's going to keep quiet for now, but it's understood I'll have to tell the rest of the family about this eventually."

"Maybe you won't." Emma tilted her face up to catch the sun. She might be a creature of the night most of the time, but she loved the feel of warm summer sunshine, even when it was responsible for baking the Southie garbage until the entire barricaded area smelled like rotten vegetables. "Maybe a demon ate the body and it will never turn up. Or maybe the cops found it and they'll get my fingerprints from the state database and come arrest me."

"One can always hope," Andre said, the husky note in his voice making her turn her head and catch him looking at her.

Or she assumed he was looking at her. She cursed dark glasses and fought the flustered feelings swimming around inside of her. She was Emma Quinn, a demon-marked predator—she didn't do fluster.

"Ha-ha." She turned back to look at the sidewalk, counting the squares in the cement, anything to keep her mind off the fact that Andre might be feeling the same way she was feeling—inappropriately lustful and stupidly unfocused, considering the situation they were in.

"I doubt it was the police, but even if it was . . . why would your fingerprints be in the database?" Andre asked. "Have you been taken in for public intox on an illegal substance or—"

Emma stopped and spun to face him, ignoring the frustrated grunt of the Mohawked man behind her who nearly ran her over before veering to the side with a few choice cusswords. The guy could get over it. He shouldn't have been following her so closely. She couldn't deal with Andre's calm assurance that she was a drug addict for another second.

"No, I've told you several times that I don't do drugs. My fingerprints were taken when I was admitted to the hospital when I was a baby. Along with blood samples and DNA that they used to search the public databases," Emma said, staring up at her own reflection in Andre's glasses. "The doctors were using genetic fingerprinting to see if they could track down any of my close relatives. For a while they thought I needed a kidney transplant."

"This was when you were taken from the cult?"

"No, it was a year or so after." Emma wished for the third or fourth time that she could see Andre's eyes. Not that it would really help. When he was in lawyer mode, she couldn't read a thing in those dark brown depths, and he was definitely in the mode now. His voice reeked of practiced impartiality. "I was in the hospital until I was three."

"They found a way to help you."

"I found a way to help myself," she countered. "I learned how to feed the demon mark with human life force. I—"

"Emma, I don't—"

Emma reached up and snatched Andre's glasses off his face, shocking him into silence and giving her a glimpse into the man's true thoughts. He didn't believe her, but he didn't completely *not* believe her, either. She had a chance to convince him she was telling the truth, and there was only one story she could think of that might do the job.

"It was an accident. There was a night nurse named Betty who worked the children's floor of the hospital," Emma said, willing herself to maintain control. She wasn't a person who cried often, but thinking about Betty always hit her hard, no matter how many times Father Paul had assured her that what had happened wasn't her fault. "She was so nice to all the kids, but especially to me. She'd let me sit in her lap and read me stories for hours. I . . . I really loved her. And she loved me."

Emma sucked in a deep breath and dropped her eyes to the dirty sidewalk. Thankfully, Andre stayed silent, as if he sensed the story wasn't finished.

"One day, she asked me if I wanted to be her little girl. Even though I was sick, she and her husband wanted to adopt me." Emma kept her eyes on the ground. "I remember being so excited that I turned on her lap and hugged her around her neck. My hands ended up in her hair, and . . . that was the first time the blue light came."

Andre stepped closer. "So you're saying . . ."

Emma lifted her head, a little shocked to find her lips only inches away from Andre's, troubled by how naked she felt as she looked into his eyes. "I killed her. She died of a heart attack a few hours later."

"Emma, you were just a little girl; you didn't—"

"I did," Emma said, maintaining eye contact even when the empathy in Andre's eyes made her want to turn and run. Sometimes there was nothing in the world as painful as kindness. "Right after I fed on her, I walked on my own for the first time. The man who raised me worked at the hospital and heard what had happened. He's a priest and has done a lot of research into aura demons. He's the one who figured out that I must have been marked. He took me away from the hospital a few days after Betty's death. I've never been sick a day since."

Andre shook his head, his eyebrows pulling together and his lips opening and closing at least three times before he finally spoke. "I don't know what to say."

"Say that you believe me."

"I . . . don't know if I believe you." The confusion in his tone made her want to kiss him again.

Instead, she stepped away and shoved his glasses on her own face. "Well, I guess that's a start." With a sigh, Emma turned and started back down the street. "And just for the record, I'd like to say again that I never have and never will use demon drugs. I felt fucking awful this morning."

"You looked pretty bad, too," Andre said, noticeably abstaining from any commentary on whether or not he believed her about the demon drugs, either.

"Thanks. But I don't really worry about stuff like that. Some people have more important things to do than spend half their lives primping."

"I don't spend half my life primping. Maybe a fourth, at most."

Emma snorted. "Right."

"It pays off. You should try it sometime." He nudged her arm with his elbow as they turned one last corner and her building came into view. "At least let me take you to the girl who does my eyebrow wax."

She laughed, an unexpected squawk that made Andre chuckle along with her. "Oh my god, you have your eyebrows waxed? That is so weird. Isn't that against the Conti manly man code, or something?"

"Screw the Conti manly man code. The eyebrows are the frames of the face, and look at this face." He smiled down at her, a real smile that made the corners of his eyes crinkle in a way that she found unexpectedly cute. "*Of course* I have my eyebrows waxed, Emma."

Despite the heat, a shiver whispered across her skin. There was just something about the way he said her name. "You are . . . unbelievable."

"I know." He winked and his smile took on a predatory edge that made Emma's body resume its foolish tingling. "That's what all the women tell me, anyway."

This doesn't mean anything, Emma's internal voice warned. *This man would flirt with a dog as long as it was female.*

Still, she couldn't help but smile back at him. The bastard really was *almost* irresistible.

"I moisturize, too, every day," Andre continued, playing to his grinning audience. "And exfoliate. The ladies can't get enough of this girly man stuff."

"Hmm, so I've seen." Emma debated whether to tell him she knew about his addiction, that sleeping around wasn't just recreational for him, but a compulsion he couldn't always control.

In the end, she decided to give Andre a break and a chance to believe her story before she pulled out the big guns, detailed all the things she'd seen in his mind, and forced him to believe her. After all he'd done for her, he deserved that chance. Besides, they were nearly at the door to her apartment. It was time to quit flirting and start watching out for bad guys who might have returned to the scene of the crime.

They really had been *flirting*. It was a first for Emma. She'd lured men into dark corners with a seductive look plenty of times, but she'd never laughed and teased like this before. It was . . . nice.

"You stay down here. I'll go up and make sure it's safe." Andre moved ahead of her to open the door to the apartment building. It was ajar, as usual, the dent in the metal rendering the first barrier to potential intruders completely useless.

Emma darted forward, shouldering in front of Andre, her body thrilled to be this close to him once more. "No, I'm coming, too."

"No, you're not."

"Yes, I am. You might run into someone up there and need protection."

"I brought protection," Andre said, discreetly opening one side of his suit jacket, revealing a small stun gun tucked in the inside pocket.

"You know how to use that?" Emma asked, shocked to see the weapon. She was used to seeing her sister's husband, Jace, with stun weapons and the occasional automatic, but he was a demon killer, not an exfoliating, eyebrow-waxing lawyer. Andre would probably end up stunning himself and she'd have to carry *him* down the stairs.

"I do. I worked demon bounty for about five years."

"Really?" That was . . . surprising. Maybe he'd once used those muscles for something other than flexing in front of the mirror. "I didn't know that about you."

"There are a lot of things you don't know about me, little girl."

"Not as many as you think, old man." She turned her head, lifting her chin, giving him access to her lips should he choose to take it.

Andre leaned into her, and for a breathless second Emma thought he was going to kiss her again. Instead, he shifted his head, turning his attention back to the door in his hand. Apparently his self-imposed embargo on twenty-year-old women with unplucked eyebrows still stood. Emma would have felt the snub more keenly if Andre's breath wasn't coming faster. She *was* affecting him, and it was only a matter of time until he gave under pressure.

Now she just had to decide whether she wanted to keep applying that pressure. Was she ready for a one-night stand with a man she'd be forced to see with an endless stream of other women at family dinners every Thursday?

Of course, that was assuming she wasn't killed by gang members in the next day and a half. She might not have the luxury of worrying about things like jealousy and the stupidity of taking a sex addict as her first lover. If she didn't want to die a virgin, she might need to take her persuasive efforts to another level.

"So we're agreed I'm coming inside?" she asked, watching the way the pulse in Andre's neck beat faster as her breath puffed against his throat.

He swallowed, hard, before speaking. "Fine. You can come inside, but stay behind me and get ready to run if there's trouble."

"I don't run from trouble, Andre." Emma handed him his glasses and nudged him out of the way with her hip when he tried to move in front of her. "*That's* something you should know about me."

She stepped into the cramped, moldy-smelling foyer and started up the stairs, grateful for the sunlight streaming in the door, illuminating the bottom steps. She didn't need light to climb stairs she'd trekked up and down a hundred times, but Andre would need it if he was going to stare at her ass while she did it.

She could be seconds away from a confrontation with real

criminals, and she was focused on some guy and the chances that he'd be checking out her backside instead of the potential danger ahead. It was wrong on so many levels.

But then, where Andre was concerned, Emma was starting to think she didn't care that much about being right.

CHAPTER NINE

*S*he's *crazy and young and off-limits. She's crazy and young and off-limits.*

Andre repeated the silent litany half a dozen times as he followed Emma up the stairs, but it didn't stop him from staring at her undeniably fine backside. The jeans she wore clung to every curve, tempting him, teasing him as her hips twitched back and forth with each step.

It was all he could do not to reach and grab a handful of that ass. Or maybe two handfuls. He remembered how perfectly she'd fit in his hands, how good it had been to pull her thin body against where he was thick and hard and—

Shit. This kind of thinking was an excellent way to put a tent in his damned pants. For the first time in ages, Andre wished he were wearing jeans. At least the thicker fabric would offer some help concealing the obvious evidence of his arousal.

As they reached the top of the stairs and moved down the dim hallway, Andre did his best to talk himself down, but even thinking about the story Emma had told him in the street didn't help. He still didn't believe in her "power" or that she'd accidentally killed the woman who'd wanted to adopt her, but he believed that Emma thought she was telling the truth. The pain in her eyes had been real. It had made him want to pull her into his arms and hold her, whisper into her hair that everything would be okay, that *he* would make everything okay.

But he hadn't. Emma didn't want comfort; she wanted his faith and trust—two things he hadn't given anyone but family for too long to remember.

The optimist in him wanted to believe that Emma had really made the choice never to use again, but they could never be just good family friends. The attraction between them was already too strong and was getting worse with prolonged exposure. He was starting to think it was cute that she didn't wear makeup, that she was beautiful in a fresh, natural way he'd been stupid not to appreciate before. And talking to her was so easy, like goofing with his cousins, but with an undertone of sexual tension that drove him crazy.

Even when she was telling him things he didn't want to hear, he couldn't help but be drawn to her. This tough girl had captivated him in a way none of the models or society darlings he'd dated had come close to. He could develop real feelings for her in a short amount of time. If he allowed it.

But he wouldn't. Not now, maybe not ever.

The only way he kept his life running smoothly was by not getting attached to the women he bedded. It was sex, pure and simple.

The more intimate things got, the more likely someone would get hurt. Maybe one of the women, maybe him. Even if he was capable of falling in love again, he didn't know whether he'd be able to stop sleeping with other women. It was a compulsion, an irresistible drive, a monkey on his back that hadn't responded well to attempts at therapy.

Emma deserved better than that. If they were together, he wouldn't want it to be a one-night stand, but he could tell she wasn't the type to stay with a man who slept around. In the end, one or both of them would end up hurt.

By the time they reached the door to Emma and Ginger's apartment, Andre had revived his flagging resolve, at least enough to refrain from staring at Emma's butt as she cursed and strode across the trashed living room.

"Shit. Someone's been here. The television's gone, and the box." She stomped a booted heel on the floor and cussed again before spinning around and crossing to one of the bedrooms. "And Ginger's boots are all gone." She spun around, hands pressed to her face. "She's going to lose it! Half her life savings was invested in those stupid boots. We should have closed the door on the way out."

"You were a little incapacitated," Andre said, picking his way across the broken glass littering the floor.

"Okay, so *you* should have closed the door on the way out." Emma propped her hands on her hips and pinned him with an accusing glare.

"The wood near the handle's busted. It wouldn't have done any good." Andre stopped a few feet away, having had enough experience with the women in his family to know it was best to give an angry female her space. "Besides, I didn't think there was anything in here to steal. Don't most people have their own crappy TV?"

"Our TV wasn't crappy. It was a flat screen."

Andre grunted. "A thirty-year-old flat screen that probably has the picture quality of—"

"So what?" she asked, stepping closer and kicking at one of the many books lying on the floor. "Not everyone can afford zillion-dollar electronics or trillion-dollar suits."

"I have never paid a trillion dollars for anything," Andre said in a light tone, "and zillion isn't a real number."

"I don't care if it's a real number. You know what I mean."

"I do. Point taken. Now can we move on to more—"

"Is it really? Is the point really taken?" she asked, her voice rising. "Do you even understand what I'm—"

"Oh, please, give me a break with the teenage angst."

"I am not a teenager!" she shouted. "And this is not angst; it is anger."

"Fine. I'll pay to have everything replaced," he shouted back. "I'm sure I can do so for a tiny, minuscule fraction of a zillion dollars. Does that make you feel better?"

She crossed her arms and the frown remained on her face, but at least her volume level was significantly lower when she spoke again. "No, it doesn't."

"Then what do you want?" Andre asked, struggling to be patient.

Emma's frown faltered, and uncertainty crept into her eyes. "I want this not to have happened." She sighed, looking as overwhelmed as she probably felt. Her arms fell limply to her sides. Poor kid. She had every right to be angry and scared, and he hadn't done much to help alleviate those feelings. "Aside from that, I want to know that my roommate is okay."

"We'll figure that out. Don't worry." Andre stepped closer, unable to resist the urge to offer some kind of comfort. He reached out and took her cool hand, squeezing it between both of his own.

"And who took the dead guy from the alley."

"We'll find that out, too."

"And who trashed my apartment," she said, curling her fingers around his hand.

"Ditto."

"And who came back and stole my television," she said, looking up at him with those amazing eyes that made his chest ache for inexplicable reasons. "And why you think it's such a bad idea to kiss me."

Damn. She'd gone there, and now he had no choice but to stare at her full lips, to imagine how amazing it would be to taste her again. "Emma, I told you—"

"Shut up," she whispered. "I don't want to hear it."

And then she kissed him, without hesitation or uncertainty, with a passion that gave him no choice but to kiss her back.

His arms went around her, hands finding that delicious ass and molding it with his fingers as he pulled her close, angling his head, opening his mouth, and welcoming the sweet slip of her tongue between his lips. She tasted vaguely minty again, but beneath that was the taste of Emma, the bright, fresh, compelling taste of this woman who made his body come alive in a way it hadn't in years.

He'd had so many women, so many different ways, that he'd been certain that overwhelming sexual thrill he'd felt when he was a younger man was a thing he'd never recapture. Sex still felt damned good, but it didn't knock him off his feet, didn't make his blood rush so fast his heart had to work to catch up.

But kissing Emma, feeling her slim arms twine around his neck and her hips push forward to rub against where his hard-on had returned with a vengeance, made him feel like he was sixteen again. He was breathless and dizzy, consumed with need and overwhelmed with longing, not certain whether he'd survive to get his clothes off and his cock sunk deep inside that hot, seductive place where he was dying to be.

"Emma," he groaned into her mouth as one of her legs wrapped around his hips, not knowing whether he was asking for permission to continue or help in stopping before this went any further, only knowing he loved the sound of her name.

"Touch me," she said as she circled her hips, grinding against his cock. "Touch me everywhere. I want to—"

Her words ended in a moan as he slid one hand up to cup her breast, teasing her nipple through the thin fabric of her shirt. Andre rolled the tight tip between finger and thumb as he kissed his way down her throat, reveling in the light scent of soap clinging to her warm skin, nipping at her shoulder as he transferred his hands to the buttons of her shirt.

Screw his honorable thoughts and realistic fears. He wanted this woman. He wanted his lips on her breasts, her tight nipple in his mouth; he wanted—

"There's somebody here—run!" The harsh whisper came from the open front door. He and Emma leapt apart, as if they were the ones who'd been caught stealing.

Seconds later, footsteps thundered down the hall.

Emma clutched her shirt together and ran to the doorway. "Hey! Come back here! I want to talk to you!"

Andre rushed after her, grabbing her around the waist and tugging her back inside the apartment. "What the hell are you thinking? You don't go running after a bunch of men who—"

"They're not men. I bet they're some of the kids who hang out down the street by the liquor store." Emma cursed but didn't pull away from him. Instead, she leaned closer, softening a bit as her hands moved to rest on his arms. "I thought they might know something about who did this, but they probably just heard the word on the street. An unlocked apartment with stuff still inside is big news around here."

"I bet." Andre refrained from making another crack about the worthlessness of most of the junk still left in the apartment. This was her place, after all, and she must find at least some of these things valuable.

"I'm amazed there's anything still left. Even the books—" She broke off and her eyes widened before she pulled away from him and hurried over to the bookshelves in the far corner of the room.

"What's up?" Andre asked, following her.

"The books." Emma knelt and began sorting through the torn pages covering the ground. "Why would someone tear the pages out?"

"Um . . . because they enjoy destroying property?"

"Maybe . . ." But Emma didn't sound convinced. She intensified her efforts, pulling out the books that remained and piling them on the floor.

"Maybe they resent your refusal to make the transition to digital like everyone else," he said, squatting beside her, a part of him wanting to bring up the kiss they'd just shared. Instead, he made another joke. It never paid to be the first one to start talking. "Or maybe they never learned to read?"

"Hmm . . ."

"And they're bitter about it, and find book ripping cathartic."

"You're funny," she said with a sigh.

"Then why aren't you laughing?"

"Because not all the books are here." The eyes she lifted to his were genuinely troubled.

Who would have guessed Emma would be so into old books? In an age where almost everyone used some sort of digital reader, it was unexpected and rather . . . adorable. He was finding a lot of things about this tough girl adorable, not the least of which was that adorable ass, that ass he might have had out of those tight jeans given a few more minutes.

It was a good thing they'd been interrupted. Once the heat of the moment had passed, he still didn't think sleeping with Emma was a good idea . . . did he?

"Some of the books are missing. Some of *my* books are missing."

Andre struggled to keep his thoughts on books, not more flesh-and-blood matters. "Thugs who steal books. That's . . . odd."

"That's *bad*. They took the books on translating demon lexicon." She stood and drove her fingers through her hair. "But I have a feeling they didn't find the book they were looking for."

"What do you mean?"

"I have a demon grimoire," she said, pacing around the room, glancing down at the few remaining books she hadn't checked yet. "It's an ancient text on aura demons and demon marks. It has spells in it, too. Ezra used it to help him summon the demons last spring."

Andre sighed. So they were back to the invisible demons. Again. Just when he'd started to hope Emma was a seminormal woman with a love for reading.

"I should have destroyed the fucking thing. I should have known better. Now Ginger's probably in danger. If Ginger even has the book." Emma's voice rose as her obvious panic increased. "What if someone else has it already? What if someone stole it from the pub?"

"What? Why would—"

"None of the artifacts on the wall were stolen, but what if they weren't after artifacts or money? What if they were after that book the entire time?" She froze for a second, her nose and eyebrows wrinkling into what he assumed was her thinking face.

She looked a little like a pug dog, which he also found strangely adorable. This was not good. *At all.* He didn't do adorable. Sexy, yes. Adorable, no. Finding someone adorable led to adoring them, which led to a depth of feeling he wasn't ready to approach at the moment.

"But then, they wouldn't have trashed the apartment if they already had the book," she continued. "Unless there's more than one person looking for it. But that—"

"Emma, hold on." Andre angled his body in front of hers. "Calm down for a second. I can't help you if I don't understand what you're talking about. And I'll admit it, I'm lost."

She took a deep breath. "My purse. I had my purse in the safe at the pub. The book was in my purse. I thought Ginger had taken it home for me, but it looks like she never came home, and I can't get in touch with her."

"And she ran off instead of coming to the safe house," Andre said, silently admitting that the chain of events seemed strange.

"Right!" Something sparked in Emma's eyes. "I bet she didn't know that those men who came for—"

"Women. Little Francis sent two women to meet her."

"Still, I bet she didn't know they were Conti people. What if she thought they were someone else? People who were trying to get her?"

"But they're not after her; they're after your purse?"

"The *spell book* that's in my purse."

"Okay, so assume you're right and some nut job wants this magic book," Andre said, doing his best to keep his tone neutral. "Why would they go after Ginger? Wouldn't they assume you have the book?"

"Not if they'd already searched my apartment and found it wasn't here." Emma paused, her tongue darting out to dampen her lips as she thought. "And not if they had seen me this morning."

"What do you mean?"

"I mean, I don't have a purse or a pocket big enough to hold a book." She gestured down at herself, drawing his attention to the fact that her top two buttons were still undone. If he leaned forward the slightest bit, he'd be able to see the lace of her bra. Somehow, he managed to resist the urge. "So if someone were following me, they'd know I don't have it."

No matter how unlikely, the thought still made Andre's jaw clench. He didn't like the idea that someone was following Emma, spying on her, hoping to steal from her.

"I have to try to call Ginger again. Could I use your bud?" Emma asked. "Our wall phone was broken when we moved in."

"I'll call her for you. I programmed it into my bud this morning after I met with Little Francis, just in case we needed it again," Andre said, ordering his phone to call Ginger Spatz.

He wasn't going to tell Emma that he had another Ginger programmed into his bud. Or two other Emmas, for that matter. He was suddenly feeling more ashamed of his collection of numbers than usual.

"She's not answering?" Emma asked.

"No . . . and no voice mail."

"Shit! What if they've got her? Or what if they killed her and—"

"Emma, relax. Who is 'they'?" He reached for her, but she danced a few steps away, nearly tripping over the ruined couch. "You're blowing this theory out of pro—"

"Don't talk to me like I'm crazy!"

"I'm just saying you shouldn't get ahead of yourself," he said. "Right now, the only 'they' you have to worry about are the Death Ministry members who think you had something to do with their friend's disappearance."

For a second she looked ready to blow, but then her arms fell to her sides. "You're right. I do need to worry about that."

"As well as who really took that body."

She nodded slowly. "Right . . . and how all these events are related. Because they *have* to be related."

"They do?"

"Yes. It can't just be a coincidence that a dead body disappears, my apartment is trashed by people looking for my grimoire—"

"You don't know that for—"

"And that my roommate is on the run for her life," Emma continued, ignoring his attempts at reason.

"Ginger could be fine," he said, the lawyer in him determined to show her the holes in her logic. "What if she's just wasted and confused? What if your spell book was stolen by one of the people who came to loot the apartment after—"

"It wasn't stolen. It was in my purse. If you'd been listening, you would remember that." Without further commentary, she headed toward the door.

"Jesus Christ," Andre whispered under his breath as he followed her. "Emma, where are you going?"

"Out to look for Ginger."

"But you have no idea where—"

"She was uptown a few hours ago. I'll find her."

"But what about the Death Ministry?" Andre asked, grabbing her arm just before she reached the door. "What about—"

"They can wait."

"Right. I'm sure they'll be fine with—" She twisted from his grasp and disappeared into the darkened hall. "Emma! Damn it!" Andre leaned out the door, calling after her. "Do you want me to try to lock the damned door this time?"

"I don't have a key," she threw over her shoulder.

"So the key on this nail is—"

"What?" Her footsteps grew louder as she hurried back to where he stood. "What key?"

"This one." Andre pointed to the small blue key hanging on the nail next to the door.

She stared at the wall before shaking her head slowly. "That's not mine. Or Ginger's."

Andre paused. Her conspiracy theory still seemed far-fetched, but why would someone break into her apartment, trash the place, leave the few valuables, but place a key on the nail near the door

ANNA J. EVANS

before they left? It was . . . suspicious, to say the least. "Was it here before?"

"I don't know. I don't remember." Emma grabbed it and turned it over. "St. Anthony's. Number 127."

"There's a church with a homeless shelter called St. Anthony's."

"And I bet they have old-fashioned lockers with keys," Emma said, looking up at him. "You want to go check it out?"

"I don't know. This seems . . . off."

"Like a trap?"

"I wasn't going to go there," he said, "but yes, I suppose it could be a trap."

"Or maybe Ginger came back and left it."

"Maybe."

"Either way, we've got nothing else to go on."

"You were ready to leave me a second ago," he said, leaning closer, sneaking that peek down her shirt he'd nobly abstained from a moment before. He just couldn't help himself. For all her crazy talk, Emma was smart and brave—the combo turned him on more than he would have dreamed possible.

"I wasn't going to leave." She shrugged and her eyes drifted down to his lips, giving him hope that he wasn't the only one affected by the chemistry between them. "I was just mad. I was going to wait for you at the bottom of the stairs."

"You were?"

"Yeah. Like it or not, I need you."

"So do you?" He cocked his head, smiling his signature grin. "*Like* needing me?"

She shook her head, but he saw the slight curve at the edge of her lips. "I like it all right. So far. But right now I've got shit to do." She held the key up between them. "So are you coming or not?"

"Why don't we head back to the Conti offices and get Douglas to search the police database first, see if they're looking for anyone matching your description. That way we could rule out the possibility that Greg's body is down at the county morgue, and then we—"

"Why don't we call Douglas and have him do that while we're on our way to the homeless shelter? That way, we kill two stones with one bird."

He laughed. "Isn't that two birds with one stone?"

"Does it really matter?" she asked, poking him in the chest with her key. "*Two* things are dead from throwing *one* thing. I think I've made my point."

"I really like you," Andre said, shocking himself and Emma. Two birds with one stone, indeed.

She actually blushed pink before blowing air through her lips hard enough to make them vibrate. "You're okay. Better than I thought."

"Better in what way? In the—"

"Oh, just shut up and come on." She turned and stormed down the hall once more, leaving Andre to follow, strangely pleased by the fact that he'd made Emma blush.

CHAPTER TEN

S t. Anthony's gray stone facade was crumbling and in need of a good deal of repair, but there was a certain nobility to the way the church shrugged its way out onto the street, forcing everyone who passed to take notice of its last remaining stained-glass window. The collection of panes was twenty feet wide and nearly as tall, depicting Jesus washing the feet of the disciples.

It was beautiful . . . haunting.

Emma had been raised Catholic—Father Paul was serious about all of the kids in his house dragging their butts to Mass at least once a week—but she'd never been sure what she believed as far as the spiritual realm was concerned. She knew there was supernatural evil in the world, so it made sense that there was also supernatural good.

But was that supernatural good God . . . or something else? And no matter what or who it was, would it ever truly listen to her, a person marked by demonic evil?

"Are you sure you want to go in here?" Andre asked. "I imagine it's going to be a rough crowd."

"You'd be surprised." Emma led the way around the church, headed toward the back entrance where a sign urged people in need of a meal or a bed to check in with the volunteer on duty. "At the Lutheran shelter where I stayed last spring, there were some really great people. Even some families with little kids."

"You stayed at a shelter?"

"I did. For a couple days. It was either that or the street."

"Wow. That's . . . tough," Andre said, with that look of genuine concern that was still so new to her. She'd never seen Andre be genuine about much of anything. But something had changed between them in the past few hours, something that drew her to him just as powerfully as the physical attraction simmering between them.

Physical attraction. God, his kiss, his hands on her breasts, making her feel things she'd never dreamed she could feel. The need pumping through her veins had been even more intense than it had been the first time they'd touched.

It had left her wanting more. And more and more and more, until it was hard to look at Andre without plotting ways for them to be alone. She was past ready to see what else she'd been missing— and not willing to wait much longer. She'd waited long enough, and who knew how much time she had left.

If someone had found the spell book, her life could be in danger again. Most of the serious spells in the grimoire required the aid of a person marked by aura demons. Not just anyone could pick up the book and start casting—even if they could properly translate and pronounce the demon lexicon. They would need Emma or someone like her.

Should they come for *her*, she would have options—refuse to help them the way she'd refused Ezra, or take a chance and attempt to use her curse as a weapon. One of the spells she'd been translating talked about casting out the demon hunger onto one's enemies until the "unmarked perished from the inability to feed." But honestly, she wasn't sure even a life-or-death situation could tempt her to speak any of the grimoire's words out loud.

What if she wasn't translating the spell correctly? She feared becoming something worse than she was already—like the monster her brother Stephen had been at the end—too much to take the chance. Dying would be preferable to becoming something even closer to demon than human.

Emma shuddered but forced a tight smile for the men hanging out near the back entrance, smoking hand-rolled cigarettes that smelled like they contained something other than pure tobacco. The poor could get the ashes left over from burning Inuago demon pellets for a few dollars per ounce. The high wasn't nearly as strong and was especially hard on the liver, but it was far cheaper than a shot of whiskey.

Just the thought of demon drugs made Emma's stomach roll. She held her breath until she and Andre reached the door.

"Let me do the talking, okay?" Emma asked as Andre held open the heavy glass and let her pass. "You're too lawyery."

"I'm not too lawyery."

"Okay, fine, then you're too mobby," she said, stepping into the warm, clammy lobby . . . if you could call it that.

It was certainly nothing fancy. A dilapidated green couch squatted in a corner, three sets of double doors—one on each wall—led to destinations unknown, and a yellowed sliding-glass window offered a view into a small office space with desks crammed together and a half dozen wall phones packed haphazardly behind the woman working the desk.

The walls of the space were flat beige, and the tile looked like it hadn't been replaced since the demon emergence. Great cracks slithered beneath their feet, letting in tufts of something black and fibrous. Probably the source of the moldy smell lingering beneath the pungent aroma of grilled onions coming from the dining hall.

"Sometimes mobby gets answers." Andre wrinkled his nose at the tile.

"Let's try friendly person from the neighborhood first. If that doesn't work, you can go mobby," Emma whispered as she got in line behind a man and a woman signing up for meal vouchers.

"Goody," Andre said, making her smile despite the smell of days' old dried sweat clinging to the man in front of her.

The man snagged his voucher and made way for his companion to sign for hers. It was only nine thirty, so they must be after breakfast. Emma's stomach growled at the thought. It had been a long time since she'd eaten . . . well, eaten *food*, at least. Her supernatural fix would tide her over for a time, but she'd eventually need something real as well.

"You want to get something to eat after this?" Emma asked. "Eggs maybe?"

"Are you asking me out?"

She snorted. "I'm asking if you want to eat eggs," she said, willing herself not to blush. This blushing and flirting and tingling was all so *distracting*. How did the average woman make it through years of this mating-dance business?

"Yes, I'll eat eggs with you." His grin made her think he'd

guessed how he affected her and was rather enjoying the mating dance. "But we're going someplace clean. The Southie filth isn't working for me."

The woman in front of Andre, whose face and hands were spotless despite the fact that her clothes had clearly been worn for several days, turned and shot him a look that would have killed a lesser man. Even Andre shrunk inside his suit and guiltily dropped his eyes to the floor.

Emma waited until the man and woman had disappeared into the dining hall before muttering to Andre beneath her breath. "Good work. Way to bond with the people."

"Sorry," Andre whispered, seeming ashamed to have been so thoughtless. Maybe there was hope for this man yet. He wasn't nearly as snobby and elitist as she'd assumed.

"Can I help you?" The dark-skinned woman behind the desk sported even darker bags beneath her eyes. She was wrapped in a purple crochet sweater despite the summer heat creeping into the windowless room. Just looking at her made Emma start sweating.

"I found this. I think it's for one of your lockers here," she said, pulling the key from her front pocket. "I was wondering if you could help me return it to whoever had it last?"

The woman held out a gray palm. "I'll take it and figure out who—"

"Actually, we're going to need to take a look inside the locker and get copies of any paperwork that will identify who used it recently." Andre moved to stand beside her.

"I can't do that. Our records are—"

"This key was found at a crime scene," Andre said in his mobbiest, most lawyery voice. "It won't be hard to get a warrant to search the locker, but then I'd have to bring the police into this, and why inconvenience us all like that?"

So much for letting her take the lead. But she should have known better. Andre wasn't very good at taking orders. It was frustrating, but it was also one of the things she respected about him. She was finding that the man had several admirable traits. He was dedicated, smart, and compassionate, and he knew his business. Add all that to the fact that he knew his way around a firearm, and it was almost enough to make up for the womanizing and the eyebrow waxing.

Almost.

"Can't we work something out without involving the authorities?" Andre asked.

The woman sighed, obviously not thrilled with the idea of policemen roaming around the shelter. She was in the business of helping people who were—on the whole—as scared of the police as they were of the gang members who ruled the Southie streets after dark. Bringing in the police would dramatically impact her ability to provide food and shelter to people who needed them.

In the end, her concern for her people won out over her need to follow the rules.

"I can let you look inside this locker. *If* the key works, which a lot of times they don't," she said. "But you'll be supervised by one of our staff, and none of the contents of the locker can be removed without a warrant. You got that?"

"I got it." Andre smiled his lady-killer grin, but the woman didn't seem amused.

"Stewart!" she yelled over her shoulder, summoning a thin young man from the desk behind her. Stewart wore thick glasses that looked at least half a century old and had skin so dark it made his faded black T-shirt look gray. "Take these two back to the lockers and let them try their key. Don't let 'em take anything."

Stewart nodded a little too long before jerking his head toward Emma and Andre. He ambled out the narrow door to the office and over to the double doors on the left wall. Emma followed with Andre close behind her as they entered a short hall and approached a second set of doors. Stewart paused in front of them, fiddling with a ring of keys on his belt. His hands trembled as he chose the appropriate key. It took several tries before he managed to slide it into the lock and give it a double turn to the right.

His unsteadiness made her think of one of the girls Father Paul brought back to the halfway house a few years before Emma ran away. Her demon mark had made her tremble all over, like a Chihuahua left out in the snow. The only thing that could calm her down was skin-to-skin contact with other marked people.

Needless to say, she'd been really popular with the boys at the house, despite the fact that she was barely sixteen. Emma had tried not to judge, but a part of her had hated the girl out of simple jealousy. In her heart, Emma believed she'd die a virgin. She never thought she'd be interested in sex. Even if her own mark hadn't made intimacy dangerous to others, the horrors she'd seen in other people's minds would have turned her off to the idea of getting naked with a man.

But for some reason, touching Andre didn't bring back any of those stolen memories. He made her feel safe in a wild, erotic, out-of-control sort of way. But could she really afford to let herself get any more out of control than she had already?

Under normal circumstances, she had to position her fingertips at the base of her victim's skull in order to feed, but she'd fed with her hands in other positions once or twice. Sometimes the dark craving didn't want to wait for its next meal. What if that happened while she was with Andre? What if she accidentally fed on him? Even if she only took a little of his life, it would be too much. He was a good guy, maybe even a great one, and didn't deserve to lose a single day to her demon mark.

But then . . . she could always make sure she didn't touch him with her hands. There were positions where her hands would be sure to be busy elsewhere.

Holy Moses, she was thinking about *positions*. She really wanted to go through with this. With Andre . . . assuming neither of them was killed first.

"This way, all the way to the back. Don't touch anything." Stewart motioned for them to enter a large, cavernous room Emma guessed had once been a sanctuary.

It was filled to capacity with twin-sized cots instead of rows of benches. Some of the beds were perfectly made with clean, white sheets and faded blue blankets, but most were piled with scruffy backpacks, duffel bags, and assorted clothes items. It brought home how very many people had no place to call their own and made Emma grateful for her grungy little apartment. Even decades after the demon emergence, there were still families who hadn't recovered from the losses they'd suffered. Second and third generations scrabbled to rebuild their lives in the shadows of the ruins that had changed their lives forever.

"We're looking for number 127," Andre said as they moved into a smaller room lined with lockers on every side, and more down a hallway to the right.

There were hundreds of them, far more lockers than there were beds for people to sleep in. But some of those beds were probably sleeping more than one—Emma had seen as many as three small children curl up close to their mother for the night. And some of those using the shelter left their belongings in storage. It was easier than bringing everything onto the streets when their seven-day bed pass expired and they had to clear out for a week before applying for another.

"This way," Stewart said, leading them down the hall, past entrances to the men's and women's changing rooms before stopping at number 127.

"Let me open it." Andre plucked the key from her hand before she could fit it in the lock. "Just in case."

"In case of what? In case a bunch of snakes jump out and try to eat my face?"

Andre moved her firmly behind him, next to where Stewart leaned against the wall opposite the locker. "Yes. In case of face-eating snakes. Better my face than yours. You're younger and prettier."

Emma crossed her arms and rolled her eyes, trying and failing to pretend she didn't enjoy hearing that Andre thought she was pretty. Thankfully, Andre had the locker open seconds later, giving her something else to think about.

"It's empty," she said, a part of her wanting to kick the damn thing. How could it be empty? What the hell was going on?

"It is. I was thinking it might be." Andre stood and handed the key back to Stewart. "We won't be needing this, but we will be needing the records of the last several people who checked out this key."

"Sure thing." Stewart started back down the hall, followed by Andre and then Emma. Of the three, she was apparently the only one frustrated by their wild-goose chase.

"Why did you think it would be empty?" she asked, giving the scuffed wall a kick or two as they walked, venting her frustration.

"Well . . . if your crazy theory isn't crazy, the person after your book probably wants to talk to you pretty badly. If they haven't figured out that Ginger has what they're looking for, they're going to think you can tell them where it is."

Emma bit her lip for a second, realizing the truth in Andre's words. "Even if they found Ginger and have the book, they're probably going to want to 'talk' to me. They'll need someone with a demon mark to help them perform most of the spells," Emma said, continuing despite Andre's grunt at the word *spell*. "There aren't that many of us around."

"And why's that?"

"Most of us die young. I would have died if I hadn't figured out how to feed myself when I was little. I probably still would have died after that if Father Paul hadn't taken me away from the hospital and kept me safe." Emma lowered her voice as they entered the big room and the stained-glass window they'd seen from the opposite side of the church came into view. She hadn't noticed it on the way through, but now her eyes were drawn to the way the bright colors made the humble beds beneath seem both sad and beautiful at the same time. "My parents' cult was destroyed, but there are thousands of demon cults out there and more of them forming every day. A lot of people think it's part of the buildup to the final battle between good and evil."

"Armageddon?" Andre asked.

"Maybe. That's what the man who raised me thought. 'First Timothy, chapter four, verse one: In later times some will abandon the faith and follow deceiving spirits and things taught by demons.'"

"You quote Bible verses." Andre shot her a look of surprise out of the corner of his eyes. "My mother would love you."

"Mary already loves me. She always gives me extra garlic bread."

"That's right." He smiled, as if pleased by the fact that she and his mom got along.

"She's Catholic?"

"She is and a big believer." He sighed as they stopped, waiting for Stewart to open the locked doors once more.

As he bent over, Emma caught the slight shimmer of gold lingering behind the man's ears, stuck to the arms of his glasses. Hamma claws . . . That's what was making Stewart tremble. He was probably starting to go into withdrawal. It happened with users who'd been on the stuff for years.

Still . . . it was strange to see a man like Stewart sparking. Hamma wasn't cheap, and the man couldn't even afford basic laser eye surgery, which had become cheaper than most bicycles.

"But she also talks to her houseplants and thinks they talk back," Andre said, "so you have to take that into account."

Emma edged closer to Stewart, continuing to talk to Andre. "But you seem to get along well." Yep, that was definitely gold dust. She backed away as Stewart opened the door and led them back into the lobby.

"I love my mother." The tightness in his tone hinted that his family wasn't as perfect as it seemed. "But sometimes I think I'm a disappointment. She really wanted grandchildren."

"Kids aren't in the picture for you, huh?"

"Nope. What about you?"

"Me?" she asked, shocked that he'd even ask. "Of course not . . . I . . . No, I've never even thought about it."

"Because you're still a kid," he said.

"I am not. I—"

"It will take some time to look up those records." Stewart interrupted before she could finish her protest. "You want to come back in an hour or so? There's a coffee stand at the next corner."

"Sure, no problem," Andre said, leading the way to the door. Emma followed him out into the bright light, but not without a final look back over her shoulder at old Stewart.

He was standing there, trembling, watching them leave. When he caught Emma's eyes, he turned and hurried back through the narrow door into the office, but it was too late. Her instincts were screaming that Stewart knew more about that locker than he was letting on. And that he might just feed that Hamma habit with Death Ministry drugs.

Maybe the gang did have something to do with this, after all. But what?

She had a feeling she'd be able to find out . . . but only if she ditched her escort. Whoever wanted her at the homeless shelter, they'd wanted her here alone. Emma knew it wasn't the smartest idea to go back by herself, but she couldn't see that she had a choice.

She needed to know what was going on. Sooner rather than later.

Besides, she wasn't going to be stupid. She'd make sure she went in armed and dangerous, equipped with her demon mark and something a little more conventional if her pickpocket skills were still up to snuff. She hated to steal from Andre, but then . . . was it really stealing if you intended to give what you were taking back at the earliest convenience?

Emma hoped Andre wouldn't have the chance to consider that question. After all, how long could it take to get the information she needed from Stewart when she was holding him at gunpoint?

CHAPTER ELEVEN

*T*here had been times when a line for coffee fifteen people deep would have sent Emma into a state of abject despair. Today, the tour bus that had just finished its morning trip through the ruins, dumping a load of caffeine-deprived tourists near the coffee kiosk, was the bit of luck she'd been hoping for.

"I'm not going to make it through this line," Emma said, crossing her arms and looking anxiously up and down the street. "I'm going back to the Laundromat to find a bathroom."

"I'll come with you. I like to watch women pee."

Emma laughed despite herself. "You're sick."

"I'm kidding. Let's go. I—"

"No, you'll lose our place in line." She stopped him with a hand on his chest that she almost immediately moved away. Even that small connection made her self-conscious, aware of all the other ways she wanted to touch him. "And I'm a big girl. I can make potty all by myself."

"I don't want you going anywhere alone," he said, humor fading from his expression. "Just in case."

Emma's conscience pinged, but she ignored it. "It's just the end of the block. You can see it from here. Stay. Get me a triple shot of espresso with three sugars and a sandwich with lots of meat."

"A triple shot? Are you sure your body can handle that much caffeine?"

"My body can handle lots of things," she said, leaning in to give Andre a good-bye hug that seemed to shock him.

He was so surprised, he didn't notice that she'd slipped the stun gun from his suit pocket and eased it down to a not-so-great hiding place on the outside of her thigh. Thankfully, none of the tourists surrounding them noticed that she'd pulled a gun, either. Of course, they'd all been lured into a false sense of security by the shiny brochures and Southie maps handed out by their tour guide. They probably had no idea there was a major gang stronghold a few blocks away or that demon drugs were being sold out of the basement of the souvenir shop across the street.

Still, shocked by her hug or not, Andre was smiling as she turned to go, pleased with the unexpected intimacy. He looked almost sweet when he smiled like that. It made it harder to shove her stolen weapon down the front of her jeans with one hand as she waved good-bye with the other.

How would Andre look at her once he learned she'd lied to his face?

Hopefully, if luck—and complicated coffee orders—were on her side, he would never have to find out.

Emma walked straight to the door of Soaps Up and went in, taking a few steps down the rumbling rows of washers and dryers before turning and moving back to the window. As she'd hoped, Andre had spun around and was once more facing the front of the line. Moving fast, she slipped out the door and hurried around the corner, retracing their steps back toward the shelter.

Now all she had to do was figure out a way to get Stewart alone. He didn't seem that interested in women—he hadn't even glanced at her shirt, which she'd deliberately left unbuttoned after her and Andre's interlude in the apartment, perversely enjoying catching Andre sneak glances at her chest. But Stewart had barely noticed that she was a woman, let alone a woman with a bit of cleavage showing and skintight jeans.

So luring him with the usual seduction routine was probably out. She'd have to think of some—

Like a shaking, twitching answer to an unspoken prayer, Stewart himself appeared, emerging from the basement of one of the tenement buildings a few feet ahead. He looked as surprised to see her as she was to see him. And guilty. Very guilty.

Emma pulled the stun gun from her jeans. Even before her logical mind figured out the *why*, her gut knew the *what*. Stewart was up to no good; that was what. And he didn't seem surprised to see her gun, which was more bad news.

She didn't realize how bad until a pair of meaty arms grabbed her from behind, pinning her arms to her sides, giving her no choice but to move her finger away from the trigger of the gun, or risk stunning her own legs into painful immobility. Her mouth opened to cry for help, but Stewart was suddenly there in front of her, pushing his thin fingers into her mouth, grabbing her bottom teeth in his fist like she was a dog he'd bring to heel.

She gagged at the taste of salt and sickeningly sweet lotion, her eyes tearing as whoever held her from behind tightened his arms, lifting her off the ground. Together, the two of them dragged her down the street, toward the basement steps from which Stewart had emerged. Emma thrashed and kicked, but the man behind her was enormous and unbelievably strong. She'd never felt so small and powerless, so very aware of her delicate human body.

Or *mostly* human body.

Despite the two hearty meals it had been fed in less than twenty-four hours, the dark craving rushed to life beneath her skin, responding to her fear. Emma could feel her cells opening up, surging with demon power, searching for the energy they craved. She twisted her arms, willing to dislocate her shoulder if it meant she could get her hands on the monster of a man behind her, but it was impossible. Every wiggle made him squeeze her tighter, until her forehead felt like it was swelling to twice its normal size.

Pulling in her next breath became her first priority, followed closely by somehow maintaining her hold on the stun gun as her hands tingled and grew numb. She was going to need that gun. When the time came, it might be her only shot at escape. She couldn't take down both of these men with her demon mark, even if she managed to get one hand on each of them.

Emma coughed and gagged again as Stewart pulled on her jaw. Behind her closed eyes, the world darkened. Seconds later, knees jabbed into her dangling legs as the man holding her descended the stairs.

They were taking her down to a basement, just like the basement Ezra had trapped her in for what had seemed like years. Even with books to read and a small radio that Ezra's girlfriend had brought down to her in a moment of empathy, her captivity had been almost unbearable, and she knew these men wouldn't worry about making her a happy prisoner.

If they cared about keeping her alive at all.

Emma's nerves sizzled, and a jolt of adrenaline dumped into her bloodstream. She wasn't going to become a prisoner or a casualty. Not now, not when she'd lived through so much.

Arching her back until it felt like her spine would snap and her lower jaw would be ripped from her face if Stewart didn't loosen his hold, Emma managed to slip one hand behind her and grab a handful of Strong Man's crotch. It wasn't what she'd been aiming for, but she fisted her fingers and held on tight. Even if the dark craving couldn't find the memories it needed from this particular position, she still might be able to do some damage, to injure the man just enough to force him to loosen his hold.

She squeezed with every last bit of strength in her body even as she willed the dark craving into her fingertips, sending it to seek out the evil it needed. Seconds later, the Strong Man's memories flew into her mind so quickly, she could barely focus on one image before the next flashed in its place.

The interior of a place made of concrete, old showers on the wall, and the man who held her crouched on the ground with another man pinned beneath him. It was . . . Stewart. Emma caught a flash of Stewart's face, fear and pain in his wide eyes as the Strong Man smashed his huge fist into his abdomen again and again. A few feet away, a man in a suit watched the beating, pacing back and forth and screaming words Emma couldn't hear.

The Strong Man couldn't hear anything when he was like this. The blood rushing through his head when he delivered a beating was too loud, overwhelming, the only thing that made him whole.

The violence of skin and bone connecting with flesh was what he lived for, the reason he'd joined the Death Ministry. He was ready to earn his second kill scar, ready to pound Stewart into the cracked tile beneath him until he was nothing but blood smeared on the—

The man with the suit punched the Strong Man in the face, his large gold watch catching him under the nose and tearing away a patch of skin. The Strong Man growled and lunged for the man's feet, intent on cutting his fancy shoes right off his body when another DM member grabbed him from behind and pulled him to his feet, screaming that he *can't beat the boss.*

More images flooded Emma's brain, less coherent, shifting back and forth with a speed that made her head spin.

Stewart crying as the man in the suit shoved a child's sand sieve into his hands; the Strong Man running outside and into the ruins, hunting for something upon which to unleash his unspent rage. Stewart shivering and cold on the floor, shaking uncontrollably; the Strong Man using his knife on an Inuago demon, gutting the large creature with a few swift jerks of his blade. Stewart slipping the key from the collection at the homeless shelter; the Strong Man helping to rip apart her apartment.

It took some time for Emma to assimilate the meaning of the contrasting memories, to realize not all of them belonged to the man whose arms were now growing limp around her.

Some of these memories weren't Strong Man's. Some of these memories were Stewart's.

Emma cracked her eyes and sucked in a surprised breath around the fingers still curled softly into her mouth. Her entire face was glowing blue. The craving was feeding on the man *through her mouth.* She supposed there was no reason that shouldn't happen—just because she'd always fed through her hands didn't mean that was the only way for it to be done. There was so much she didn't know about her power, so much she'd never wanted to learn. She'd always tried to survive by doing the bare minimum, giving the darkness only enough to keep it sated. She'd never wanted to give it free rein to explore just how far it could go, how much of her humanity it could consume.

But now she didn't have the choice. Adrenaline dumped into her bloodstream in response to fear. The demon mark sensed danger—and it was rising to fight back.

Still, seeing Stewart's second face, the face of his soul, shrivel in the blue light sickened her—terrified her. It made that part of her that feared the craving would someday take over scream for her to stop feeding no matter how dangerous these men were.

Emma spit Stewart's hand from her mouth as she twisted from Strong Man's arms. With a guttural cry, she shoved Stewart away, sending him flying down the stairs to crumple at the bottom. Without waiting to see whether Stewart would be getting up again, she turned, lifting the gun that still remained in her hand, ready to finish off the man who'd grabbed her.

Instead, she found herself aiming at the face of another man, a very pissed-off man in a perfectly fitting suit.

Andre.

The Strong Man was at his feet on the narrow landing, passed out cold but still breathing, if the light snuffles erupting from his crooked nose were any indication. Emma's fingers went limp. When Andre reached for the gun, she handed it over without protest.

"What the hell—?" His words ended in a light grunt as Emma threw her arms around him, burying her face in his suit, inhaling his safe, clean smell.

———

All the angry words he'd been planning tripped on their way out of his mouth and fell into the softness of Emma's hair. Andre hugged her tight, squeezing her to him, dropping his lips and pressing a long, hard kiss to her forehead, willing her to realize how stupid she'd been to ditch him.

"I'm sorry. I was going back to talk to Stewart. I thought he'd tell me something if I was alone, but I shouldn't have—"

"Damn straight you shouldn't have." Andre pulled away from Emma when a groan sounded from the bottom of the stairs. Looked like Stewart would live, unfortunately. Andre wouldn't have been sad to see the man dead. He'd heard the struggle and looked down the stairs in time to see Emma spit the man's hand from her mouth.

The fact that the man had dared to touch her in any way made him want to smash someone's head in. Luckily, the thick-armed bastard holding Emma had been in the perfect position for a fist to the back of the head. He too was going to live, however, which meant he and Emma should move. Now.

"Come on. We'll talk about how dumb you are later," Andre said, taking Emma's hand and trying to pull her up the stairs, but she snatched it away before he could take a step.

He turned to see her fingers clutched to her chest, her breath coming faster. "I'm sorry, I just . . . I don't want to touch you right now."

Andre's jaw clenched, and hurt tightened his chest. "Fine. But we need to leave. I'll call Francis and ask him to send a team over to pick these two up and take them back to headquarters for questioning. We need to find out why they were—"

"I have a good idea why they were after me." Emma turned and ran to the bottom of the stairs.

"Emma, stop. Get your ass— Shit." He hurried after her as Emma stumbled over Stewart's writhing body and opened the door leading to the basement of the apartment building. Andre reached her side in time to grab her around the waist and keep her from taking another step. "We're not going in there. We don't know—"

"I do know. Look." She pointed into the darkness. Across the hard dirt floor, on the opposite side of the low, cramped space, a lamp stood on a wooden table next to a cage big enough to hold a midsized demon.

Or a small human woman.

"There really is someone after you." Andre's arm tightened around Emma's waist instinctively, everything in him insisting that he had to keep her safe.

"There is. And I'm betting money it's because of the spell book. But here's the kicker—the Death Ministry is involved in some way. Look at that guy," she said, motioning to the giant man still lying on the landing above them. "He's got a kill scar."

"But how is this sack of shit involved?" Andre glanced down at Stewart, who was conscious but not saying a word. He looked like he was in too much pain to do much more than groan.

Good. Andre hoped his goddamned neck was broken.

"I don't know, but he's the one who stole the key to plant in my apartment. He and the other guy wanted to get me down here. I'm guessing they were planning to put me in that cage and wait for whoever's calling the shots to tell them what to do next."

Andre was pretty sure his teeth were going to crack if his jaw got any tighter. He grabbed Emma's wrist and held tight as he started back up the stairs. This time, she didn't pull away. "Okay. So we're going to find out who that is and we're going to make sure he or she realizes what a very bad idea it was to fuck with our family." Andre ordered his bud to call Francis.

"It's a man in a suit, the guy in charge," Emma said softly as they emerged onto the street and started back toward the homeless shelter. "I saw him when I was feeding on the guy you hit. I couldn't see his face, but I saw . . . his shoes. I think."

Andre shot her a look but didn't have a chance to say anything before Francis answered on the second ring.

"What the fuck, Andre? Where the fuck are you? Where the fuck is Emma? What the fuck are you—"

"Shut the fuck up and I'll tell you," Andre said, a little louder than he'd intended. A pair of young women in faded brown maid's uniforms scurried to the other side of the sidewalk as he and Emma passed by.

Andre took a deep breath and lowered his voice as he detailed their search of Emma's apartment, finding the key, and Emma's attack to his cousin. By the time he finished, he and Emma had reached the end of the block. He stepped to the side of the building and paused, wanting to keep an eye on the basement steps to make sure neither of the men who'd attacked Emma was going to try to make a run for it. He didn't want to think about what would have happened to her if his gut feeling that she was headed back to the homeless shelter had been wrong.

"Shit. Is she okay?" Francis asked. "Did the bastards hurt her?"

"No, she's fine. But they would have locked her in a cage if I hadn't found her in time." Andre lowered his voice further and did a scan of the immediate area. Aside from an older man with a walker on the opposite side of the street, they were still alone. "One of them was Death Ministry and the other one a guy who worked at the shelter. We need to find out what they know and who they're working for."

"Where are they?"

Andre gave him directions and the street address of the apartment. "It's number ten. They're both on the stairs leading down into the basement. One was unconscious a few minutes ago, and the other one fell down the stairs and is pretty messed up." Andre shot a glance at Emma, who huddled next to him, her arms wrapped around herself as if she was cold despite the increasingly brutal heat of the day. "He wasn't moving, but—"

"I'll have two men there in ten. Get Emma back here so we can keep her safe."

"I think we should wait to make sure these guys are here when the—"

"Doesn't sound like they're going anywhere, Andre," Francis interrupted. "And what if there are more where those two came from? You got nothing but a stun gun. You need to get out of there."

"You're right," Andre said, though it pained him to say the words. Francis was making sense.

He, on the other hand, was still too disturbed by seeing Emma in danger to form any kind of real plan. He just wanted to reach out to her, to put his arms around her and pull her close, but he kept seeing her face when she'd told him she didn't want to touch him—so serious, so disgusted, as if she'd suddenly realized he was as repulsive as the rest of the men on earth.

But could he really blame her? When she'd just had two guys roughing her up?

"We'll be back at the office in twenty minutes."

"Make it less if you can." Francis sighed. Even before he spoke,

Andre knew he wasn't going to like what Francis had to say next. "The police found that Death Ministry kid who went missing this morning down near the park."

Shit. And shit again. This just kept getting worse. "Dead, I assume?"

"Yep. His stomach was ripped open. The rumor is that it was a demon attack, but I'm not so sure the rest of the DM is going to go for that explanation," Francis said. "They may decide a revenge killing is in order. The girl this dude was last seen with would be a good target."

"This goes deeper than that, Francis. I don't know how, but Emma has a few ideas. She can tell you about them when we get to the office." And Andre was going to have to tell Francis about his phone call to Mikey, as well. *That* wasn't going to be fun. But at this point, he needed to be absolutely honest with his cousin. Emma's life might depend on it.

"Sounds good." Francis shouted something to Douglas. "Okay, two of ours just left the building. You get back here and start working that big brain of yours. Whatever shit's going down, we need to head it off before it gets any worse."

"You're right. Have you thought about calling your dad?"

Francis made an unhappy sound. "I put a call in when I got the news about the Death Ministry guy, but he's not answering his fucking phone."

"You don't think something's happened, do you? Do you think—"

"No, he's fine. We talked earlier. He was getting on a plane to Vancouver for a meeting. They're probably still in the air. I left a message. He'll call me as soon as they land."

"Okay. We'll see you in a few," Andre said, ending the call as Emma tugged on his sleeve.

"You didn't tell him about the man in the suit," she said, her voice unusually soft.

"I figured you could do that when you explain to him about the spell book. The supernatural stuff is your territory." He tried to take her hand, but she pulled away again, so Andre stuffed his hands in his pockets and took off down the street toward Conti Bounty, leaving her to follow. It was only a half dozen long blocks, but he wished he hadn't sent his driver home earlier in the day. The sooner he got Emma off the street, the better he'd feel.

"So do you believe me now?" She stayed close to his side, though still kept very much to herself.

"I do. Obviously those guys were after you. Probably because of that book, just like you thought." He turned to look at her as they walked. "You're a pretty smart kind of crazy, turns out."

Emma nodded, her long lashes sweeping down as she dropped her gaze to the ground. She really was so beautiful, and she kept getting prettier with every minute he spent in her company. It had been like that with Katie, but not nearly this intense. He'd fallen for Katie over the course of several weeks, not several hours.

Oh, hell no. He couldn't believe he was even *thinking* about emotions like that. He wasn't ready, and Emma certainly wasn't willing. She might be attracted to him, she might flirt with him, but she didn't particularly like him or trust him—she'd proven that.

"Can we stop by Sam's shop on the way to the office?" Emma asked. "It's only a couple blocks over."

"No. We don't have time. They found that missing Death Ministry guy you were with last night. He'd been gutted."

"What? But when I left him, he was fine." Emma shook her head. "I mean, not fine, obviously, he was dead, but he was whole."

"All I know is what Francis told me, and he said the body was ripped open," Andre said, dropping his voice as they turned a corner onto a busier street. "For now, the police are calling it a demon attack, but—"

"But they'll know better once they do the postmortem," she said. "It will show that he was cut open after he was already dead."

"Maybe a demon did do it." Andre hoped his words would prove true. Demon violence was so much easier to deal with than the human variety. "Maybe something found the body and pulled it away for a snack."

"Except that demons big enough to drag a full-grown man out from between those Dumpsters and into the ruins don't usually eat carrion, only things they've killed themselves. And they wouldn't have left anything behind."

"True."

"Shit," she said, suddenly veering to the left. "Come on, let's go to Sam's. Really quickly."

"No!" Andre grabbed at her arm, but she easily avoided him.

"Then I'm going to have to stop somewhere else," she said, the hint of her usual hardness in her tone. No matter how much he loathed her stubbornness, he was glad to hear that surly note return. The soft, deferential Emma had been scaring him. "I really do have to go to the bathroom."

"Well, you can wet yourself, then, because we're not going anywhere except—"

"I will not wet myself." She stopped dead in the street, turning to him with her hands on her hips. "I'm sorry I stole your gun and pissed you off, but I thought I was doing what I had to do. And we *are* closer to figuring out what's really going on than we were before. So give me a break. A pee break. Is that too much to ask?"

Without another word, she spun on her heel and headed in the opposite direction from the Conti Bounty offices, clearly intending to take her potty break in the comfort of her sister's shop. Andre sighed and followed, but for the first time he wasn't tempted to stare at Emma's ass. Right now, he didn't want to fuck her; he just wanted to hold her. To have her *want* him to hold her.

The realization was nearly as frightening as seeing Emma locked in that Death Ministry guy's arms.

CHAPTER TWELVE

*E*mma took her time washing her hands and splashing water on her face, soaking in the smell of fresh flowers and the light, ginger-scented soap Sam kept in the staff bathroom. The shop didn't open until two o'clock on summer days, so she still had a few hours until Sam's assistant, Paige, arrived to start filling orders and sorting through the new deliveries.

Emma wished she and Andre could stay here until then, sitting in the silence of the sunny stockroom, surrounded by buckets of cool, peaceful flowers soaking in the water and vitamin solution Sam swore kept her blooms the freshest in the city. She was so tired. She hadn't slept in twenty-four hours, and sooner or later the adrenaline high was going to wear off and she was going to crash. Hard. She wished that she could crash here, in this sweet-smelling haven Sam had created.

Sam. Emma was suddenly possessed by a powerful longing to see her sister, to talk to someone who understood.

"Are you almost finished?" Andre knocked on the door, a light but impatient rapping that made her fingers curl around the cool porcelain of the sink.

"Just a second." She pulled in another deep breath.

Instead she had Andre . . . who didn't understand at all. She could tell he was taking her reluctance to touch him the wrong way. But it would be pointless to explain to him why she was afraid to hold his hand. He didn't believe in her demon mark and would only think she was even crazier than he did already if she told him she was afraid all the drama and danger of the past hours had made the darkness inside her harder to control.

If only he'd come down the stairs a few seconds earlier. Then he would have seen the blue light shooting from her hands and face and realized just how dangerous it could be for him to touch her. Then there wouldn't be this awkwardness between them, this horrible feeling that something good was going bad.

She stepped out of the bathroom, expecting to find Andre lurking outside the door, ready to haul her down the street to the Conti offices. Instead he was across the room near the kitchenette, slicing an orange. The bright smell of orange peel cut through the sweetness of the flowers, making Emma's mouth water.

"Hope you're planning to share that," she said, circling around the wooden table that dominated the room where Sam compiled her arrangements.

Her sister was blind, so she chose the flowers for her projects by selecting complementary textures and smells, which made for some unique works of art. It looked like she'd left instructions for Paige before she'd left. The purple and yellow and orange flowers erupting from the four vases in the middle of the table bore Sam's distinctive stamp.

"Actually, this is all for you." Andre pushed a plate filled with orange slices and a toasted bagel across the counter.

"Thanks." Emma grabbed the bagel and took a huge bite, sighing with relief as she chewed and swallowed and went for another. "You sure you don't want some?" she asked around a mouthful of bread, beyond worrying about good manners.

She hadn't realized how starved she was. But then, if you didn't count supernatural feedings, she hadn't eaten anything since the handful of stale pretzels last night at the Demon's Breath. It was a wonder she hadn't passed out from low blood sugar.

"No, thanks," Andre said. "I had a bagel while you were enjoying the world's longest bathroom break."

"Hm." Emma swallowed and reached for the other half of the bagel. "I needed a second."

"More like fifteen minutes." Andre wiped his hand on a towel and circled around the counter. "We should go as soon as you're finished."

Instead of coming to stand next to her, he moved to the wooden table a few feet away, keeping his back to her, staring at the flowers. Emma couldn't help but feel a little sad that he'd so easily accepted that she wanted her space. Still, it was for the best. She didn't want to hurt him, and what had happened with Stewart had only proven that she couldn't be sure kissing Andre was safe right now. Hell, it might never be safe. Even on a good day, the darkness was still there, waiting to come out and play, struggling to triumph over her human side.

The thought made it hard to swallow her last bite of bagel, and the orange slices still on her plate weren't nearly as appetizing as they'd been a moment earlier. She might never kiss Andre again.

Even five hours ago, she couldn't have imagined that would make her so very sad. But it did.

"Thanks for the food," she said, wanting to reach out and smooth her hands along the lines of Andre's shoulders. Instead, she grabbed his discarded towel and brushed the last of the crumbs off her hands. "That was nice."

"That's me. Nice."

"I think you're nice."

Andre turned, nailing her with a hard look. "You think I'm an asshole."

"Yeah, but a nice asshole," she said, uncomfortable with the strained laugh that followed her words. "I mean it. I appreciate everything you've done for me today."

"Right. Appreciation made you decide to steal my gun and—"

"I explained that. And I said I was sorry."

"I don't want to hear that you're sorry, I want to hear that you're going to stop putting yourself in danger," he said, closing the distance between them in two long steps.

Emma stood a little straighter, unable to ignore the closeness of his body. He was only a few inches away. No matter how determined she was to keep this man safe, she couldn't stop thinking about the fact that they were alone for the first time. In a private place where they wouldn't be interrupted, surrounded by bright colors and seductive smells that seemed to heighten all of her senses, making her crave that intimate connection she'd nearly allowed herself to believe would be possible.

But it wasn't possible. Not for her. Not now, not ever.

"I can't stop putting myself in danger. I've been putting myself in danger since I was a tiny little kid," Emma said. She knew it was the wrong thing to say, but she couldn't help herself.

The unfairness of her mark was hitting hard today, harder than it had in years. But then, she'd never been so keenly aware of what she was missing as she was right now, staring up into the dark eyes of a gorgeous man she wanted to kiss so badly it hurt.

"You're talking about the demon mark again, right?" Andre moved even closer, his hands coming down on either side of her, pinning her between him and the counter.

"Yes." Emma tried to move away, but Andre refused to move his arm.

"You're going to have to show me."

She shook her head, dropping her chin, refusing to look at him. "No, I won't."

"I want to believe you, Emma, I really do, but—"

"No, you don't. If you wanted to believe me, you would," she said, increasingly breathless as he pressed even closer, the hard planes of his body molding against her, making her light up from the inside, like the face of one of her victims.

Her victims. She didn't want Andre to become one of them. She had to maintain control, no matter how tempted she was to twine her arms around his neck and pull his lips down to her own.

"It's not that simple," Andre said, one hand leaving the counter, wrapping around her waist.

Despite herself, she relaxed against him, sighing as she felt the hard ridge of his growing arousal against her hip. God, she wanted to see him, to touch him, to feel that part of him pushing inside her, easing the unfamiliar ache he'd awakened. She'd never wanted anyone like this.

All the more reason to put as much distance between you as possible.

The dark craving had responded to her fear in powerful ways

today—what if it responded to her desire, as well? What if it decided Andre would make the perfect snack and began to feed while they were . . . in the middle of something?

The thought of the blue light shining from between her legs was almost enough to make Emma laugh, but not quite. No amount of ridiculous imagery could banish the awareness of Andre's body so close to her own, Andre's mouth teasing near her ear.

"Come on, Emma, show me."

Emma lifted her chin, shivering as he pressed a soft kiss to her neck, his tongue flicking out to taste the place where her pulse raced beneath her skin. She reached up, careful to keep her hands fisted as she pushed against his chest, forcing him back a few precious inches.

"I can't show you." She stared into his eyes, heart beating even faster at the need she saw there.

It wasn't just physical need. It was something else, something more. Andre really *did* want to understand, but nothing in his realm of experience had prepared him for her. Sadly, her experience *had* prepared her for him. She knew how to convince him she was telling the truth. She also knew that the words she'd have to speak wouldn't be easy to hear.

"Come on, let's go." She tried once more to break out of his arms, but he only held her tighter. Once he'd set his mind on something, the man was like a pit bull—utterly intractable and determined to the point of being dangerous.

"Don't you think Francis is going to want some kind of proof of what you can do?" he asked. "Don't you think he'll have the same doubts that I have? Wouldn't it be easier to go in there with me on your side, able to confirm your story?"

"It's not a story," she said, his condescending tone finally pushing her to say things she'd hoped could be avoided. "When I touched you this morning, I saw inside your mind. I looked into your memories. I saw Katie. She was a redhead with—"

"You didn't see anything." He stepped back, cutting the physical connection between them.

"Then how did I know? How would I be able to describe—"

"Jace told you," he said, pacing back and forth in front of the table, his anger clear in his pinched features. "Or Jace told your sister, and she—"

"Jace and Sam have nothing to do with this. I saw her. In your mind. I saw the way she was crying the last time you saw her before she died," Emma said, hating every word she spoke, but knowing she couldn't stop now. She had to finish this, to make sure this was the last time Andre ever questioned her about her mark. "She was crouched in a corner near a bed with a . . ." Emma closed her eyes, searching her mind for the specifics she needed. "A blue comforter, with some sort of white pattern on it. She was reaching out to you, begging you not to leave, but you—"

"Stop it." Andre's sharp tone made her eyes fly open. He'd stopped his pacing and stood frozen in front of her, one accusing finger pointed at her chest. "However you found out about Katie, it's none of your—"

"I know it's none of my business, but that's the question you have to answer, Andre. How did I find out?" Emma asked in her softest voice, the pain on Andre's face making her wish he'd left well enough alone. "Did you ever tell anyone about those last few moments? Did you ever tell anyone that Katie was crawling across the floor to you when you slammed the door in her face?" Emma tensed, half expecting Andre to strike her. The violence simmering in his eyes was making his hands shake—it was terrifying.

But not nearly as terrifying as what happened next.

Instead of lashing out, Andre crumpled. He dropped his face into his trembling hands, his back hunched, and seconds later, those broad shoulders began to shake. He didn't make a noise, not so much as a gasp for breath, but there was no doubt about it—Andre was crying, weeping like his heart was breaking all over again.

And it was all her fault. She'd known how much he'd loved Katie, how it had killed him to lose her, but she'd ripped the scab away from the wound anyway, hurting him in the name of proving her stupid fucking point. Her worries about the dark craving faded to background noise as a more powerful need surged inside her. She *needed* to comfort this man, needed to help take away some of the pain that she had caused.

She went to him, wrapping her arms around him, holding him as best she could, the act of offering herself to someone in such an intimate way making her awkward and unsure. Andre must have felt her doubt. For a moment, his body stiffened and she was certain he was going to pull away. Instead, his arms parted and he engulfed her, hugging her so tight, she could barely breathe. He buried his face in her neck and continued to sob in absolute silence while she smoothed his hair, stroked his strong neck, ran her hands in comforting circles on his back.

Emma had no idea how long they stood there, holding each other, before Andre finally lifted his face, but she knew for certain that the darkness was as dormant as it ever was. Touching Andre with empathy and compassion hadn't summoned the beast from its rest. It gave her some small hope.

Maybe . . . if Andre didn't hate her for the things she'd said . . .

"You made me cry. I can't remember the last time I cried," he said, wetness still shining on his cheeks, though he forced a small smile. "What a jerk you are."

"I know," she whispered, threading her fingers through his hair, marveling at how soft it was. "I'm sorry."

"You don't have to be sorry. I'm the jerk. I should have believed you." He brought one hand to cup her face, smoothing away a tear she hadn't realized she'd shed. "I'm just . . . not very good with faith. Or trust."

"Me, either." Emma's chest tightened with an emotion as foreign as the desire Andre inspired. "But for what it's worth, I'd like to get better. I would . . . I'd try to get better."

He curled his fingers at the back of her neck, making her shiver. "Me, too." The expression on his face the second before he kissed her was enough to make Emma forget how to breathe.

Was *that* what love looked like? Was that the way a man stared at the lips of a woman who meant more to him than a way to scratch the most ancient of itches?

She'd seen into Andre's mind and knew better than anyone that women were his fix. He might *need* his fix, but he didn't love it. Sometimes he even hated it, hated the weakness his compulsion shoved in his face every night of his life.

She should have known better than to think there was anything but lust and addiction in his eyes. But when he kissed her, she could *feel* the emotion there. There was hope in the way his lips moved against hers, tenderness in the way his tongue swept into her mouth, tasting her with an intensity he hadn't before. He wanted to believe she was different. He wanted to believe that *he* could be different.

More than anything in the world, Emma wanted to believe those things, too.

She didn't hold back when Andre moaned and kissed her harder, his hands roaming over her body, opening buttons and un-snapping snaps as he went. Instead, she shoved his suit jacket off his shoulders and down to the floor, then went to work on his buttons, stopping only when he leaned down to catch her behind the knees and hoist her up around his waist.

Emma tensed her arms and held tight to his shoulders as she spread her legs and wrapped them around his hips, pulling him closer, sighing as Andre's hard-on pressed against where she ached.

"I want you." She kissed his neck, his jaw, his lips, any part of him that came close enough for her to taste.

"I want you. Way too much," he gasped against her lips, spin-ning around, setting her ass down on the wooden table behind him.

His hands were on her boots a second later, pulling them off and throwing them to the side, knocking over a stack of wicker bas-kets without pausing to assess the damage. He was too busy at her blouse, ripping open the last two buttons, sliding it off her shoul-ders before coming back for another kiss.

This time the meeting of their mouths was frenzied, wild, making it impossible to concentrate on the small buttons on Andre's shirt. But she needed her hands on his bare skin. Now. Ten minutes ago. Emma grabbed two handfuls of fabric and pulled. Buttons flew, and Andre let out a rough sound of approval that made her smile against his lips.

"I've got protection covered. Don't worry," he said, "I'll put a condom on."

"The sooner the better." Electricity shot across her skin as the true impact of their words hit and spun through her addled mind. She was going to sleep with him; he was going to be inside her within minutes, and her virginity would be a thing of the past. The thought should have been a little frightening, but it wasn't. It was thrilling, perfect, and made her sex ache until she squirmed against Andre, desperate to dispense with the rest of her clothes.

She reached for the waist of her unbuttoned jeans, but Andre beat her to it. "Let me," he said, fisting the thick fabric in his hands and whipping her jeans down her long legs. Her socks went next with two little flicks of his wrist, and then he was kissing his way up her thigh, making her gasp when he paused between her legs, inhaling the smell of her through her black cotton panties.

"You smell . . ." He inhaled again, and his hands came to rest on her thighs, shoving her legs a little farther apart.

"Um . . . good, I hope?" Emma tried to joke, but the words came out breathless. It was a miracle she could even form words. Andre's lips teasing against the fabric of her panties were causing a full-body meltdown of epic proportions.

Her nipples puckered tight, aching for his touch, while her pussy . . . well . . . the poor thing might never be the same. She'd never been so plump and swollen and wet. Every inch of her cried out for his touch—his tongue, his fingers, his cock—anything would do. If only he would touch her and ease the need that made her innermost walls pulse and her clit stand up and beg for the attention it had never been given by anything except Emma's own hand.

It didn't want her hand now. It wanted Andre, any part of Andre. Her hips arched of their own accord, pressing her crotch shamelessly into his face.

Andre's fingers tightened, digging into the flesh of her thighs. "You smell like . . . everything. So perfect." He opened his mouth and bit down lightly, dragging his teeth over the cotton covering her, making her cry out. She made a sound like she was in pain, but she wasn't, though the aching need was so intense, it was almost more than she could take.

She wanted him now. Right now, before this wild desire inside her spun any higher, before the dark craving took notice of what she was doing and surged toward the surface. So far, Andre was safe, but she could feel the foreign, demonic part of her beginning to awaken, seething through her veins, curious at this new fire burning in her blood. No matter how perfect it felt to burn, she couldn't let this go on much longer.

"Now, please." She fisted her hands in his hair, pulling his mouth back to her lips. She kissed him hard, making him groan as she worked his pants open and tried to pull down the tight waist of his boxer briefs.

No, not boxer briefs. *Tighty whiteys.*

As Andre stepped back, dispensing with the last of his clothes, Emma was treated to a sight that she'd always assumed would make her laugh—a man wearing nothing but a pair of tighty whiteys. Surely, they had to be the least sexy article of clothing in the world . . . or so she'd assumed.

But Andre made them work. Hell, he could probably make a fluorescent orange man thong work, she thought, watching the tighty whiteys slide down his thighs to join the other clothes on the floor. And then, Andre stood bare before her, taking her breath away. His body was Roman-statue perfect, with dark, olive skin that dipped and swelled in all the right places. Emma understood why no woman could resist him. He was beautiful, every single part of him.

She reached out, taking his cock in her hand before she could second-guess the urge. It was heavy and hard but covered with skin that was surprisingly soft. It sprung from closely trimmed black hair, its shaft full and thick, with a fleshy, dark-rose-colored head that, strangely, made Emma want to kiss him there. She'd never put her mouth on a man like that, but suddenly she wanted to. She wanted to lick and suck and taste. She wanted to feel that soft skin hot against her lips, taste that bit of liquid that had formed at the tip of his arousal. What would it taste like? Would it be sweet or sour? Salty or—

"The way you're looking at me right now"—Andre grabbed a foil packet he'd dropped onto the table beside her—"it's almost enough to make me come, you know that?"

"No, I don't." Emma watched with undisguised fascination as he rolled the condom onto his cock, a part of her wishing they didn't need it, wondering whether it would feel different with the thin rubber between them. "We wouldn't want that."

"No, we wouldn't." Andre reached out, flipping the clasp that held her bra closed in the front open with one practiced motion. Emma shivered as he eased the straps down her shoulders. "So maybe you should close your eyes for a while."

Emma gasped as his lips touched the bare skin just beneath her breast, and her already aching nipples pulled even tighter, until they stung and burned. But then Andre came to kiss the sting away. And lick and suck and bite and . . . *god.*

Desire surged through her body, cutting away her mistaken expectations, forging new pathways that had never been explored before, awakening every part of her—from her lips to her toes to those desperate inches between her legs—to a new kind of sensory overload. She'd always thought feeding the dark craving was the most intense, visceral experience in the world.

She'd been wrong. So very, very wrong.

This was the ultimate high, a pure, erotic thrill with none of the guilt or shame. Andre's skin on hers, Andre's hot mouth on her breasts, Andre's hands pulling her panties down to her ankles and flicking them onto the floor—were completely natural, things a man should do to a woman.

As natural as it was for Andre to push the blunt head of his cock against where she ached, as natural as it was for her to arch her hips, welcoming him inside. Emma gasped at the slight flash of pain that came as he drove to the end of her, but any discomfort faded as he moved in and out of her slick heat, each slow, controlled drive making the electricity sizzling inside her surge higher.

"Andre," she gasped his name against his lips as his thumb found her clit and circled, keeping time with his thrusts, building the tension inside her until her back arched and a wild sound leapt from her throat.

She looked up, flowers filling her vision, all those wild oranges and purples flooding in through her eyes, making her feel shot through with beauty and pleasure. And then Andre kissed lower, capturing her nipple in his mouth once more, pushing her over the edge.

Emma squeezed her eyes closed and fisted her hands by her head—keeping Andre safe from the chance of blue light her last rational thought—and came so hard and long, she feared her soul would be wrung from her body by the time she came down. Or maybe she'd *never* come down. The thought was frightening, but surely there were worse ways to spend eternity than riding this high with the man she loved.

Oh god. *Love.* It had crept in on little demon claws.

The realization dulled the edge of her pleasure. Her eyes opened and she looked up at the man laboring above her, the man whose skin glowed from within with a pale blue light.

Chapter Thirteen

*B*y the time Emma screamed, it was too late. Andre *couldn't* stop. All he could do was dig his fingers into the soft flesh of her hips and drive harder, faster, until the tight knot of pressure at the base of his spine exploded and pleasure rocketed through his every cell.

"Emma!" He called her name as he came, his cock jerking inside of her, his arms holding her close even as she pushed at his chest, trying to force him away.

But he didn't want to be away from her, outside of her. He wanted to keep his dick in this woman for the rest of his life. They would arrange for some kind of old-fashioned slave-drawn litter to carry them around the city. He'd go to court and conduct his Conti family business from their traveling bed so that he'd never have to stop fucking her. Never stop driving in and out of that sweet heat that had connected his soul to his body for the first time in years.

Fucking Emma wasn't just good sex or even *great* sex; it was something more, something he'd never dreamed he'd have again. He wasn't going to let her run away from that without a fight. He'd seen her face when she came, felt her pussy clutch at his cock as her pleasure gripped her tighter and tighter.

She'd enjoyed what they'd done as much as he had. Hell, she'd *more* than enjoyed it. There was no reason for her to act like he was some kind of rapist to be shoved away at the first opportunity.

"Get back," she said, her voice nearing hysteria. "Please! Stop!"

"Emma, relax, I—"

"Look at yourself." She pointed to the wall behind her. "You're glowing."

Andre lifted his head. Emma had left the door to the bathroom open, enabling him to catch a glimpse of himself in the mirror above the sink. He watched the shock creep across his features as he realized he was, in fact, glowing. And not some metaphoric post-coital glow, but full-on *shining bright blue* like he'd swallowed a stick of neon.

"What the hell . . ." He pulled away, struggling to catch his breath. As soon as the contact between them was broken, the glow faded. But there was no denying that he'd seen it or that—if Emma's story was to be believed—he knew exactly what it meant. "So were you . . . eating from me?"

Emma sniffed. "I don't know," she said, her voice trembling. "I'm pretty sure . . . I've never seen the blue light when I wasn't."

He looked down to see tears sitting in her eyes, making the caramel depths shimmer with pain. He reached out to her, but she backed away across the table, nearly crashing into one of the flower arrangements in her haste to get away from him. "No, don't touch me!"

"Emma, sweetheart, I don't care. It's not a big deal." He laughed, a tight sound that held no real humor. He wanted to hold her so badly, wanted to show her that everything was going to be all right. "I don't care."

"Well you *should* care. If I'd taken too much, you could have died. And now you *will* die sooner than you would have." She sobbed and covered her face, clearly devastated by what she thought she'd done. "I don't even know how much I took. I didn't realize I was pulling on your energy. I didn't see the glow until after I . . . after the—"

"After you came?" he asked, easing closer, reaching tentative fingers out to brush against her toes. Even her feet were beautiful. He wanted to kiss every part of her, from her big toe to her small, sloping breasts to the tip of her slightly crooked nose. "I loved feeling you come," he said, encouraged by the fact that she was allowing him to smooth his hand up to grip her ankle.

She mumbled something into her hands that he couldn't understand, but he decided to take it as a sign of encouragement.

He squeezed her leg, letting his thumb play back and forth across her skin. "So, are you going to tell me that was the best fucking of your life now, or make me wait until I remind you how hot it was?" he asked, his recently spent cock growing the slightest bit thicker as he spoke.

"Stop making jokes." She lifted her face from her hands and brushed his hand away before pulling her knees into her chest, hiding her nudity except for lightly bruised shins and long, bare arms.

She was almost more striking with parts of her hidden from his view. Seeing her there—surrounded by flowers, lips swollen from his kisses, hair fluffing around her face in a wild tangle—he could safely say he'd never seen a woman so beautiful. To him, at least, she was beautiful, the *most* beautiful, the only one he wanted now and maybe . . . for a long time from now.

His jaw clenched as a strangled laugh escaped his lips. He'd fallen for her, the last woman in the world he would have imagined could get under his skin this way.

"This isn't funny," she said.

"I know it isn't." Hell, yes, he knew. He knew how dangerous this thing between them could be, but he hadn't been able to stop himself. Just like he couldn't stop himself from climbing onto the table beside her and wrapping an arm around her narrow shoulders. "I just can't stand to see you so upset, especially for no reason," Andre said, breathing a little easier when she leaned against him. "I really don't feel any different. I feel great, even better than I did before."

She bit her lip and turned to look at him, surveying him through concerned eyes. "You don't feel dizzy? Or weak?"

"Not at all. Hell, I'm ready to go again." He leaned in to kiss her neck, but she pushed him away.

Still, her tight mouth quirked at one edge and her fingertips lingered at his jaw for a moment before pulling away. "Don't be an idiot."

"I'm not an idiot. I'm an addict," Andre said, regretting the words the second they were out of his mouth. His smile faded, and it was harder to meet her eyes. But it was better they get this out of the way now, before his infatuation with this girl got any worse. "I mean . . . I *really* am an addict. A sex addict. I've tried to go to meetings and—"

"I know." Her voice was soft, compassionate, shocking him into silence. "I saw those memories, too. It's . . . okay."

"It is?"

"Well, no, it's not. I can tell it's not easy for you, but who am I to judge?" She swept his hair away from his forehead with a tenderness that made his throat tight. "I don't just use people—I steal their life away."

"You didn't steal anything from me," he said, grabbing her hand and kissing her fingertips, holding tight even when she tried to pull away. "I'm fine. I feel better than I have in years. You have to believe that."

"It was different," she said, searching his face. "Your skin was glowing, but not anything underneath. Usually I see a second face beneath the skin, and I can watch it . . . waste away when I pull someone's energy inside myself. But I didn't see that with you, and I didn't get any new memories." She paused for a moment, nibbling her lip. "The energy felt different. But I obviously fed. I feel charged the same way I usually do. Although with you, it felt more like . . ."

"Like what?"

She shook her head. "I don't know. Andre, please—"

"Really, it sounds like we're good. I'm fine," he said. "I mean, none of your other lovers dropped dead after sex, did they?"

Emma's eyes darted to the side, and a flush rose on her cheeks. "Um . . ."

"That's not terribly assuring, Emma," Andre said, his stomach clenching.

What if she'd realized that there was a chance she'd feed on him before they'd started this? He wouldn't blame her—she'd tried to warn him numerous times and told him to stop when she saw the light—but if she'd known this was possible . . .

If she'd known, there was no way she could feel anything close to what he felt for her. He'd never do anything to put Emma in danger. He'd give everything to protect her. He was a selfish, shallow man who, before today, wouldn't have allowed a woman he'd fucked to spend the night, let alone risked his life to keep her safe. But here he was . . . hanging on Emma's next words, holding his breath as her troubled eyes dropped to stare at the tops of her knees.

"Just tell me. Tell me the truth," he said, scared by the need he could hear in his own voice. And it wasn't even fear for his life that made his chest ache and his pulse speed; it was fear that she'd confirm he was a fool.

God, he should have known better. He should have—

"No, I've never hurt anyone during sex." She hugged herself tighter and shivered beneath the hand he still rested on her back. "There hasn't been anyone else."

It took several seconds for the meaning of her words to sink in. Then it all fell into place with a swiftness that made his head spin— the hesitance in her touch when she'd reached for him, the slight resistance as he'd pushed inside her, the shock and panic when she'd seen his face glowing and asked him to stop. She hadn't guessed that sex might activate her mark or her power or whatever she called it because she'd never *had* sex before.

He'd been her first.

The realization made him strangely aroused . . . and terrified by the responsibility of his first virgin . . . and aroused . . . and flattered . . . and aroused. . . .

"I'm . . . honored," he said, meaning the words, even if they came out sounding like some cheesy line. He just couldn't think of what to say, how to let her know that what they'd done had been special to him, too, without sounding even cornier than he did already.

She blew a breath out through her lips. "Don't worry about it. It's not a big deal. I just figured it was time I do it and you're decent-looking and we were here alone and . . ." She let her words trail off with a shrug before scooting away from him toward the edge of the table.

"I'm sure there was more to it than that," he said, more uncomfortable than he'd been in a long time, but not regretting for a second the fact that he and Emma had been together. "There was definitely more to it for me, and—"

"Really, you don't have to stress about de-virgin-izing me or whatever."

"Emma, I—"

"You should be more worried about whether you're going to die. I fed from you, even if I didn't mean to. I have never seen that blue light when it didn't mean I'd stolen life energy from someone. Not one single time." She grabbed her bra from where it had landed on top of some lurid-looking orange flower and shrugged it on.

It was a little too big and didn't do her small curves justice, but he could imagine how drop-dead sexy she'd look in some expertly fitted lingerie. It made him want to stop everything and drive her up to the boutique on Eighty-third Street, where he bought his regular lovers the occasional gift, and outfit her with a giant shopping bag filled with lacy, silky, sexy things.

Then they'd head back to his apartment and lock themselves inside for the week, and she could wear her new lingerie during the few hours when they weren't naked, hot, and sweaty, rolling around in his bed making love. Or in the shower making love, or in the bathtub, or on top of the kitchen counter, or—

"Did you hear me?" she asked, frustrated . . . and nearly dressed.

Sometime during his imaginings, she'd pulled on her shirt and jeans and was halfway across the room gathering a stray boot.

"No, I was thinking about all the places I'd like to make love to you," he said, ridiculously pleased by the flustered expression his words put on her face, and not at all embarrassed by the fact that he was still buck naked except for the Saint Christopher medal around his neck and the watch on his wrist.

But he'd never had trouble with nudity. According to his mother, she'd had a hell of a time keeping clothes on him when he was little. As soon as he'd learned how to pull off his shirt, pants, and diaper, he'd stripped down and gone running naked through the restaurant, making the entire family laugh. For some reason, he wanted to share that story with Emma, wanted her to know what his childhood had been like, wanted to know more about the little girl she'd been. Did she have any good memories mixed in with the horror she'd endured?

"So do you think we should?"

"Think we should what?" he asked, struggling to focus.

"You're impossible," she sighed, pulling on her boot and stomping across the room to fetch the other. "You know, your dick is going to get you in trouble someday. Maybe today . . ."

"Nah, me and the dick will be fine." He watched her bend over to zip up her other boot, admiring the curves of her ass inside her snug-fitting jeans. She just kept getting prettier, sexier. It was impossible to believe he'd thought she needed makeup and highlights. She didn't need anything. If she were any more attractive, he'd have to beat other men off of her with a stick. "We'll figure out some way to keep the supernatural stuff under control next time."

Emma stood fast, her hair whipping around her head in a cloud. "What next time? We can't . . . We can't do that again."

"Of course we can." Andre eased off the table, not missing the interest in Emma's eyes when they darted to his cock. He wasn't hard again yet, but he was getting there. If only they had even another hour to waste . . . He couldn't wait to show her that they'd only brushed the surface of the pleasure he could give her. "As soon as we get this Death Ministry situation sorted out and make sure you're safe, I insist on fucking you properly. In a bed, with some lube and maybe a few—"

"No." She shook her head. "I won't hurt you again." Her hand clutched at her stomach as if the very thought of hurting him made her ill.

No matter how much he hated to see her upset, her distress was vaguely thrilling. It meant she cared, maybe even the same way he cared. A relationship between them wouldn't be easy—with his addiction and her . . . strange appetite—but at least they'd stand a chance. Maybe, if he got serious about therapy, and they talked to Sam about some way to help Emma with her mark, then maybe—

"I mean it, Andre," she said, holding up a warning finger, as if she could read his big plans on his face.

Andre smiled and reached for her, letting his hands smooth down her bare arms. "Listen, we don't have to make that decision now. Just tell me you'll think about fucking me again . . . assuming I don't shrivel up and die in the next few hours."

She sighed. "You wouldn't shrivel. You'd have a heart attack."

"Okay, so assuming I don't have one of those."

"It doesn't always happen in a few hours. Sometimes it takes months, or even years."

"But I feel fine," he said, squeezing her hands, willing her to sense the life in him. "I feel great. I don't think you hurt me."

"And maybe I didn't—it's never happened before, but maybe— but are you willing to bet your life on it?"

"Maybe."

She shook her head, exasperated. "Well, I'm not, and Francis is going to have a heart attack if we don't get to the office," she said. "I'm surprised he hasn't been calling your bud nonstop."

Andre's smile faded. She was right. "I'm sure he has. I turned it off while you were in the bathroom."

"You did?" She pulled her hands away from his. "But what if—"

"You're not the only one who needed a few minutes. I'm not nearly as tough as I look."

Emma snorted. "I don't know who told you curls and flashy jewelry were tough, but—"

"I don't have curls. It just . . . gets wavy when I perspire."

"And you use the word *perspire*. That's really tough, too."

"Okay, you win. I'm a big cream puff who turned off his phone so he could pull his girly-man shit together," Andre said, the thought of the anxiety he and Emma would cause his family if they didn't show up soon making him scan the ground for his clothes. "But you're right. We should hurry."

He gathered his pants, socks, shirt, and suit coat in a matter of seconds, but ended up one article of clothing short.

"Looking for these?" He turned to see a grinning Emma with his briefs dangling off one finger. "I can't believe you wear tighty whiteys."

"What's wrong with briefs?"

"They look like adult diapers."

"They offer support," he said, snatching them from her with a smile. "And these aren't just briefs— they're very *expensive* briefs."

"Even if they were made of solid gold, they would still be . . ." Her words trailed off, her grin faded, and her eyes dropped to his arm, suddenly very interested in counting how many hairs were growing from his elbow to his wrist.

Surely, his underwear couldn't be *that* bad.

"You okay?" Andre hurried to pull on his pants. "Emma? Are you—"

"Yeah, yeah, I'm fine," she said, but her smile was forced—a flash of teeth in her tight face. "I think I forgot something in the bathroom. Be right back."

"All right, but I'm going to call Francis and tell him we're on our way," Andre called after her as he pulled on his shirt. "So don't take long."

"Two minutes," she said, slamming the door shut behind her.

Andre dressed in record time, his gut telling him something had soured between him and Emma, though he had no idea what he'd done. He couldn't believe this was really about his choice of underwear—though the vain part of him did wish he'd grabbed a pair of boxer briefs instead.

Maybe she was just feeling awkward. Pillow talk was never easy, especially when there hadn't even been a pillow involved and it was your first time.

God, he still remembered his first time—fifteen years old in the basement of his parents' restaurant. He and one of the much older waitresses had gone at it on some cardboard boxes they'd laid down in the corner. It had been over in thirty seconds. Afterward, he'd barely been able to look her in the face while he'd hitched up his pants.

It wasn't that he'd been embarrassed about his lack of staying power—he'd heard enough from his older, male cousins to know the first few times were a bust for most guys—it was more the shock of the whole thing. It had been so different from what he'd imagined—better and worse all at the same time. Overwhelming, really. He'd run home and holed up in his room all weekend playing video games he hadn't touched since he was twelve. The familiar characters and endless bleeping noises had made him feel safe.

Emma had nothing to make her feel safe. Her only family was out of town, her apartment was wrecked, and someone was trying to kidnap her because she'd been marked by a demon when she was a baby. He shouldn't have been teasing her or demanding another fuck session; he should have been offering her comfort and reassurance.

Andre cursed his own lack of sensitivity and headed toward the bathroom. "Emma? Are you ready?" he asked. When his words were met by silence, he wracked his brain for something that might make her feel better. "I thought you might want to try to call Ginger again. To see if we can make sure she's safe." More silence. Damn it. Being reminded her roommate could be in mortal danger probably wasn't the best call.

"And we could call Sam, too," he added, leaning his forehead against the cool wooden door, willing her to hear the concern in his voice. "I'm sure she'll want to know that you were attacked. She's safe with Jace, but she should know that there's another nut job out there looking for someone with a demon mark."

Still nothing. Even the mention of her sister hadn't provoked a positive response.

He was going to have to go in there and look her in the eye. He'd apologize for pressuring her and make sure she knew that he was going to back off and give her some space. But not too much space ... He didn't want her to doubt his interest.

Damn it, why did relationships have to be so complicated? And why did he suddenly have to decide he wanted a *relationship* with a girl who didn't trust him as far as she could throw him?

If Emma had trusted him, even a little bit, he wouldn't be opening the door into an empty room or an open window with its pale pink linen curtain waving tauntingly in the slight breeze. She was gone. Again. And this time he had no clue where she'd gone or why she'd run. He knew only that the thought of losing her made him ill.

Chapter Fourteen

*T*hank god for fire escapes.

Emma was through the third-story window, down the curling metal steps, and dropping to the ground into the narrow space between Sam's building and the restaurant next door in less than a minute—making her second bathroom-based escape in less than four hours. By the time Andre came to check on her, she hoped to be far, far away.

She had to get out of Southie. Hell, she had to get out of New York City. The watch on Andre's arm had confirmed there was no one she could trust. No one except Sam, and she was a million miles away.

So what? It's just distance, and there are planes and trains and cars.

Emma didn't have the cash for a plane, but she might be able to afford a train ticket. She could head up to Penn Station, get on the first train headed west, and find a way to contact her sister along the way. Hopefully, she could meet Sam and Jace between the two coasts.

Assuming she could trust Jace. He *was* Andre's cousin, after all.

Andre, whose memories evidently *hadn't* shown her everything she needed to know about the state of his soul. She couldn't believe that he was the man in the suit she'd seen in the minds of the pair who'd attacked her, that *Andre* was the leader who'd made Death Ministry thugs cower and Stewart cry. But then, she hadn't *wanted* to see something like that in Andre.

She'd wanted to believe that he was a good guy, a man worthy of the stupid crush she'd developed, a man she wouldn't mind remembering as her first . . . maybe her only. She must have simply tricked herself into seeing only the not-so-bad in Mr. Conti, because there was no doubt Andre was the one she'd seen ordering Stewart's beating.

The gold watch on his wrist was *exactly* the same, down to the gaudy diamonds on the band and the gold and black C etched into the face. There was even a slight crack in the glass . . . probably from where he'd backhanded the Death Ministry thug.

Emma's heart raced and her stomach punched at her lungs until she had to pause for a moment to swallow the bagel rising in her throat. She leaned against the cool stone of the building on her right, sucking in deep, calming breaths, refusing to lose what little sustenance she'd managed to ingest.

She didn't have time to get sick or to think about what Andre might really want from her. If he was the man behind all this and had ordered the trashing of her apartment, then he had to be after the spell book. Which meant he'd been playing with her all along, worming his way into her confidence in order to steal what his thugs hadn't been able to find.

It was . . . sickening.

Emma's gut pitched, but she shoved away from the wall and started running again anyway, weaving her way through the tangle of streets surrounding Sam's building, heading in the general direction of the barricade's exit. If only the city allowed people to cross over into Manhattan on foot, she could be at Penn Station within an hour. Instead, she'd be stuck in a taxi for half the afternoon, a sitting duck for any of Andre's minions who might be looking for her.

For the first time since moving to Southie, she felt trapped by the walls surrounding her, the hunted instead of the hunter. Andre had done that. He'd betrayed her and let her down, just like everyone else she'd ever trusted.

She couldn't believe she'd slept with him, or felt so guilty for losing control of her demon mark. She was a fool, a dumb, horny fool. Just the memory of how Andre had made her call his name as he pushed inside her made her face hot with shame. What had she been thinking? How could she have gotten naked with a man she didn't even like?

But then, if she hadn't gotten him naked, she never would have seen that watch. It was usually tucked up beneath the sleeve of his coat. Why he would pay so much money for a status symbol and then hide it under his jacket was a mystery to her, but so was just about everything else about Andre.

Everything he'd told her was a lie. *Everything.* After all she'd seen in the minds of evil, deceptive people, he'd still managed to fool her.

He was an excellent actor. For a few hours, she'd actually believed he cared. He'd seemed so genuinely affected by what they'd done. The way he'd put his arm around her and just . . . held her . . . She'd actually started to think they might have a future together:

the sex addict and the energy vampire. What a combo that would have been.

Emma was so wrapped up in her thoughts that she didn't realize she'd missed her second left until the cramped alley opened onto a dilapidated courtyard. She slowed, surveying her surroundings, the nasty feeling in her stomach getting even nastier.

Small, twisted trees and thick vines sprung from the ruined concrete yard, creeping toward the rays of sun that shot through the hollowed-out wreckage of the building across the way. The pavement beneath her feet was buckled in several places—as if some giant worm had passed this way before her—and the smell of demon waste baking in the summer heat drifted through the air.

Oh shit. This was bad. This was very bad.

Even before Emma saw the scaly alien form crouched in the wreckage of the old Spanish-style fountain dominating the yard, Emma knew she'd made a very serious error in judgment. Wandering into the ruins was a dumb call on a good day—when you'd had a good night's sleep and a solid breakfast and didn't feel like your stomach was going to leap out of your mouth if you opened too wide.

On a day like today—when her heart ached and her head spun with Andre's betrayal and her body burned with shame and fear—a stroll through the ruins might just be the death of her.

As Emma turned to run—boot sliding in a pile of demon shit she'd missed on the way in—she wondered whether Andre would find her corpse before it was too late. If he caught her before the demon ate her, he might still be able to use her body to work whatever spell he was hoping to cast. Some of the grimoire's spells called for the blood or flesh of a demon-marked human, not the human's aid in working the magic.

The thought made her run faster, legs pumping hard as the click of claws on concrete sounded behind her. That bastard had already used her body once. She'd be damned if she'd let him use it again. She was going to make it out of here alive. Demons were strong, but most of them weren't particularly fast. If she kept her head on her shoulders and ran straight back toward the more populated streets, then—

The second demon seemed to emerge from the ground in front of her, rising like smoke from a steaming manhole.

Striker demons. Like Ju Du demons, the lizardlike creatures could change the color and texture of their scales to blend in with their surroundings. Unlike most other demons, however, they hunted in packs. Still, you didn't hear many stories about Strikers killing off tourists. They were about the size of your average five-year-old, with short, stunted forearms and only a handful of teeth in their small mouths.

But if there were enough of them, they could kill a thin woman. Especially if that thin woman was suddenly dizzy and ill, her forearms shimmering with the telltale hint of gold dust.

No! She was sparking. Again! How the hell had this happened?

Stewart's shimmering neck floated across her mind's eye, and the truth cracked like a whip through her clouded thoughts. The Hamma claws. She'd pulled the claw venom into her body when she'd fed on Stewart and the Strong Man. She should have realized the truth sooner! Greg hadn't slipped Hamma into his tequila; he'd had it in his bloodstream and she'd sucked in a contact high.

The same thing had happened once, years ago. One of her victims had been tripping on Inuago pellets at a rave. After she'd fed, she'd gone back inside and danced until she threw up, then fed on one of the women who bent to help her up off the bathroom floor. It was the only time she'd ever danced—or fed—in public. She'd suspected she was as high as a kite. She should have learned her lesson and kept her hands off anyone who might have touched demon drugs. More important, she should have fucking understood what was happening this morning from the get-go.

Most important, she should stop wasting time beating herself up. She had to get out of here and find a suitable human snack before she ended up passed out on the concrete, Striker demons nibbling her flesh from her body while she was still alive.

Emma grunted as she darted to her right, narrowly avoiding the snapping teeth of the second demon, but she didn't dare cry out for help. She wasn't going to find help in this part of Southie. All she'd find were more demons or bounty hunters who might very well be working for the man she was trying to avoid.

She just had to stay quiet and move quickly. If there were only two of the Strikers, she would be okay. There was another alley on the opposite side of the courtyard. It had to lead to somewhere better than where she was now. If she just kept moving, she would—

The third demon was crouched on the opposite side of the fountain, waiting for the other two to herd their prey in the right direction. Out of the corner of her eye, Emma spied a flash of gray but barely had time to turn her head before the third Striker was on her, knocking her to the ground.

If she'd been steadier on her feet, she wouldn't have fallen. But she wasn't, and so she did, crashing into the concrete shoulder first. Her head came next, pain shooting from the back of her skull to slam between her eyes. The agony was so intense that it took several seconds for her to regain awareness of the body still attached to her throbbing head, to feel the hot noses snuffling at her stomach as the three Strikers scrambled on top of her, each searching for soft flesh to bite.

Emma sobbed and pushed at the wriggling bodies, but the Strikers didn't even bother to snap at her trembling fingers. They could tell she was weak, easy prey. There was no need to fight her when they'd be eating her in a few more moments. She tried to turn over, to protect her vulnerable stomach, but her writhing only seemed to excite the creatures.

She'd nearly accepted the fact that she was going to die when a sharp blast of stun fire crackled through the air, and one of the Strikers screamed and fell heavily on top of her.

The other two scattered like cockroaches in a newly lit room, scuttling away across the courtyard as the stun gun continued to fire. Emma thought she heard one of them fall but couldn't be sure. Her pulse was pounding too loudly in her ears, her heart struggling to overcome the trauma of her close call and the drugging effects of the Hamma claws.

Still, it didn't take her long to guess who had shot the gun that had saved her life. Even before his face appeared above her, lit from behind like some dark angel come to earth, she knew it was Andre. He'd found her, and now he was going to scoop her up and drag her back to that cage near the shelter.

If he wanted you in the cage, why didn't he help Stewart and the Death Ministry guy put you in there before?

The thought made her pause, but only for a second. Andre needed the book and knew her well enough to realize she wouldn't let him anywhere near it if she suspected he was going to use it for some evil scheme. That must have been why he'd let her roam free for so long. But now that he knew she was onto him, that she'd run from him the same way she'd run from the doctor and Little Francis, he—

"Is Little Francis in on it, too?" she asked, shoving at Andre's hands when he flung the limp demon off her stomach and tried to help her into a seated position.

"In on what?" he asked, angrier than she'd ever seen him. He looked like he wanted to shake her teeth loose. Finally, she was seeing the real Andre, and she didn't like what she saw one bit. "What the fuck are you talking about? Why did you run from me?"

"You know why." She tensed as he grabbed her arms and hauled her onto his lap. He swiped at the gold on her skin with a rattled sigh.

"You needed a fix? Is that it? You had to go get—"

"Give it a rest. You know I don't use drugs," she said, energized by the anger coursing through her veins. She managed to sit up a little straighter. She couldn't quite stand, but there was no way she was going to lean against his shoulder. "Why don't you tell me why you're after the book?"

He froze, a look of genuine confusion marring his face. He was good; no doubt about it. "The spell book? What are you—"

"Don't lie to me. Not again," she said, cutting him off before he could. "I know, Andre, so you might as well tell me the truth."

"You're out of your mind," he said, angry again, his fingers digging into her hip with a contained violence that would have been scary if she hadn't just nearly been eaten alive.

"Tell me," she said, ignoring the heaving of her stomach as the Hamma venom worked its way deeper into her bloodstream.

"I told you, I—"

"Fine, then I'll find it myself." With the last of her strength, Emma drove her hands into Andre's hair, fingers digging into the pressure points at the base of his skull. She expected him to fight her, to rip her arms away and haul her body to her feet and off to whatever holding facility he deemed fit. Instead, he sat completely still, only flinching slightly as her fingers dug deep into his skin.

After a moment, his lips parted and his face muscles relaxed; then, she was inside his mind. Frantic and enraged, she rifled through his memories, throwing pieces of him in the air as she hunted for the proof she sought.

She watched him running through the ruins, desperate, looking for her; she saw herself through his eyes as he kissed the curve of her breast; she saw her own smile as they walked down the street, the sun glinting on the gold in her hair. Emma pushed the pretty images aside, probing deeper, shoving into every corner of Andre's mind, scattering memories of beautiful women and childhood hurts and Katie in her wake.

For what seemed like hours she scoured the contents of his soul, finding every little sin he'd ever confessed into the quiet booth at Saint Mary's and a few dozen he'd been too ashamed to tell anyone. But nowhere in those secret shames did she find anything about Death Ministry connections or Stewart or great plans involving demon spell books and supernatural evil.

She did, however, find a hazy memory of the watch on his wrist, the one his Uncle Francis had given all the male cousins for their twenty-first birthdays, the special watch designed just for the Contis. Andre had cracked the face a few months ago when he'd dropped it on the marble floor of his bathroom. He'd been hiding it under his suit jacket until he had a chance to get it fixed, knowing how important the watch was to his uncle.

His uncle. All the male cousins.

That meant at least five men had this exact same watch. It also meant that—if his memories were to be believed—Andre was innocent. Unfortunately . . . one of his cousins was not. One of the Contis was up to his eyeballs in shady drug connections and big, bad plans of the demon-spell variety. One of the Contis wanted her in that cage, and she had a pretty good idea who that man was.

But she couldn't tell Andre, not until she had some kind of proof. He'd never believe that one of his family members had tried to hurt her, especially not now, when he assumed she'd run away from him to get high only hours after nearly overdosing.

Emma pulled her hands from Andre's hair. "I'm sorry," she said.

"Can you really see inside my mind when you do that?" he asked, for once his tone more curious than disbelieving.

"I can." Emma took a deep breath, fighting another wave of nausea. She was going to have to find someone to feed on, quickly, or she wouldn't be investigating anything except the inside of the nearest toilet. "But I didn't find . . . what I thought I'd find."

"You really thought I was the one after your book?" he asked, having evidently put two and two together and figured out what she was raving about. The hurt in his eyes made her wince.

"I had reasons to believe you were," she said.

He shook his head, his disappointment making the air even harder to breathe. "You had more reasons to believe I wasn't."

And . . . he was right. *Completely* right. He'd given her no reason to doubt him. He was angry and hurt, and he had every right to be. She'd been horrible to him.

But then, she was horrible to everyone . . . sooner or later. She could blame it on her childhood, she could blame it on her time locked away in a madman's basement, she could blame it on the dark craving and every life it had driven her to steal from the time she was too little to tie her shoes . . . but it didn't really matter *why* she was the way she was. It only mattered that she was broken, useless to other, normal people. She'd tried to warn Andre that she was bad news, but he hadn't listened. It was his fault that he felt like his favorite puppy had pissed in his shoes.

Too bad blaming him didn't make her feel any better. Nothing she could do would make either of them feel better. . . .

Unless . . .

Andre had said he wanted to try. Had he meant it? Could he really care about her enough to give her his trust? And could she put aside all her bullshit, all her issues, all the fear that she'd never be able to have a normal, human relationship, long enough to give him that same chance?

She didn't know. But she suddenly realized how much she'd meant those words in her sister's shop. She did want to try. With Andre. And there was no better time than the present.

"I've never been on Hamma claws."

Andre sighed. "Emma, I—"

"I think I sucked the drugs into my body when I was feeding on Greg this morning and then again with Stewart. Right before the Striker demons attacked, I . . . I had a memory of a time when the same thing happened," she said, watching Andre's face for some sign that he thought she was lying or crazy or both. Instead, he was quiet, waiting for her to go on, for her to give him a reason to believe. "That time it was Inuago pellets. They made me sick, and I had to feed again to get the drugs out of my system, the same way I had to feed this morning."

She told him about Dr. Finch, about what she'd seen in his mind, how she'd pulled his energy inside her to banish the torture of the venom and antivenom warring it out in her body. She shared everything she'd seen in the Strong Man and Stewart's memories, even the things she couldn't make sense of yet. It was only when she got to the part about the watch that her voice faltered and the words didn't come so easily. She was ashamed of how she'd reacted. So ashamed.

Now Andre would know that—even for a few minutes—she'd suspected he was a truly evil man.

Andre shook his head as she trailed off and swallowed hard. The strained silence stretched on and on, broken only by the scuffling of tiny claws somewhere in the shadows around the courtyard.

Squat demons, most likely, or something equally harmless. Still, they should get out of here before something bigger came along or the Striker demons decided to come back for their stunned friend. Not to mention the fact that Emma needed to feed. Now. But she couldn't seem to say any of those things to Andre. She couldn't say a word, not until she knew if he could at least *try* to believe her.

"What about all the other bad guys you've fed on? Why hasn't this happened more than once before?" Andre asked, shocking her with his choice of questions. Of all the things she'd told him, she'd assumed he'd be more interested in the fact that someone in his family was working with the Death Ministry. "Weren't a lot of those people on demon drugs?"

"Not where I grew up. People in our town were too poor to afford fancy drugs. We had to stick to alcohol and cigarettes and the occasional bowl." She winced as another cramp hit her stomach but forced herself to talk through the pain. "But you'd be surprised—a lot of the really bad guys, and girls, don't do drugs."

"Too dedicated to their evil work to cloud their mind with toxins?"

"Something like that," she said, searching his shuttered face again for some sign that he'd heard and understood the implications of the watch she'd seen in the men's minds. "I think, for most of them, violence is its own drug."

"Kind of like sex." He laughed a humorless laugh and shoved a damp clump of hair off his forehead.

His words made her think. Sex and violence—two extreme human emotions, one capable of creating life, the other all too often dedicated to destroying it. She'd always known that she could feed on anger and evil, but apparently she could feed on sex, as well. Father Paul had never mentioned such a thing, but he *was* a priest and hardly an expert on sexual energy.

But just because she *could* feed on sex didn't make it okay. As far as she knew, the consequences of her feeding would still be the same for her victims, and she certainly didn't want to make victims of her lovers. Especially *this* lover.

God, was there a chance they really could be lovers? Could he forgive her? Could she find a way to control her demon mark and make sure he was safe in her arms? She hoped so, hoped so hard it made her ache all over.

"My money's on Little Francis," Andre finally said, proving he'd understood what that watch meant for the Conti family. He stood with her in his arms as if she weighed no more than the small demon lying stunned on the concrete a few feet away. "I think his eagerness to work a deal with the Death Ministry must have been a cover for his real agenda."

"Dealing drugs? But why would he want the spell book if this is all about drugs? Why try to kidnap me?"

"I don't know."

"Do you think your uncle knows? Do you think—"

"I doubt it, but I can't be sure. And we can't go back to the offices or to your sister's shop or anywhere else Francis will think to look for us until we know who's turned traitor and who hasn't. We're going to have to find someplace else where you can rest and—"

"I know somewhere we can go," she said, seizing on the first idea to float through her spinning head. She didn't need rest; she needed food, damn it. Whether Andre believed that part of her story or not, she knew it was the truth. "You know the strip club behind Yang's Curiosity Shop?"

"Boudreaux's?"

"Yeah. Jeremiah, the manager. He has rooms for rent," she said. "No one will look for us there."

Emma held her breath, hoping he'd agree that Boudreaux's was a good choice. The manager, Jeremiah, would perfectly suit her current needs. He'd raped at least three of the strippers at the club since Emma had moved into the area last spring.

Ginger volunteered at the rape victims hotline and had warned Emma against getting anywhere near Boudreaux's. She'd even insisted on accompanying Emma to buy her miniflamethrowers since the back room of Yang's shared an alley with the front entrance to Boudreaux's. Ginger, for all her faults and flightiness, was a good person and a very good friend.

Emma had to find some way to contact her and make sure

she was safe and—hopefully—still had the spell book in her possession. Thank god she'd run from Little Francis and his people. If anyone could be trusted with a demon grimoire, it was Ginger. She had no lust for supernatural power; she just wanted to expand her boot collection and find a guy who wasn't a complete scumbag or married or both.

"Please, Andre. It's not far and—"

"I know where it is, and I can guess what you want there," he said, turning right into a narrow street that ran alongside the main road. "What exactly did you see in Dr. Finch again—what was he doing?"

Emma closed her eyes, pulling up the memory of the dark room and Dr. Finch's hands deep in the insides of a man with a bloated stomach. She swallowed hard, eyes flying open to meet Andre's. "Organ harvesting, I think. Definitely illegal surgery of some kind, and he didn't care whether the man on his table lived or died. He wasn't even wearing gloves when he reached inside his—"

"Sh." Andre hugged her tighter to his chest. "You're going to make us both sick."

"I'm probably going to be sick, anyway."

"No, you're not," Andre said. "We're going to get you what you need. I promise."

"So you believe me? You really do? About all of it?" She was almost afraid to hope, but there was no doubt he was headed toward Boudreaux's and away from the Conti family offices.

"I do. I just wish I'd believed you sooner. Then maybe you would have believed in me."

"I'm sorry. I really am." She looked up, catching him gazing down at her. What she saw in his eyes made it even harder to breathe. He was still angry, but there was another emotion in those dark depths, something that looked like a word she was too afraid to think for fear of jinxing their future.

"I forgive you," he said, the three words a promise she knew he would keep. They were in this together now, for better or for worse. Hopefully, they'd get around to the better part one of these days, after all the madness and mayhem.

"Thank you." Emma dropped her head to Andre's shoulder.

"I should call Little Francis," he said, "just so he doesn't get suspicious."

"No, you shouldn't." She lifted her head again. "It's better if he has no idea where we are or what we're up to. But we should call Ginger from one of the wall phones at the club. Maybe she'll answer if it's a Southie number."

"After we take care of you," Andre said, casting a concerned look down at her bare arm. "You're getting worse."

"I don't feel as bad as I did last time." *At least not yet.*

The unspoken words hung in the air between them, making Andre pick up his pace as they eased into the alley behind Yang's, and Boudreaux's pink neon sign came into view.

CHAPTER FIFTEEN

*T*here was a time and a place for strip clubs. That time was not eleven thirty in the morning, when he was stone-cold sober. That place was not some Southie dive where the girls swaying listlessly on the miniature stages looked like they were about to pass out or throw up from whatever combo of demon drugs they'd sniffed, swallowed, or injected before starting their shifts.

The madly pink walls—covered with black velvet paintings of rock stars from the 1980s that glowed neon yellow and orange in the dim light—only made the strippers look more tired and worn. They also gave Andre a splitting headache. That particular shade of pink should never be used for anything. Ever. It was an aggressive, testosterone-killing color. It made it hard to imagine any man had gotten a boner in this room in the past ten years, no matter how up close and personal the girls at Boudreaux's were alleged to get.

But then, he was a little pickier than the average Southie client.

There were only a couple of men slouched in the black, wrinkled, faux-leather chairs crowding the space, but if they were anything to judge by, the patrons here weren't any more sober than the women who danced for them. They were probably so high they couldn't even see the walls.

Hell, for all he knew, the glowing portraits of Billy Idol and an aged, bloated Elvis added to their experience.

He didn't doubt that the manager here was dealing demon drugs and probably bribing law enforcement officials to keep them from raiding the club. If he didn't, this place would have closed down years ago.

What he didn't know was whether that made Jeremiah a suitable source of energy. Now that Andre believed Emma, the reality of what she was churned in his gut. She *killed* people. Bad people, yes, but what was her definition of bad? And did any definition or any code make it okay for her to stand judge, jury, and executioner to other people?

All he knew was that he was falling for her, fast, and needed to believe there was an alternative to more death. There had to be a safer way for her to feed. Or had he been wrong when he assumed their lovemaking hadn't harmed him? For all he knew, he could be ready to drop dead on the damned stairs up to Jeremiah's office.

Still, he was willing to risk it. For her. No matter how angry he was, or how hurt by her assumption that he was as evil as every other bastard she'd ever laid her glowing hands on.

Speaking of evil bastards . . . he wondered when Little Francis would get around to returning his message. Despite Emma's veto vote, Andre had left Francis a quick voice message while he was paying their admission to the club, telling him they'd been delayed because Emma wasn't feeling well. He'd assured his cousin they were in a safe place and would be back soon, but that wouldn't appease him for long. Andre had to figure out what to do about his turncoat cousin ... as soon as he made sure Emma was going to live to see the sun set on this shitty day.

"I don't know if I can make it up the stairs," Emma said as he stuffed his wallet back in his coat and fetched her from the faded couch by the door. She leaned heavily against him, her skin sparkling even in the dim light.

But the man he'd paid for their admission didn't blink an eye, only grunted that Jeremiah's office was at the top of the stairs, past the bathrooms.

"I'll carry you," Andre said, but Emma pushed his hand away.

"No, it's too narrow. I'll get up there somehow. It will be easier if I'm alone." The way her fingers trembled made his throat tighten. He hated to see her like this, so fragile, poisoned by the drugs rushing through her system. If he hadn't run after her, she would have been too weak to defend herself from the Striker demons. They would have eaten her alive.

The thought enraged and terrified him all at the same time.

It upset him that she'd run. No matter how damning her vision, she shouldn't have doubted him after all they'd been through together in the past few hours. It terrified him that her safety already meant so much to him, that his stupid heart was so eager to make excuses for her behavior. In the short time it had taken them to reach Boudreaux's, he'd found at least a dozen reasons to give Emma another chance.

Could he blame a woman who'd been through everything Emma had been through for having trust issues? He should have expected that her first instinct was to run away and anticipated her need for more reassurance than the average person. He should have believed her about her demon mark sooner. He should have talked more and teased less, he should have, should have, should have, blah, blah, blah, until he wanted to scream.

In less than a day, Emma had him thinking like a man in love. Worse, she had him thinking like a *woman* in love, second-guessing himself to the point that he'd let her talk him into coming to this cesspit to kill a man.

He knew that's why she wanted to be alone. She didn't want him to see what she'd do to the man at the top of the stairs. The thought made his stomach roil. He couldn't do it, not even if the alternative might mean risking his own life.

But would she agree to what he had in mind? Probably not. So maybe he'd pull an Emma and refrain from telling her the entire truth until it was too late for her to protest. . . .

"I'm not letting you go alone," he said. "It's not safe."

"It's perfectly safe." She nodded to the tall, dark shadows skulking in the corners of the room. "There are three bouncers down here to protect you."

"No," he said, his tone clipped and final, refusing to acknowledge her attempt at humor. "Let me help you walk up, or I'm going to carry you up. End of discussion."

She sighed and looped her arm around his shoulders. Andre could tell she didn't like it, but that was fine. She didn't have to like that he was looking out for her; he was still going to do it. Andre started up the stairs, pulling Emma beside him, praying harder than he'd prayed in a long time that he'd be able to help her. He wanted her to know that she didn't have to spend the rest of her life looking for her next victim, that she could get what she needed in another way, from another man, if it came to that.

Damn. The thought made him physically ill. He didn't want to think about Emma with another man. He couldn't help remembering the look on her face after they'd made love, when she said she'd "like to try." There had been something in her eyes, something amazing that made him pray even harder as they reached the top of the stairs and shuffled down the hall.

Mercifully, the walls on the second floor were a relatively innocuous light blue, but the stench was as aggressive as the decorating scheme downstairs. A thick, lurid odor hung in the air, a mix of unwashed flesh, sex, and . . . meat. Barbecue chicken, to be specific. It was almost enough to make Andre gag, even when breathing through his mouth.

"God, it's like . . . I can *taste* that smell," Emma said, echoing his thoughts. The gold shimmer of her spark did nothing to conceal the unhealthy green that tinged her skin. She was going to be sick if they stayed up here much longer.

Andre had nearly decided to screw Jeremiah's rooms and seek out another private place when the man they were looking for stepped out of his office. Jeremiah Boudreaux was even more repellent than his stench. As the obese black man oozed out into the hall—the front of his gold T-shirt smeared with barbecue sauce and the close of his pants not quite zipped—it became clear he was the source of the stink in the hall.

Behind him, in his equally filthy office, two of his employees—still dressed in nothing but gold thongs and matching tassels—crouched on top of his desk, digging into a bucket of chicken as if they hadn't eaten in days. And maybe they hadn't. They were both as painfully thin as Jeremiah was fat, their ribs standing out clearly beneath their skin.

Andre turned his eyes back to Jeremiah, finding him the less disturbing of the two sights.

"Raymond said you wanted to see me?" Jeremiah bared a mouthful of even, white teeth that were at odds with the rest of his appearance.

"We need some antivenom for Hamma claws and heard you were the person to ask. We also need a room, and we need you to make sure no one knows we're here, not even my family," Andre said, feeling the man saunter up behind him. A glance over his shoulder revealed a giant bald guy with a stun gun on his hip standing at the top of the stairs.

He should have known Jeremiah wouldn't talk to anyone without security. He was a shady, disgusting bastard, but he was a rich bastard with a prime piece of Southie real estate several people would kill to see back on the market.

"But, Andre, I—"

"Emma, I'll take care of this." Andre shot her a pointed look, silently willing her to trust him. She pressed her lips together, then thought better of it and opened them again, the better to breathe through her mouth.

"Yes, sir, Mr. Conti. I believe that can be arranged." Jeremiah drew the words out into a half dozen syllables. Whether real or affected, his Cajun drawl sounded like the genuine article. "I most certainly can help you. Tyrone." He motioned to the man behind them with two thick fingers. "Take these fine people up to a sweat room, the best available. I'll have that antivenom sent right up."

Without another word, he turned and waddled back into his office, shutting the door behind him. Seconds later there came a grunt and a giggle from one of the women still inside. Tyrone strode past them on the right, continuing down the hall to another set of stairs, hopefully leading to a floor unaffected by Jeremiah's profound personal odor.

Emma cursed beneath her breath. "What are you doing? I don't need the antivenom."

"I know."

"Then why are we going to the sweat room?" she whispered, pulling away when Andre tried to lead her down the hall. Clearly she was aware that the sweat rooms were where the strippers took clients who could afford a "private dance"—the kind where the thong came off and the customer had his turn to work up a sweat.

"Relax." He reclaimed her arm, the very thought of "sweating" with Emma arousing him, despite the stench lingering in the hall and the knowledge that the room they were being led to was probably extremely unhygienic. "I told you we'd take care of you."

"Andre, please." Her eyes darted down the hall to where Tyrone waited for them at the bottom of the second set of stairs. Her next words were so soft he could barely hear her. "Listen, I thought I could . . ." She paused, taking a deep breath through her mouth, fighting the effects of the venom. "I know Jeremiah's done a lot of bad things to the girls here. I know he'd work, but I'm not sure about Tyrone. I don't know if he's done anything to deserve what I'd do to him."

"Just trust me."

"I can't. I—"

"Then what are we doing here? Why did you tell me all those

things you told me in the ruins?" he hissed, anger flaring to life inside him once more.

"I ... I thought I could try, but I don't know. I—"

"Well, I know. So shut up and let me help you," he said, his harsh words shocking even himself.

He couldn't remember the last time he'd told a woman to shut up, or whether he'd ever. He'd been raised to treat women with respect, to consider them fragile and sensitive in ways that made them both finer than the male of the species and lesser at the same time. But Emma was different. She wasn't nearly as delicate as she looked. She was tough, hard, strong—his equal in every way, including her nearly debilitating fear of trusting another person. He knew what she was going through, and he knew they could get past that fear. Together.

"But what are we—"

"Trust me, and keep quiet." Andre hustled her up the stairs behind Tyrone and followed the large, silent man down a narrow hallway to the right.

Once again, Boudreaux's underwent a dramatic shift in character from one floor to the next. Instead of bright pink or baby blue, the walls were covered in simple wood paneling interspersed with black, numbered doors. The music playing downstairs pumped through speakers in the ceiling, presumably to cover the sounds of the people busy in the sweat rooms to their right and left. At this early hour, the rooms all seemed empty, but Tyrone still led them down to the last door on the right, lucky number thirteen.

Outside the door, a girl in a green silk wrap thrown hastily over her stripper gear stood with a silver tray holding a cup of steaming liquid, a dish of silver powder, several small mixing bowls, and a hypodermic needle still in its plastic wrapping. Just looking at the needle made Andre's skin crawl.

"She can take the powder in the tea or mix it with a little water and inject. Shooting will be faster, but it might make her sicker. If she starts having convulsions, stick the wooden mixer between her teeth so she doesn't bite her tongue," the girl said, swift and non-chalant with her instructions, as if she talked to people on the verge of overdose every day. She slipped into the room ahead of Tyrone, leaving her tray on a small table by a tidy, twin-sized bed.

The bed was made up all in white, with a simple comforter and sheets that smelled of bleach and cheap laundry detergent, topped with a red pillow like the cherry on a sundae. The floor was bare except for a thick brown and red shag rug, and the walls were painted a deep red with a swirling pattern in dark brown that swept from the floor to the ceiling.

On the whole, it was far nicer—and cleaner—than Andre had anticipated. It would make the testing of his latest hypothesis a whole lot more comfortable now that he and Emma could actually sit down somewhere without catching a venereal disease.

"You've got two hours," Tyrone said as the girl in green left the room. "But if you take longer, it's no big deal. We don't get many people using the VIP room."

"Thanks," Andre said, all but carrying Emma into the room and sitting her down on the bed.

She was getting weaker with every passing minute. If his plan didn't work, he would have to take her down to Jeremiah's office, no matter how the thought terrified him. He wasn't going to let her die, not even if it meant being an accessory to murder.

"Credit card or cash deposit?" Tyrone asked, holding out one meaty hand. "It's two grand for the room and another two for the antivenom."

Emma gasped at the numbers, but Andre didn't blink. Demon drugs themselves might be relatively cheap, but the antivenom went for ten times the price of an equal amount of Hamma claws. It was cheap to party. It was a lot more expensive to live.

He handed over his credit card.

"You can sign and pick it up at the front desk on your way out," Tyrone said before turning and leaving the room without a backward glance, apparently unconcerned by the low moaning sound Emma made as she fell to her side on the bed.

But then, he'd probably seen worse. The bodies of the people who didn't survive the antivenom didn't get down all those stairs and dumped in some trash bin on the other side of Southie on their own. Someone had to carry them, and Tyrone was the biggest guy he'd seen around the club so far. He might suit Emma's needs after all.

The thought comforted him. The more potential energy sources, the better, though he still hoped with everything in him that they wouldn't need that sort of "food"—that Emma might not need that sort of food ever again.

Andre waited until Tyrone closed the door and then went to turn the two locks, ensuring them at least a few seconds' notice if Tyrone or someone else with keys decided to interrupt. Andre didn't anticipate interruption, however. From everything he'd heard about Boudreaux's, the establishment was known for its discretion . . . at least in everything except decorative choices for their first-floor showroom.

"Please, Andre," Emma moaned, trying to sit up but failing.

"Let's just go. I'll find someone else. We can go out the window, down the hall, and—"

"No more sneaking through windows. You've done enough of that for one day," he said, crossing back to the bed and easing her onto her back, unable to keep from noticing how beautiful the spark could be.

Lying there, shimmering like some golden goddess, Emma looked too perfect to be real. Even with her hairline damp with sweat and her lips pressed together in pain, she was gorgeous. Katie had been gorgeous, too, but for the first time in years, thinking about Katie didn't hurt quite as much.

"Andre, please. You don't understand—"

"I understand." He shrugged off his coat, letting it drop to the rug, making a mental note to burn this suit at the first opportunity. "You sucked the life out of a drug addict and it's giving you a bad Hamma trip. You need something to counteract the venom."

"Yes, but the antivenom only made it worse last time." Her brows drew together as she watched his fingers work open the two buttons left on his shirt, the ones she hadn't popped off when she'd ripped it off of him earlier. "I promise you, I . . ."

His shirt joined his suit coat on the floor, and his hands went to his belt, working the leather through the tight loops. Emma's eyes grew large with understanding.

"Andre. We can't. I—"

"You said you felt charged after we had sex. Right? So why don't we see if I can help you out." He pushed his pants to the ground along with his briefs, until he stood before her completely naked, his cock thickening at her soft inhalation. She might not feel her best at the moment, but she still wanted him. He could see it in the way her lips parted, in the way her fingers dug into the blanket beneath her. "Now, take off your clothes."

Emma's wide eyes grew even wider. "No! I'm not going to let you take that kind of risk when—"

"Fine. I'll take them off for you." He reached for the close of her belt. For a second, he thought she would fight him, but the look in his eyes must have made her think better of it.

Instead, she lay back, breath growing shallow as he unbelted and unbuckled and pulled her jeans and panties roughly down to her knees. For a second, he thought about taking off her boots so that he could finish stripping off her clothes, worried about making her more comfortable. But then he saw the look in her eyes and knew she couldn't care less about comfort. She wanted to feel better, yes, but she wanted him to fuck her nearly as much. He'd seen that hooded look of desire on dozens of female faces, but it had never aroused him as much as it did right now.

"Roll over. Lift your hips," he said, growing hotter, harder, as he realized he'd be balls deep in Emma Quinn in a matter of seconds.

"I can't." Emma's lips parted and her tongue flicked out along her dry lips. "You have to help me."

"Not a problem." He reached for her again, but this time she lifted her hands, warning him away.

"Do you know what you're risking? Really? Do you know—"

"I know. Now, roll over."

"Andre, I—" Her words ended in a grunt as her gripped her hips and flipped her onto her stomach, then pulled her legs around until they dropped off the edge of the narrow bed. Her boots hit the floor with a thud Andre could barely hear over the pounding of his pulse. Emma's new arrangement put her pussy in the perfect position, her slick opening pressed tight against the base of his cock. All he had to do was pull back and adjust himself the barest inch and he'd be inside of her, shoving into her heat, banishing the fear and hurt flooding his body in a frantic pleasure that just might kill him.

What if he was wrong about sex creating the energy she needed without hurting him? What if there was a heart attack in his immediate future? More important . . . what if fucking didn't give her enough fuel to fight the poison in her body? What if this was a potentially deadly waste of time for both of them?

"Please," Emma whispered, her voice breathy and her body trembling lightly beneath the fingers he rested on her hips. "Don't make me . . ."

"Don't make you what? Fuck me?" Even the thought that she might not want him reopened the painful hole in his chest.

The same hole she'd ripped open when she'd described the last moment he'd seen Katie alive, the one she'd made even deeper when she'd run from him, having the nerve to suspect him of trying to steal that stupid book.

"No." She turned to look at him over her shoulder, caramel eyes filled with such raw need that he felt the echo of it screaming across his skin. "Don't make me hate myself any more than I already do. I don't want to hurt you. . . . I . . ." Her voice broke and her fathomless eyes shone with unshed tears. "I think I love you."

His anger slipped away, the string on a balloon escaping into the sky. "I love you, too." His voice was so choked with emotion, it was hardly recognizable. What she made him feel . . . it was more than he could handle, more than his mind could process with Emma bent over in front of him, vulnerable and yet still so far beyond his reach.

So he didn't try to process or understand; he simply positioned himself at her entrance and pushed inside, fear melting away as he sank deeper and deeper, until he was completely encased in her heat, her body, the core of her that was by far the most addictive place he'd ever been. But it wasn't his addictive personality that gave him the control he needed to move slowly, to wait until Emma cried out in pleasure and lifted her hips before he quickened his thrusts, until he drove into her faster and faster with a force that made her groan and shove back against him, as hot and ready and desperate for the pleasure they would find together as he was.

No, it wasn't addiction. Or experience. Or compassion. Or the fact that he was a decent man who would never hurt a woman.

It was love. It was love that made him hold back his own release, to keep driving when Emma's back arched and she came with a long, low moan. It was love that urged him to thrust harder, faster, even when the blue glow came again, illuminating the curves of Emma's pale flesh, highlighting her golden hair with streaks of sapphire.

Almost immediately he could see Emma's vitality begin to return, but the light didn't hurt him any more than it had the last time. If anything, it made the last few seconds before he lost himself even more intense. He was climbing to the top of the world with this woman, taking in the humbling beauty of creation from a pure, perfect place he'd never dreamed existed before toppling off the edge into wonder with Emma by his side. He'd never felt so free, never known making love could be as much a spiritual pleasure as a physical one.

Only with her, only with Emma, had he ever been liberated by desire rather than chained to its side. It made him love her even more, made him certain she was worth this risk, worth any risk. Her power might be the work of evil demons, but there was nothing wicked or bad in Emma Quinn. Despite the lies, he believed that with everything in him.

If he didn't die of a heart attack in the next few hours, he was going to do his best to make sure she believed it, too.

CHAPTER SIXTEEN

*E*mma fought the driving need to come again, but her body was quickly spiraling out of her control. She'd never felt so damned *good*, so satiated, so drunk on sex and love and life. Inside her addled cells, the dark craving fed with a vengeance on the sexual heat she and Andre created, just as it had in the flower shop. There were still no memories, no sense of sin or bad karma flowing from Andre into her. There was only fullness. So much fullness. She was full to the brim with him—his passion, his energy, his spirit. The world spun and pitched and tossed her in the air like a doll, and she never, ever wanted it to end.

But she didn't want to come again, either. She couldn't. Hell, she *could*, she *could* in a heartbeat, but there was some good reason she *shouldn't*. In the fever Andre inspired, it was hard to remember what that reason was, but—

Andre cried out, his cock jerking, the liquid heat of his release flooding inside of her, sending her over the edge.

Emma's head fell back as she lost the battle against bliss. She came, her back arching with the force of her orgasm, her fingers clawing into the blanket beneath her. She screamed—a wild, feral sound—and wiggled her hips in a shameless attempt to force him deeper, to draw the moment of mindlessness out a little longer, to lose herself in the magic of what he did to her.

She'd never imagined sex could be like this. That she could feel so subjugated, yet so powerful, at the same time.

When Andre had shoved her pants down and taken her without the expected foreplay, without a kiss or a caress or any of those pre-liminaries she'd always heard were the best part of sex for a woman, she'd expected pain or at least discomfort. But there hadn't been any pain. Only bone-deep satisfaction. It had been even better than the first time. Hotter. Wilder. And unexpectedly . . . sweeter, somehow.

Her jeans were bunched around her knees, and her ass pre-sented like an animal in heat, but she'd never felt so treasured. This moment wasn't just about pleasure or affection. This was about a man risking his life. For her.

A part of her truly believed that this new method of feeding the darkness was what she'd been searching for—a way to sustain her own life without stealing from others. It was amazing, the miracle she'd prayed for before she'd grown too tired and angry to pray. The way Andre had glowed in the shop was so different from anything she'd ever seen before, as if he was as charged up by their encounter as she was. As if the sexual energy they created together nourished him instead of stealing his life away. It truly hadn't felt like she was hurting him.

But what if she was wrong? She could be. They both knew the danger, but he'd made this decision regardless.

It boggled her mind, made her thoughts race faster than her pounding heart as Andre collapsed on top of her, breathing hard. Seconds later, he rolled to his back beside her, severing their connection. The blue light vanished, but the feeling of goodness, of satisfaction and health, remained. The poison in her system was gone, burned away in the heat of the fire between them.

"You are . . ." His words trailed away as he brushed her sweaty, sticky hair to one side and pressed a kiss to her neck, sighing as if her Hamma-tainted skin was the sweetest thing he'd ever tasted.

"I am?" she asked, voice husky.

"Yeah. You just . . . are." He sighed and rolled back onto his back, staring at the ceiling. "And I do."

She sucked in a shaking breath and pressed her face into the blanket beneath her, his simple words affecting her even more deeply than his admission of love. Surely, he couldn't care that much. Maybe he had a death wish she hadn't seen in his memories. Maybe that wild streak in him was wilder than she'd assumed. Maybe he hadn't truly understood the risk he was—

"How do you feel?" he asked.

"Better. Good." She lifted her head, daring a glance at his face. He looked entirely healthy, happy, and relaxed in a way she'd never seen him before, even in the flower shop. It was amazing, especially considering he was half naked in the kind of establishment that would have usually kicked his clean-freak phobia into high gear.

"Good." He smiled. "Me, too."

"Good. Great. Thank god." Emma swallowed and considered sliding off the bed and pulling up her jeans. But she didn't. She stayed there beside him on her stomach, the evidence of what they'd done sliding down her thigh. It made her want him again, that messy bit of real life that he'd left behind. "And you're sure you're okay? You're not dizzy or—"

"No. I'm . . . perfect. I can't remember the last time I felt this good after sex." His eyes stayed on the ceiling, though she could tell he was aware of her watching his emotions play out on his face. The fact that he allowed the intimacy without feeling the need to pin her with his usual assessing glare made her want to kiss him. And then kiss him again. "It's usually . . . sad at the end. The second it's over . . . it's like . . ."

"It's like what?" she asked, wanting him to know that she cared, that she craved his confidence as much as his body. She'd seen inside his mind, but there were still so many things she wanted to know about Andre Conti. "Tell me."

"It's like . . . the emptiness comes back." His tongue slipped out to wet his lips, making her fingers itch to trace the curves of his full mouth, to tease inside the sweet hollow beneath his nose. "I can't even enjoy the release. I'm too busy thinking about the next time." He turned to face her, the vulnerability in his expression making Emma struggle to catch her breath. "It's not like that with you."

"It's not?"

"No, it's not."

Emma bit her lip, overwhelmed. The cynic in her screamed that he was feeding her a line, but her heart knew better. Andre wouldn't lie to her, not about this. He wasn't a liar. She'd known that on some gut level even before she'd searched his mind in the ruins.

Unfortunately, the same couldn't be said of his cousin.

Shit. Now that the poison in her blood was gone, the full weight of the mess they were in hit hard. What if Little Francis already suspected that she and Andre knew too much? Ginger's behavior, her own flight from Conti headquarters, and the fact that she and Andre were still out and about and not firmly nestled in the family bosom would have all conspired to make him suspicious.

But how suspicious? Enough to take steps to cover his tracks? Or enough to make damn sure she and Andre didn't tell anyone that he was the man after her spell book? Did Little Francis have it in him to order the death of a member of his own family? Even in the name of acquiring supernatural power?

LF's face flickered on her mental screen, full of false confidence and suppressed anger that Jace was favored to take over the family business. He wasn't the smartest man, but he was clever, ambitious, and lacking that certain thread of moral fiber that kept the rest of the Contis from being the kind of criminals Father Paul would have urged her to add to her feeding list.

She had her answer.

Now she needed to know why Little Francis wanted her spell book, why he was getting in the drug business with the Death Ministry, and how the two were related.

"Emma? You still with me?"

"I . . . I am," she said, focusing in on Andre's face.

She *was* with him, more than he knew. Protecting the Conti family was something she wanted to do for him, because she cared, because she . . . loved him. Emma blushed, even the *thought* of loving a man enough to make her cheeks heat. She wasn't ready for this, not by a long shot, but if she'd learned anything in her life, it was that life didn't wait for you to be ready. She was simply going to have to rise to the challenge. Because she wanted to love Andre, more than she could have imagined even a few hours ago.

"I just . . . don't know what to say."

"You don't have to say anything," he said. "I know I'm amazing in bed."

Emma smiled. It was past time to throw the man a bone. "You are. Completely amazing. I had no idea it could be like that."

He grinned so hard his dimples popped. "It *wouldn't* be like that with anyone else. So if I die of a heart attack, don't even think about sleeping around."

"You're not going to die," she said, smile slipping at the sobering thought.

"I know I'm not. And you're not going to sleep around."

"No. I'm not." Even if sex was the answer to her problems, even if she could have been feeding on sexual energy instead of evil since she was old enough to have intercourse, it didn't matter. She didn't want anyone else. She wanted Andre. Fussy, vain, loyal, brave Andre. And he seemed to want her as well.

But would he still want her if her demon mark were responsible for turning him into a killer? If Little Francis had been up to the very bad things she suspected, and Andre was the one to out his plans, then Andre would have to take care of the problem. The Contis were a kinder, gentler breed of mobsters, but they were still organized crime. If LF had betrayed his family, put the lives of Conti women and children at risk, and tried to make a deal with gang members and demons behind his father's back, he'd have to be dealt with. And as the senior Conti in town, that would be Andre's job.

Emma had seen in his memories that he'd never killed anything before, not even the demons he'd helped hunt as a younger man. Taking a life—especially the life of one of his own—would destroy something inside him, that core of faith in his own goodness that made him the man he was.

She shivered, though the air-conditioning in the small room was hardly functioning at top capacity. She had to get to Little Francis and have a hands-on conversation. Now. Surely she and Andre would be safe if they went directly to the Conti family offices. Little Francis couldn't hurt Andre with half the family there to witness it.

And once she had confirmation, she'd find a way to take care of him herself.

"We should go." She stood and reached for one of the white towels on the table near the bed, trying not to think about how many other people had used them to mop up various excretions. At least the rag smelled like bleach; surely it was clean enough.

Her thoughts made her laugh beneath her breath.

"What's funny?" Andre came to stand beside her as he adjusted his clothes.

"I was wondering how clean this was." She held up the towel before tossing it in the linen basket near the table. "I think you're starting to get to me."

"I know you're getting to me. I don't plunk down four thousand dollars for just any woman." He stared at the tray filled with all the trappings of the antivenom. "I'm just glad we didn't . . ." He paused, slowly reaching for the dish containing the silver powder, tilting it to the light before letting it fall back onto the tray with a curse. "Dr. Finch."

"Dr. Finch?" Emma echoed as she buttoned her jeans.

"That's why you suspected I had something to do with all this, isn't it?" he asked, turning to pin her with one of his most piercing looks. "Because of Dr. Finch. Because I was the one who told Little Francis to call him."

Emma's mouth opened and closed without a sound as she struggled to understand where Andre was going with this.

"Don't lie to me," Andre warned. "No more lies."

"I told you about Dr. Finch," she said. "I saw him performing some kind of back-alley surgery . . . something that made him a lot of money, but that's all I could see for sure. I was so out of it by the time I touched him that I couldn't—"

Andre cursed again. "I should have realized."

"Realized what?"

"I'd never seen anyone suffer through the antivenom like you did this morning. I thought about how odd it was before I went to talk to Francis, but I didn't— Shit! He has to be in on it."

"What are you saying?"

"I'm saying that Dr. Finch is working with the Death Ministry and probably my fucking cousin," Andre said, scooping his coat from the ground and shrugging it on. "The antivenom he gave you this morning was silver, but not like this. I'd forgotten the antivenom powder was so bright before it was mixed with water. Whatever Dr. Finch gave you was something else."

So Finch was in on this, too. It made sense that Little Francis had recruited other members of Conti Bounty, but how many? Just how deep did this go? What if . . .

What if this went all the way to the top? What if the Contis weren't what she'd thought them to be? Maybe Uncle Francis had decided it was time for the family to get in on the lucrative drug trade and had given his son directions to get the ball rolling in his absence. She didn't know the exact nature of the business that had taken the elder Francis out of town, but she'd heard mention of "new revenue avenues." What if one of those avenues was running demon drugs?

Still, that didn't explain the ransacking of her apartment or her attempted kidnapping.

"It was probably some sort of spasm-inducing drug," Andre said, still thinking aloud. "If you'd gone into convulsions, you would have been transported to his clinic uptown. From there, it would have been easy for him to administer the antivenom and do what he wanted with you."

"Or let me die. Some of the spells don't require the demon-marked person to be living," Emma said, pushing away the anxiety that rose in her chest.

She couldn't believe that the Contis were crooked. Jace would never do anything to hurt Sam, and Andre had proven he would risk his life for hers. This had to be something Little Francis had cooked up on his own.

"I can't believe this," Andre said, his expression darkening. "We trusted that man. He knows the Death Ministry has terrorized half the . . ." Andre froze again, his attention focused inward before he turned back to where Emma still stood by the bed. "You said you saw Dr. Finch cutting someone open."

"Yeah. A man."

"And he wasn't wearing gloves?"

She paused a moment, searching her memory, wondering what Andre was getting at. "No, he wasn't. I'm positive he wasn't."

"But if he were harvesting organs to sell on the black market, he'd be wearing latex gloves. He wouldn't want to risk contaminating the organs or himself."

Emma nodded. "Riiight."

"So why wasn't he wearing gloves?"

"I . . . don't know." For the first time in this conversation, she was the one who was out of the loop. Why would Dr. Finch put himself at risk like that? It didn't make sense.

"He wasn't wearing gloves because he didn't care about preserving the organs, and what he was pulling out of the man would be ruined if it made contact with latex." Andre paused again, giving her the second she needed to catch up.

"Oh my god. Demon drug mules." Plastics and demon drugs didn't mix. It was why everything on the table next to her was in a ceramic or metal container. It was also the reason the rate of blood-borne diseases had skyrocketed along with the popularity of demon highs, as addicts shared expensive all-glass needles.

Andre nodded, obviously pleased that she'd come to the same conclusion he had. "The new police chief's narcotics team has been cracking down on the Death Ministry's runs to the pleasure islands, searching boats, confiscating any demon drugs they find. But still, somehow the pleasure islands haven't experienced any dips in their supply."

"They've been using drug mules." The image she'd seen of a weeping Stewart being handed a child's sieve suddenly made an entirely new—and repulsive—kind of sense.

"And Dr. Finch has been helping them retrieve their drugs when whatever they're using to pass them through the human body fails. The guy that Little Francis said was found cut open—he must have been a mule. He had the drugs inside of him. . . ." Andre trailed off, fingers coming to play along his bottom lip in a movement that was oddly sensual. Who knew watching a man think could be so sexy? "And we're guessing that whatever your power does to people drew it out of him and into you?"

"And the same thing happened with Stewart," Emma confirmed. "It hit about an hour and a half to two hours after I fed both times."

"But the first time, Dr. Finch had to go in to fetch the drugs after Greg kicked the bucket," Andre said. "Maybe your power made whatever the drugs were wrapped in burst?"

Fear clutched at Emma's throat as her certainty that she hadn't killed the man in the alley faded away. "So I might have killed him."

"If you did, it certainly wasn't your fault. Still, we need to know what happened to Stewart. We should—" He broke off as his bud pulsed in his ear. She hadn't even realized he'd turned it back on. "Just a second—my cousin Michael's calling. Don't worry, I won't tell him anything until we know who we can trust."

Emma's heart raced as Andre ordered his bud to answer the call and the man on the other end of the line began to speak. She knew before Andre said a word that he was getting bad news.

"Michael? What's wrong? What are you . . ." He trailed off, eyes going wide. "You did? You're not? Why the hell not? Have you contacted Francis or— Oh, he did?"

"What? What is it?" Emma asked after the tense moment of silence stretched into three minutes, then four. She'd never seen Andre so pale. "Andre, tell me—"

He silenced her with a gentle hand in the air. "I understand. I'll take care of things on this end, but we have to talk later. Yeah. About this morning, and . . . some other stuff. You haven't talked to Francis about—" Emma watched Andre's shoulders relax the slightest bit. "Good. Don't. I'll take care of that, too. And Emma is going to need to talk to Ginger." He grunted his disapproval of Michael's response. "Well, figure something out. Try giving her a Xanax or something.

We'll touch base tonight." He tapped his bud, ending the call before Emma could say a word.

"Wait! What happened? What happened to Ginger?" Emma asked. "Why did you hang up? I should—"

"Ginger was kidnapped," Andre said, his dark eyes full of a rage she didn't understand until he spoke again. "By people who thought she was you."

CHAPTER SEVENTEEN

*E*mma's lips parted in shock. "What? But how—"

"Michael said they were members of your parents' cult." Andre double-checked the location of his wallet and gun, obviously preparing to leave their unexpected sanctuary. "They didn't know what you looked like. Only that you were a blonde who worked at the Demon's Breath. Two of them, men, showed up at closing time and shoved Ginger into a van while she was out on the street, looking for you. She got away but ran from our people because she thought—"

"She thought they were working with the men who'd taken her," Emma said, cursing beneath her breath. She'd suspected as much.

"Most likely." Andre sighed. "But I guess it was good she didn't go with our people, either." Knowing that his family couldn't be trusted was weighing heavy on his shoulders.

"Do you think Mikey . . ." She let her words trail off, not wanting to voice the suspicion out loud. "Do you think Ginger's safe?"

"I think Mikey is one of the good guys, but . . . I can't know for sure."

"But he saved Ginger, right?"

He nodded. "The cult members found out they had the wrong girl and stopped at a hotel. She managed to escape. Michael and our team found her walking on the side of the road and convinced her they were the good guys. She's okay but pretty messed up by whatever happened. She's refusing to come back to the city. Little Francis told Michael to stay with her."

"Little Francis?" Her skin crawled. "I don't like the sound of that. Call Michael back. I have to talk to Ginger. I have to see if she's really okay," Emma insisted.

"Mikey said she's hysterical and won't talk to anyone. That's why I told him to give her a—"

"I don't like this, Andre. I need to know Ginger is safe, and I have to find out what happened to my purse."

"Well, I can help you out with the last part. Ginger had your purse. You were right," Andre said. "Michael sent it back to New York with a couple members of his team. It should be here within the hour."

"What about the spell book?"

"It's in there. Before she broke down, Ginger told him that the people who kidnapped her were after your book. They took it from her, but she managed to get her hands on it before she escaped. She knew it was something you'd like returned," Andre said.

"She knows it's dangerous. For everyone. That's why I don't let it out of my sight." Emma sighed, the knowledge that her grimoire was in the possession of the Conti family members not giving her much comfort. "What about the men transporting it? Do you think they're working for Little Francis?"

"I doubt it. I know Mikey's team. They're good guys. Besides, if cult members were the ones after you, Little Francis probably doesn't even know about your book."

"But we don't know for sure. And we can't let Little Francis get his hands on it," Emma said, frustrated with Andre's dismissive tone. "You should call the men. We can try to meet up with them ourselves."

"Emma, relax. These guys are solid, and they're going to the safe house. I'll get up there and get your book and keep it safe. I swear it to you. Trust me."

"I do trust you. I just . . ." She buried her face in her hands, fighting to gain control of the anxiety pulsing through her veins. Something wasn't right about this story. If former cult members were the ones after her and the grimoire . . . "Andre, cult members taking Ginger by mistake doesn't explain why two guys working for your family were trying to kidnap me. Why did Stewart leave that key in my apartment to lure me down to the shelter? He and that Death Ministry guy weren't working with the cult."

"They must think you know about the drugs. They must think that Greg guy told you he was a mule for Little Francis . . . or something," Andre said, beginning to pace the tiny space.

"But why kidnap me if it had nothing to do with the spell book? Why—"

"Not all drug mules are volunteers, Emma." Andre turned to face her. "They might have decided to volunteer you themselves, especially after you threw off whatever drug Dr. Finch gave you and walked out of Conti Bounty under your own power. They probably figured you had the perfect mule constitution."

"So they wanted me because of drugs," she said, the explanation still not sitting well.

"And they probably still do." He pulled his gun from his coat and pressed it into her hand. "That's why you're going to stay here with my stun gun while I go sort through this fucking mess."

"Here? You want me to stay here? But what about—"

"I know it's not ideal," he said, his brown eyes shifting to the rumpled bed and the tray of demon antivenom. "But I don't want you out on the street until we make sure you're safe. Now that we know the Death Ministry has a contact in our organization, it isn't safe for you to go back to the bounty office. Not until I have a long talk with Francis."

"No, Andre." She couldn't let him walk into Conti Bounty alone. "He could hurt you, even kill you. You can't go—"

"I'm not going to go in there alone. I'm going to meet the rest of Michael's team at the safe house uptown, get your purse, and make sure that book is locked away in a safety-deposit box. Then me and a few of the guys I'm sure I can trust will head back down to the office."

"What if the team is in on it?"

"I don't think they are."

"But they could be. Michael could be lying. He could—"

"That's a chance I'm willing to take to get this book off the street. If no one can touch it, then no one's going to want to touch you. Right?"

Emma nodded, comforted that her safety was Andre's top priority, even at a time like this, when his family could be falling apart.

"So I'll have an armed escort for that talk with Francis. As soon as we're done, I'll come back here to get you." He walked to the door, pausing to flip open the two locks. "I'll be an hour and a half. Two at most. I'll drop another grand at the front to make sure you're not disturbed."

She hesitated, torn between continuing to argue with Andre until she convinced him he couldn't handle this alone, and jumping through the window he'd just opened. It would take him an hour to get uptown and back. That was more than enough time for her to get to the Conti offices, have that hands-on chat with Little Francis, and make sure he never hurt anyone again. There was a chance Andre wouldn't be able to forgive her for taking out his cousin, or that she might not be able to handle Little Francis and his thugs on her own, but those were risks she was willing to take.

She owed Andre two or three, and she knew that being forced to take out his own cousin would destroy an important part of him. He was a lover, not a killer. No matter how tough he tried to play it, Emma could see how horrified he was by the thought of taking a life. She, on the other hand, had experience dealing death. If one of them was going in there alone, it should be her. She'd just have to be more careful, shoot first and ask questions . . . never.

It would have been a no-brainer if it weren't for one thing. "But what about Francis? Isn't he going to be expecting both of us? If you show up uptown, he's going to get suspicious and—"

"Little Francis is busy in the basement with Stewart and the Death Ministry guy they just picked up. That's why Mikey called me. Douglas told him I was free to meet the team at the safe house."

"But Francis is expecting us both at the office," Emma said, still confused by the fact that Andre *wasn't* confused. "He knows you're with me. Why would he—"

"I left Francis a message while I was paying for our admission," Andre said, hand lingering on the door handle as if he'd leave any second, as if he hadn't just confessed to telling her one thing and doing another. To *lying*, when he'd insisted she tell nothing but the truth. "I told him we'd been delayed because you were ill but that we were in a safe place. I'm assuming he thought I'd taken you to the safe house, so it won't be a big deal for me to meet the team and fill them in on what's been going on. And if that's the case, it doesn't seem he thinks we know anything about his . . . extracurricular activities."

"I thought we agreed it was dangerous to call Francis," Emma said, keeping her voice low and controlled.

Andre shrugged. "I didn't want him to get suspicious. I'm sure that phone call bought us more time. I did what I thought was best."

"Right. Of course." His intentions were in the right place. And now she'd do what *she* thought was best, minus the guilt about lying to the man she loved.

Love him. She really did love him. Even knowing he'd lied didn't make her as angry as it usually would have. But then, she was hardly in the place to judge.

"It's not like you haven't misled me once or twice today," Andre said, reading her thoughts in that uncanny way he had.

"I know. I've apologized. I'll apologize again if you—"

"No, I don't want an apology." His hand slipped from the door, and for a second, Emma thought he was going to reach for her. Instead, he crossed his arms at his chest and stared, peeling her secrets away with his eyes. She'd thought she'd been on the receiving end of his most piercing look before, but she'd been wrong. *This* was piercing. She fought the urge to squirm. "I want us to be honest with each other from here on out."

"Me, too," Emma said, managing not to wince as the words left her mouth. She *did* want that; she just wouldn't be able to deliver for a little bit longer.

"I . . . I care about you. I want this to work."

"Me, too." And she did.

If she didn't know firsthand how awful it was to take the life of another human being, there was no way she'd lie to him again. She wanted to trust Andre, and she wanted his trust in return. In an hour or two she would do her best to earn that trust, even if that meant telling him that she'd killed his cousin.

Of course, there was a chance her search of Francis's memories would prove he was innocent.

There was also a chance that pigs would fly. Out of her ass.

Emma crossed the room in two steps and pressed her lips softly to Andre's. "Just hurry back."

"I will. Stay safe." Andre kissed her again, his tongue teasing against hers for the barest second before pulling away. "Don't open the door for anyone but me, and don't be afraid to use that gun."

"I won't be." She watched him slip out of the room, then closed the door behind him, sliding the locks closed once more. They clicked in their chambers, a sharp sound she knew would carry. Good. Andre would assume she was locked in tight.

She leaned into the door, closing her eyes, listening to his footsteps fade away down the carpeted hall in time to the music throbbing from the speakers in the ceiling. Amazing how she hadn't noticed the music when they were together. She'd had ears only for Andre's voice, for the sharp intake of his breath, for the sounds of skin upon skin echoing through the room as they came together. The memory made her light up, electricity dancing across the previously undiscovered territory Andre had awakened with his touch.

They'd be together again soon. She was sure of it. In a real bed with nothing but time on their hands and pleasure on their minds. This last lie would help ensure their future happiness. It would preserve that part of Andre that had never known what it was like to commit the ultimate sin.

Emma used another towel to wipe away the last of her spark as she counted to one hundred and then back down to one, giving Andre plenty of time to exit the building. Only then did she slide the locks back into their open position and ease out into the hall.

All was clear and quiet. She turned right, moving swiftly past the empty rooms to the top of the stairwell. A peek around the corner revealed that the stairs were deserted. The only sound beneath the music was the faint rumble of Jeremiah Boudreaux's laughter drifting from the closed door of his office.

She could have slipped down the stairs, past that door, and gone out the way she came, unobserved. Instead, Emma padded softly toward the window at the end of the hall. Windows had been good to her today. She saw no reason to buck a successful trend. Besides, she could do without another encounter with the ground floor of this establishment. If she never saw another hot pink wall or black velvet painting again it would be too soon.

Andre lingered near the back entrance to Yang's Curiosity Shop for as long as he dared, staring at the entrance to Boudreaux's across the street, the cynical part of him expecting to see a mop of messy blond hair emerge from the door any second. There had been something in Emma's eyes when he'd left . . . a glimmer of trouble he was beginning to recognize.

She was up to something. But what?

He'd known better than to ask, but his suspicion made him hide in the shade of Yang's awning for several long minutes after he should have been on his way. Michael had said the rest of the team would arrive in the city within thirty or forty minutes. Andre needed to hurry if he wanted to reach the safe house when they did.

The sooner he got there, the sooner he could take care of the dreaded encounter with his cousin and get back to Emma. He wanted her in a car with an armed guard on her way to his apartment as soon as possible. It could be days, even weeks, before he and the family members he could trust got to the bottom of what was going on with the Death Ministry, the drug mules, Dr. Finch, and Little Francis and finally ensured that their organization was traitor free. Not to mention sorting out this cult business and making certain there weren't any other crazies out there looking for Emma or her spell book. During that time, he wanted her by his side. In his arms. In his bed. It wasn't as if she had a safe place to go home to, and she seemed as intrigued by the idea of starting something real as he was.

Then why is she still lying to you?

Andre tried to ignore the nagging voice, but it echoed, bouncing around inside his head, making him watch the door for just one more minute. And then one more. And then—

He caught the slight movement out of the corner of his eye. If he'd been looking in the other direction, he wouldn't have. He would have missed the blur of white and the flash of long legs hurrying down the street. He would have continued on his way uptown without confirmation that the woman he was in love with had lied to him. Again.

Some part of him wished he hadn't seen her, that he still believed she cared enough about him to tell him the truth. But she didn't. And maybe she never would. This thing between them was probably doomed before it even started.

"Conti Bounty office." Andre ordered his bud to make the call as he eased from the shade, tailing Emma down the street. Doomed or not, he had to follow her. He had to know what she was hiding this time.

Douglas answered on the second ring. "Conti Bounty." Andre breathed a small sigh of relief, grateful that Francis hadn't answered the phone. He didn't want to talk to that bastard until he could look him in his flat, greedy eyes.

"Douglas, this is Andre. It's going to take me a little longer than expected to get uptown." He moved faster, turning the corner just in time to see Emma disappearing around another corner. "I'll get there eventually, but—"

"Oh, no, sir! Mr. Conti was very insistent that—"

"I'll get there. Don't worry. I'll do what needs to be done," Andre said, his tone making it clear that they were at the end of their discussion. Thankfully, the underling in Douglas recognized an order when he heard it.

"Yes, sir. Just a moment. I'll tell Mr. Conti."

"No, wait. I don't—" Andre cursed as the Conti Bounty promo message droned softly into his ear, assuring him that the Contis were the most experienced, professional, and successful hunters in the United States.

Shit.

He watched Emma turn right on East Tenth, greatly narrowing her destination options. There was nothing down East Tenth anymore except a few warehouses, a block of low-income apartment buildings . . . and the Conti Bounty offices.

Shit again. What the hell was she doing? She'd warned him against coming back here without backup and yet here she was, on another solo mission. Hadn't she realized the whole "lone cowboy" bit wasn't working for her? She'd nearly been killed or kidnapped half a dozen times in the past year.

But even as a part of him cursed her for being a fool, another part of him felt the marrow-deep joy of being loved for the first time in way too long. She was doing this for him, to protect him, because she loved him enough to put her own life at risk to ensure his safety. It made him love her even more.

And it made him angry, too. They were going to have to have a talk about the lying and putting herself in danger. A serious talk. Right now.

He raised his hand, preparing to call out to her, when a big man in a black T-shirt crossed the street, trotting to catch up with Emma. He was following her; he had to be. There were only a handful of people on the street, and no one headed in Emma's direction. She'd acquired a tail, one who just might draw that gun tucked into the back of his pants if Andre called out to warn her that she was being followed.

Damn it. He had no choice but to keep quiet, to fall back and hope the man in black didn't notice that he was being tailed, as well.

Andre kept his distance as Emma closed the final blocks to Conti Bounty and turned right into the alley just before the Conti building. Her shadow lingered near the bricks at the alley's entrance. Apparently Emma didn't plan on taking the front door, preferring to make a surprise appearance through whatever window she'd used to escape Dr. Finch the first time. It would have been a decent plan . . .

If it weren't for the man following her and the armed guards tracking her movements from the roof of the building across the street. There were always at least one or two men on duty there, keeping watch. It was a minor miracle she'd slipped past them unnoticed the first time, one Andre could guess they'd been appropriately reamed out for.

They certainly weren't letting their guard down now. One man was already on his bud reporting Emma's presence, while the other trained his gun down the alleyway. Andre's heart squeezed unhealthily in his chest even after Trace—the sniper on duty—gave him a curt nod of recognition. The knowledge that a gun was aimed at the woman he loved made him crazy. He was about to shout for the men on the roof to disarm—and hope they actually listened to him instead of whatever order his cousin had given—when a breathless Douglas came back on the line.

"Mr. Andre, are you still there? Is that you outside?" Douglas asked, his usually high, thin voice stretched so tight, it made Andre wince.

"Yes. Emma Quinn is coming in the back," he said, hoping Douglas wouldn't ask for an explanation he didn't have. "I'll be at the front entrance in a few—"

"Thank god. Please hurry. Something's wrong with Mr. Francis. He's cuffed me to the desk," he said, confirming all of Andre's suspicions in one horrible, screechy stream of words. "And the scary men he brought in after your phone call are walking around the ground floor. With guns!"

Andre broke into a run, racing the last block to the Conti Bounty entrance.

"What about the rest of our people?" Andre asked, nearly to the door.

Douglas sucked in a deep breath. "I don't know. I don't know what's going on. Trace called for backup, but I want out of here! I've got a miniflamethrower in my bag that could cut through the cuffs, but I can't reach it. Please help me!"

"Are you being guarded? Is there—"

"A couple men are patrolling the ground floor, but there's no one near the front desk right now. You can get in and get out before—"

"I'm here, I'm here." Andre hurried through the double doors and the metal detector, stopping only when Douglas and two men in Conti guard uniforms stood up from where they'd been hidden behind the main desk.

He froze. Douglas had lied to him, he thought, noting that the two guards were men he'd never met before. By the time he realized that the second man on the roof had also been a new hire and begun to theorize that a hostile takeover was in progress, the two guards in front of him had pulled their guns and trained them on his chest.

"So sorry, Mr. Andre," Douglas said, his voice as polite as ever. "But I'm going to need you to give me any weapons you have, please."

For a split second, Andre debated lunging for one of the guards. His combat training had been a long time ago, but he was still in excellent shape and damned fast. There was a chance he could take care of the guards and Douglas before he was shot.

"We've already got Miss Quinn, so it would be best if you'd cooperate." Douglas was the picture of smiling, deferential servitude as he issued threats like a criminal mastermind. Even when he motioned for the guards to advance on Andre, it was hard to believe that Douglas was a traitor. "Guns, please, Mr. Andre. I know we'd all hate to see something bad happen to Emma, because—"

Rage bloomed inside him, moving his feet forward despite the guns still aimed at his heart. "You son of a bitch. If you hurt her, I'll—"

"Save the threats, smart guy," came a familiar voice from down the hall. Andre turned, betrayal punching him in the gut as Little Francis ambled toward him, hands in his front pockets, as at ease as he would be on any other day at the office. He'd suspected his cousin of duplicity, but the smug note in his voice brought home what he'd done in an entirely awful way. "We're not going to hurt her. At least not right away. You, on the other hand . . ." He trailed off with a shrug and a smile. "You should have gone to the safe house like I told you. I was going to leave you out of it, but now you're here, and . . . Well, sometimes the transfer of power has certain consequences."

"Your father's going to kill you," Andre said calmly, stating the facts. Firstborn son or not, Uncle Francis would kill Little Francis for this.

"My father's already dead." Francis smiled again, his satisfaction at sharing the news making the bottom drop out of Andre's stomach.

If what his cousin said was true, then he was a walking dead man, and a number of the people he loved might not be too far behind him.

CHAPTER EIGHTEEN

*L*ittle Francis was expecting her.

Exactly how he'd known she was sneaking in through the bathroom window—security cameras, a silent alarm, or a good old-fashioned tail—Emma didn't know, but it didn't really matter. The end result was the same. The big man with the kill scars still had a gun pressed into the middle of her back. He'd been waiting for her in the bathroom, hidden inside the second stall, and he moved so fast, she hadn't had time to think about running.

Now she met his eyes in the bathroom mirror, silently counting how many people he'd killed in the lines covering his face, watching him watch her with a respect he hadn't the first time they'd met. Maybe she wasn't just another dumb blond bitch he'd been ordered to kill.

She recognized him. He'd been at the bar last night, one of the men sitting with Blue Eyes.

"Keep your hands to yourself, *chica*, and we won't have any problems," the man said, making contact only with his gun, careful not to touch her with any part of his body.

He knew her touch was dangerous. It made her wonder what had happened to the men who'd tried to kidnap her. Were they dead, too? And if so, was there any way she could use that to her advantage?

"How's Stewart? Did I kill him?" she asked, sucking in a breath as *Chica* Hater shoved her forward with the gun.

"Shut up and move. Go to the door; open it up."

They weren't going back through the window. They were going to walk out into the Conti family offices. *Shit!* This was bad. So bad. If Death Ministry thugs were roaming freely through the building pulling guns on former Conti family friends, then things were much worse than she'd imagined. She'd been a fool to come here alone, thinking she would corner Little Francis and cut the head off this beast. The beast was too big to kill so easily and probably capable of growing another head in a matter of moments.

After everything she'd been through, she should have known better. But the Contis had lulled her in, relaxed her guard. Their generosity and love and acceptance had dulled the edge of her cynicism. Their family dinner nights and Fourth of July picnics and insider jokes had softened her distrustful inner core. They'd made her feel they were family in the true sense of the word, people she could trust and admire, people who defied the lowest common denominator. And most of them did.

Even with a gun pressed to her back, Emma still believed most of the Contis were good people. Too bad it took only one bad apple to ruin the bunch.

"Are you working for Francis, or is he working for you?" she asked.

"I don't answer questions," the man behind her said, kneeing her in the back so hard she stumbled forward. She grunted as she regained her footing.

So he was working for Francis. If it were the other way around, most men wouldn't be able to resist bragging about having an important man under their thumb.

"You're going to trust a man who would sell out his own family?" she asked as she shuffled toward the door, the grit from her boots scratching against the tile as her mind scrambled for a way out of this latest mess. "Betray his own father?"

"Walk faster."

"Francis doesn't have what it takes to replace his dad. He doesn't—" Emma's words ended in a moan as the back of her head exploded. Agony flashed down her spine, and her entire body twisted in a half circle before crumbling to the ground. She was on her hands and knees, seeing double, before her mind could process the fact that the man had struck her.

Guess he'd changed his mind about the "hands-off" policy. It wasn't what she'd intended, but it could work.

"God . . . please . . ." She moaned and slumped closer to the floor, playing up the damage she'd suffered from the blow.

"Get up." *Chica* Hater's boot landed none too gently in her gut, making Emma's next groan even more convincing.

She fell the rest of the way to the floor, curling in a ball to protect her vital organs from another boot to the stomach, and waiting for her opening. Sooner or later, he'd have to stop beating her and get her to whoever had sent him to fetch her in the first place. The second he put his hands on her, she had to be ready.

Silently, she reached for the ever-present hunger, coaxing it to the surface, promising a hearty meal. She didn't need any more evidence that this man was proper food. The hunger could have him. All of him. She wouldn't make it stop this time. This time, she'd let it feed until there was nothing left, until the darkness swallowed its victim whole. The snake could drop its jaws and pull the man inside for all she cared.

Light flared from the hands curled against her chest as the altered part of her rushed from the secret places inside. It had smelled blood in the water.

The fierce pleasure of that foreign thing almost made Emma reconsider her promise. Did she really want to leave this man dead on the floor? Did she really want to look into another set of lifeless eyes, no matter how evil a man they belonged to?

"Get the fuck up, bitch." Swift kicks connected with her spine—once, twice—bruising the knobby bones in her back, bringing fresh waves of pain. Second thoughts vanished in a red rush. The bastard was going to die. Soon. Very soon. As soon as he—

The instant his thick fingers closed around her arm, Emma struck, stomach muscles contracting, spinning her body around to face him. Her hands shot for his throat, latching on like two hungry infants and suckling for all they were worth, draining, consuming.

Her attacker screamed—a raw, shocked sound—as the blue light flooded from her fingers. It was brighter than it had ever been, strong enough to stream through the air and bounce off the bathroom mirrors, illuminating the room like some moody disco while she and the man who had beaten her danced. They swayed to an unheard beat and the dark hunger writhed between them, pulling wickedness to the surface and then down, down, down into the fathomless pit of devouring.

Emma watched the man's second face prune into his death mask with an odd detachment. Even after the beating, even after seeing the evidence of murder and mayhem in his past, viewing that skeletal soul would usually have hit her hard. But when he issued a final, thin groan and fell to the floor at her feet, she didn't feel a thing. No remorse, no regret, only a gleeful satisfaction that she'd finally done this horrible thing that she'd held at a distance for so long.

It took several minutes for the pleasure to fade, for Emma to realize that the room still pulsed with the cool, quiet color of death.

"God," she whispered, choking on the prayer as she forced the hunger back into hiding.

Banishing the darkness was harder this time, harder than it had ever been. For a moment, she feared that the wrinkles where she'd stored it had been ironed away by what she'd done, that she'd committed a sin that would forever erase the barriers between her human self and the part altered by the demons. But finally, ever so slowly, the monster crept back into hiding. The light flooding from her hands faded with a final, petulant pulse, a child angry at being told to clean up its toys.

Emma knelt down, fingers sliding through the oily flesh of the man at her feet, searching for a pulse she knew she wouldn't find. One second, two, three . . . nothing but rapidly cooling skin and a sinking in her bruised stomach. He was dead. She'd killed again. Maybe for the third or fourth time in twenty-four hours. She was a serial killer in the textbook sense of the word. Technically, she had been for years, but not like this, not at all like this. . . .

All her big talk about being the professional killer, the one who should come in here solo and take care of Little Francis, came back to mock her with a cruelty that made her skin burn.

"Okay . . . okay." She stood, hands shaking, stomach pitching in protest. This wasn't okay, but there wasn't time to think about it now. She had to get back out on the street before someone came to check on the man she'd killed.

After a moment of debate, Emma left the man in the middle of the floor and ran for the window. There was no point in hiding the body. It wouldn't buy her more than a few minutes at most and would cost her—

She screamed as gunfire exploded near her hands and face. She flinched, hunching on instinct, frozen for a few precious seconds before she dove back through the window, landing in a pile of aching bones on the floor.

Her heart slammed in her chest as her mind took swift inventory of the rest of her body: bullet hole free, for now. But there were people outside trying to shoot her. At least one, maybe two. Who knew how many more enemies Little Francis had stationed throughout the building? Her chances of getting out of here alive were shrinking. Rapidly.

"No. If he wanted me dead, I'd be dead," Emma whispered aloud, her voice echoing weakly through the bathroom.

If Little Francis had given the order to kill her, the dead man on the floor would have shot her in the back of the head when she crawled in the window the first time, before she had the chance to fight back. And in those few seconds of shock, the snipers outside had been given ample opportunity to fire a second round and hadn't taken it. They weren't trying to kill her; they were trying to keep her in the building.

But why? Why wouldn't Little Francis simply give the order for her to be eliminated? Did he intend to give her the chance to remain a friend of the new Conti family organization? Was this because of his obvious attraction to her in the past? Or was there some other reason Little Francis wanted to keep her around?

No matter what Andre had said, a part of her still suspected that this had something to do with her demon mark.

Andre. God, he could be in danger. She had to call him and warn him.

Emma rushed to the body on the floor, struggling not to think about the fact that the corpse had been a living, breathing person before she'd killed him. "Shit, shit, shit," she cursed again as a turn of the man's head revealed that his earbud was an implant. There was no way to remove it and use it herself, but maybe . . .

She tapped the bud to life, waiting for the tiny green light to flash before she spoke Andre's number. She waited for three interminable seconds, praying he had answered before leaving her message. "Andre, it's Emma. I can't hear you, so don't talk—just listen. I'm at the Conti Bounty offices. Little Francis is definitely working with the Death Ministry. He tried to have me killed, and he's got a ton of backup. You need to stay away from here. I'll call you as soon as I can."

Hopefully that would be sooner rather than later. She tapped the bud off and then on again, placing a second, hurried call to her sister, warning her and Jace that a coup was taking place at the Conti Bounty office and that they shouldn't assume they could trust anyone.

"Except Andre," she added. "He's been helping me. Talk to him if he calls. He'll tell you what's been going on. I'll call the second I'm able."

Emma tapped the bud, then did a quick sweep of her victim's body. A demon-skinning-sized knife in his belt—way more weapon than she was prepared to handle. Instead, she fetched his gun from the floor. It was heavier than she'd anticipated, making her wrist ache as she held it with one hand and flipped the safety on with the other.

It was probably smarter to leave the safety off, but something inside her insisted she put that small obstacle between her and another murder. If she had to shoot someone, she would, but she wanted that extra second to think about what she was doing, to recognize she could be taking a life. The people outside might be traitors, but a lot of them were also Andre's family.

Maybe so, maybe not. What if the Death Ministry took over the office and this has nothing to do with Little Francis or any of the Conti family?

The optimistic notion had barely crossed her mind when the bathroom door opened, and a man she recognized stepped into the room. He wasn't one of the core group of Contis, but she'd seen him at Andre's parents' restaurant on the occasional Thursday, eating manicotti and talking shop with the rest of the Conti men. She thought he was one of the several Anthonys, a second or third cousin with bronze Conti skin and pale blue eyes that didn't seem to match the rest of him. They were odd-looking, a small detail that made him less attractive than the other Anthonys at the table.

Or maybe it wasn't his eyes; maybe it was something on the inside that had turned her off. Like the fact that he was a son of a bitch who would turn on his own family.

All doubts about Conti involvement in whatever was going on evaporated as Anthony raised his gun and shouted over his shoulder to someone in the hall. "She's in here. José's down." His next words were obviously for her. "Drop the gun, Emma. I'm not supposed to shoot you, but I will."

Deep inside her bones, where marrow twined with hunger, the darkness slithered, cursing her for her weakness. If she hadn't put the safety on, there was a chance she could have drawn down on the man in front of her. Father Paul had taught all of his charges how to shoot. The normally peace-loving man believed firearms would be required when it came to the final battle of good against evil, that everyone should be prepared if Armageddon came in their lifetime. Emma had shown a natural aptitude for marksmanship from the first time she was handed a child-sized shotgun in the third grade. She had faith she could hold her own, even against a trained demon bounty hunter.

But with the safety on, she didn't stand a chance. Anthony would shoot her before she could aim, let alone fire. She saw his resolution in his eyes. The body on the floor had convinced him she was expendable, no matter what orders he'd received from his cousin.

Slowly, carefully, she held the gun out to her side and let it drop with a clatter onto the floor. The sound made Anthony jump and, for a moment, she feared he'd shoot her anyway. Her breath caught in her chest as his finger twitched against the trigger, but then Douglas, Little Francis's assistant, appeared behind him. After a nervous glance over his shoulder, Anthony lowered the gun a few degrees, aiming the barrel at her hips rather than her heart.

For some reason, Emma wasn't surprised to learn that Douglas was on the wrong side. Considering the way he'd scampered and fetched for Little Francis, it would have been more surprising to find him loyal to the true Conti leader.

Douglas peered over Anthony's shoulder, brown eyes widening when he saw José. "Oh my god. Did she shoot him?"

Anthony's eyes flicked to the floor and then back to Emma. "Doesn't look like it. There's no blood, no wound."

"But he's dead, right?" Douglas eased around Anthony, being careful to stay out of the way of the gun he still held in front of him.

"Sure seems that way."

"So cool." Douglas giggled but quickly slapped a guilty hand over his mouth. When the hand returned to his side, Emma was shocked to see a little smile on his face. "Sorry, I mean, it's not cool. But you know, it's cool. Did you kill him with the demons? Do they come when you call them? Like . . . pets or something?"

Emma sighed, for once hating the fact that her instincts were dead-on. It would have been nice not to have to worry about the demonic implications of a dangerous situation. "I don't know what you're talking about. This guy was dead when I got here."

"Oh, come on, Emma. We know about your powers. I have to admit, I didn't think—"

Anthony silenced him with a raised hand, then pressed two fingers to his ear. "We've got an ETA of ten minutes on the book."

The spell book. *Shit.* Andre wasn't picking it up, after all. Then why had Francis sent him uptown to the safe house? Just to get him out of the way? Silently, Emma sent out a prayer that Andre was even more out of the way than Francis assumed. She hoped he'd gotten her message before he'd reached the people waiting for him and found someplace safe to hide out for a few hours.

"They need her upstairs," Anthony said, moving to hold the bathroom door open, careful to keep his gun trained in her direction. It was as if he was scared she was going to put the life-sucking demon whammy on him from across the room.

Which . . . she probably *could* . . . if she used one of the spells she'd been working on translating for the past few months. If she closed her eyes, she could almost see the ancient words she needed floating in front of her. There was a good chance she could recall the spell she needed by memory . . . but did she dare?

Allowing the darkness to feed with impunity for the first time had made it so much harder to tamp down. If she cast from the demon grimoire, if she deliberately turned the hunger inside of her out onto other people with the intent to destroy, would she ever regain control? Or would the line between her human self and the demonic presence inside her be wiped away forever?

Hunger humming along the surface of her skin every waking moment of every day would drive her insane. And then there was the danger that she would physically transform and become some sort of hybrid creature like her older brother. It was the memory of his face, so human, but covered with scales and dripping liquid horror, that made her bite her lip and swallow the words tickling along her tongue. She couldn't take the chance, not now, not yet. . . .

Inside her, the hunger writhed. She could practically hear its screech of disappointment. That alien sound only confirmed that she'd made the right call. Anything that made the darkness happy was a very bad idea.

"Okay! Come on, right this way." Douglas gestured for her to precede him through the door and out into the hall. "I can't wait to see how all this works."

He pulled his own small revolver from the pocket of his suit coat as Emma passed by, but he didn't seem to be genuinely afraid. Emma stored the information away, hoping she might be able to use it to her advantage.

"Just head straight back toward the elevator," Douglas chirped.

"Everyone's waiting on the second floor. I didn't even know we had a second floor, did you? You need a special key to make the elevator go up instead of down. Apparently only the family was allowed up there before. But then, I guess you probably knew that, didn't you?"

She heard the smirk in his voice and wondered at its source, but not enough to speak to Douglas. Her past had taught her a few things about dealing with people who assumed they were in control. The less she engaged, the better. It was best if they realized up front that she wouldn't be cooperating. She wasn't going to talk, she wasn't going to bargain, and she certainly wasn't going to help out with whatever demon magic they had in mind.

Besides, why bother talking when she'd have the answers to her questions the second she got her hands on the skinny little bastard bounding into the elevator behind her? Douglas wasn't any bigger than she was. If she got him alone, she could physically overpower him and let the blue light do the rest. She'd taken down two men at once earlier in the day, and even the emaciated Stewart was taller and stronger than Little Francis's terrieresque assistant.

Two men . . . There were only two men in the elevator. Sure, there were guns, too, but in such close quarters—

"Don't move." A sharp click bounced off the elevator walls as Anthony rolled a bullet into the chamber of his weapon. "Put your hands in your pits. In your armpits. Do it!"

Emma obeyed with a slight frown. Either half the Conti men were mind readers or she'd been telegraphing her intentions more than usual today. *Shit.* She had to get her game face on. She had to calm down and focus. Despite the guns and gang members and trained bounty hunters with intentions to shoot to kill if she didn't behave, she'd been in worse situations.

The box that housed the aura demons that had marked her as a child was lost forever, its demons banished from the earthly plane. No matter what Little Francis wanted her to do, it couldn't be as bad as what Ezra had wanted. Without the box, there was no way to bring about the rule of the invisible demons and the infestation of humanity. Even if Francis captured Sam or another person with a demon bond; that could never happen.

The thought gave her comfort as the elevator doors opened and Anthony tapped her between the shoulder blades with his loaded weapon, urging her out into a lushly carpeted hall that looked more like an upscale hotel than a place where demon hunters did business.

All she had to do was refuse to cast, and everything would be okay. The worst they could do was kill her. She'd always thought that death would be preferable to a life ruled by her mark. Now it was time to put her money where her mouth was.

"Did Andre ever take you here?" Douglas asked, gaping at one of the beautifully furnished rooms on the right side of the hall. Emma pressed her lips together and pretended she hadn't heard him. "This is gorgeous. I can't believe I never knew about this."

Anthony's earbud beeped softly, and he spoke to someone on the other end. "We're in the hall. Keep your pants on."

Douglas laughed. "You are funny." He wagged a finger at Anthony before hurrying ahead to open a heavy wooden door at the end of the hall.

Emma got the joke as soon as she stepped into the giant conference room, where a shining oak table had been shoved against one wall and all its chairs stacked on top, clearing the space for the twenty or so Conti Bounty and Death Ministry men staggered throughout the room. All of whom were wearing *nothing* but underwear and a smile.

Actually, most of them hadn't bothered with the smile but were absurdly serious considering they were nearly naked in a room full of other nearly naked men. In spite of the danger and the gun still trained on her back, Emma normally would have laughed her ass off as soon as she stepped in the room.

Whatever or whoever had been schooling these losers in demon magic was a complete fraud. Anyone with real knowledge of aura demons knew nudity wasn't required to work demon magic. That was as much a myth as garlic repelling vampires. Real vampires—demon-marked people who fed on human blood and life force—couldn't care less if their victims took baths in the stuff.

But the smile teasing at the edges of her lips faded before it got started. There was nothing funny about seeing Andre—the only man in the room still fully clothed—tied to a chair with a gag stuffed into his mouth.

Her stomach cramped, and every hopeful, comforting thought she'd had on the walk into the room shriveled in the acid bath of panic soaking her brain. Little Francis was more perceptive and diabolical than she'd given him credit for. She was willing to lose her own life before she'd work demon magic.

But was she willing to let Andre die?

The second his sharp brown gaze met hers, communicating disappointment and fear and love and regret and a hundred other things she never would have understood in the eyes of anyone but the man she loved, she had her answer.

CHAPTER NINETEEN

"Let him go and I'll cast whatever spell you want," she said, the words alone enough to make her soul shrivel, even as the demonic hunger buzzed through her bones, sending messages of pleasure to some ancient part of her brain. It was like being overheated and freezing at the same time. Her nerves screamed in protest and her stomach heaved, but she forced herself to speak. "But you have to let him go first."

"Hmm. Interesting offer." Little Francis stood at the opposite end of the room, smiling like a butcher's dog. "But you don't even know what kind of spell we're looking for."

"I don't care." Emma's eyes slid to Andre's for a split second before she sucked in a deep breath and turned back to Francis.

She couldn't look at him, couldn't focus on how helpless he appeared, tied and gagged. She was going to lose it. She'd never felt so powerless, so at another's mercy. Even the darkness inside her had never ruled her so completely. But the feelings she had for Andre ... they made her rib cage feel like it was about to implode. She would do whatever it took to gain his freedom, anything, even kill again, even risk becoming something less than human.

"Well, that will make things a lot easier." Francis laughed. He wore nothing but a pair of gold and black striped boxer shorts and his Conti family watch, his rounded stomach out of place on his otherwise proportional body, his torso covered in enough hair to knit a small scarf. He should have been ridiculous, but the look in his eyes was too frightening. The man didn't care whether Andre lived or died, but he knew that she did.

Maybe he'd had someone following them, reporting back on how close she and his cousin had grown in the past few hours, or maybe her emotions were still as pathetically obvious as they'd been all day. Maybe the fact that she loved Andre was etched on her face. Either way, Francis knew he held all the cards. She didn't even have a place at the table.

"But I think we're going to have to keep my cousin tied up for a little longer," he said, strutting across the room on bare feet. Also hairy, she observed. She'd like to pull out every hair on his body until he bled and screamed. "We might need human blood to make that circle to cast the—"

"You don't need human blood. Animal blood will work," she said, deliberately keeping her tone low and even. She couldn't let him know how much the thought of Andre being bled to create a circle for black magic terrified her. "Demon blood would be even better if you have it."

"I don't know." Francis made a big show of pondering her words, but she could see the smile tugging at his lips. He was enjoying this, getting off on lording his power over her. "Douglas here was saying—"

"You're listening to Douglas?" She didn't bother hiding how ridiculous she found the decision.

"I have an undergraduate degree in demon studies." Douglas—who was undressing down to his own boxers—paused to shoot her a nasty look. He crossed his arms and stuck out his hip. "And I'm the one who thought of having the Death Ministry guys kidnap Ginger to get all the party pooper Contis out of town."

"So there are no cult members," Emma said, a statement, not a question.

Douglas rolled his eyes. "Of course not. Duh. All those people are still in jail or too old to kidnap anybody. Reggie just had a couple of new recruits do the job and say they were cult members so no one would connect them to us if they were caught. They were going to earn their first kill scar for the job."

"They're not going to earn shit now," muttered an older man whose face was a mass of ruined flesh, slashed with so many kill scars it was hard to guess at their number.

"Yeah." Douglas winced. "Reggie is going to kill them for letting Ginger escape. I mean, we ended up with the book and *you*, and I say all's well that end's well, but . . ." He shrugged and grinned at Reggie, not nearly as terrified of the other man as he should have been. To Douglas, this was just a big game.

Still, a part of Emma was relieved to hear the cult members weren't really cult members. One less pile of shit to clean up.

It was also nice to think that there were at least a few Conti Bounty employees who hadn't defected to the drug-running faction. It was still a nightmare, but not as horrible as she'd feared.

Somewhere out there were people who would be working to stop Little Francis . . . as soon as they found out what he was up to. Hopefully that would be before she was forced to work demon magic in order to save Andre's life.

Please, please . . . Sam. Emma sent out a silent call to her sister, praying Sam had received her message.

"Douglas has done some good work." Francis smiled at Douglas, who beamed under the slight praise. "And he's got a lot of good friends."

"It was my second cousin on my mom's side who blew up the family plane," Douglas said. "He's amazing with explosives."

"And cheap. I never dreamed killing the old man would be so affordable." Little Francis made the pronouncement without the slightest bit of shame, but Emma didn't miss the impact his words had on several of the Conti men. Whether they agreed with Little Francis's plans for the family or not, many weren't happy that their patriarch was dead.

God. Uncle Francis was dead. Strangely, it made her want to cry. She'd never been that close to the man, but she'd seen how much Andre loved his uncle when she was sifting through his memories. This had to be tearing him up. She wished she could have spared him that pain, spared him all of this.

The door behind her opened. Emma spun in time to see James, one of the youngest Conti family bounty hunters, a kid who couldn't be more than seventeen, bounding in the door, her purse in his hands.

"You ready for this?" James asked, shooting nervous looks around the room, as surprised by the underdressed state of the men as she'd been.

"Perfect timing. Bring it here and head back downstairs," Little Francis said, holding out a hand in James's direction. "We don't need any virgins hanging around."

"I told you, I'm not a virgin," James mumbled as he handed over the purse amid low laughter from some of the Death Ministry members. Still, he didn't seem too upset to be leaving the party.

"Yeah, right, and I'm not hairier than a fucking poodle," Little Francis said. More laughter from the gang members. Who knew they had such healthy senses of humor? "Get out of here. We don't need a cherry messing with the vibes."

Emma fought the urge to roll her eyes.

Jesus. H. Stupid. This was the most ridiculous thing she'd ever been a part of. Little Francis had no idea what he was doing. Virginity didn't "mess with the vibes" any more than clothes did. It seemed like Douglas had latched on to every television cliché he'd seen on *Demons of New York: Supernatural Victims Unit* and run straight to Little Francis without bothering to employ anything he'd learned while earning that degree he was so proud of.

"Now, Miss Emma, we're going to do two things at once here." Francis nodded to Douglas, then motioned to Anthony—who was still fully clothed and had his gun aimed in her direction. "Anthony here is going to give you your spell book."

"Sounds good," Emma said, trying to pay attention to Francis, though her eyes were all for Douglas.

The small man crossed to Andre and reached down beside his chair, pulling a pair of gold pellets from a small cooler Emma hadn't noticed until now. A part of her knew what the pellets were and what Douglas intended to do with them, even before he tugged the gag from Andre's mouth.

"Run, Emma! Get out of—" Andre's words ended in a strangled sound as Douglas delivered a sharp karate chop to his throat. As Andre choked and gasped for air, Douglas shoved the two pellets into his mouth, then forced his jaw closed with surprising strength.

"Swallow the pellets, don't bite, or that much Hamma will kill you." Douglas hung on tight as Andre tossed his head back and forth, trying to throw off the man who held his jaw closed. But he couldn't, not with the rest of his body tied to a chair.

"No! Stop!" Emma's hands fisted. "I won't do the spell if you—"

"You'll do the spell," Francis said. "You'll do it or we'll tell Dr. Finch to keep the antivenom in the cooler downstairs. Those pellets were only wrapped with half the amount of cellophane we're supposed to use."

Emma's eyes flew back to Andre. Douglas had covered his nose now. He couldn't breathe. He was going to have to swallow the drugs or risk suffocation.

"They're going to get down in his stomach and burst," Francis said. "He's got ten, maybe fifteen minutes, and I've got guards all over the first floor. If you try to work some other spell and screw us, there's no chance of you walking out of—"

"There they go! Down the hatch," Douglas said.

"No!" She had to get to Andre and find some way to get those drugs out of him. Emma made it three steps closer to the chair where he was bound before the sharp report of gunfire filled the small room. Only one shot was fired, but one was all it took.

Emma cried out and fell to the ground as the bullet burrowed deep into the muscle above her knee. Blood—hot and thick—flowed out to soak her jeans as she clutched at the area just above the wound, gasping as a fiery worm of pain squirmed through her flesh. Still, she was pushing back to a seated position, determined to reach Andre, by the time she heard him suck in a desperate breath.

Her eyes flew to his face, taking in his slightly parted lips and flushed cheeks. He'd swallowed the pellets. It was too late.

"Anthony, you son of a bitch. You shot her," he mumbled, his words thin and breathy. "I'm going to kill you."

"I'm sorry," Anthony said, real fear in his voice. "Andre, I swear I only—"

"Fuck you. You're a dead man." Andre's eyes found hers, taking what was left of her breath away. She'd never dreamed a man would look at her that way, as if he saw all the way to the heart of her and wasn't repulsed by what he saw. "Don't do whatever they're asking you to do. I love you."

"I love you, too," she said, fighting the urge to lunge for Douglas when he shoved the gag back into Andre's mouth.

Already, the slightest hint of gold shone at his temples. The drugs were hitting his system. Fast. There was a very real chance she could lose him, that he'd die right in front of her while she struggled to perform whatever miracle these fools expected her to pull out of her ass. Even the thought of it was enough to make her feel the entire world was crumbling.

She didn't realize the soft sobs filling the room were hers until Anthony knelt down beside her and laid her purse and a clean white handkerchief on the floor near her feet. At first she thought the handkerchief was to mop off her face, but then Anthony gestured toward her leg with the barrel of his gun. "Tie this above it," he said, regret in his strange eyes. "It will help stop the bleeding." He backed away quickly, as afraid of her as he'd been before, despite the fact that he'd shot her in the leg.

Good. He should be afraid. They all should.

Emma snatched the handkerchief from the floor and tied it swiftly and efficiently around her thigh. Then she reached for her purse, digging through until she felt the familiar leather of the grimoire against her fingertips. She pulled it out, sparing only the slightest attention for the intricate etchings on the front. For the first time, the swirls of the demon runes didn't affect her in the slightest. She didn't feel tempted or frightened; she was too scared for Andre to feel anything but desperation.

"What spell do you want me to cast?" she asked, lifting impatient eyes to Little Francis when he hesitated for a second too long. "Hurry. It might take me longer than ten minutes to translate the words, and if Andre dies before I finish the translation you'll have nothing left to bargain with. I don't care if you kill me. You know that, right?"

"Kind of figured. You're the depressed type," Francis said. "I was going to threaten your roommate to make sure you played nice, but she escaped and Mikey got his do-gooder hands on her. But then Andre showed up and I had a feeling he liked you a lot." He smiled, a canine baring of his yellowed teeth. "I didn't realize you two were in loooove, but—"

"Tell me what you want," she said, hating that Francis and the rest of these wastes had heard words she'd wanted to keep between her and Andre.

He'd become so incredibly important to her in such a short amount of time. She could feel the connection they'd forged humming in the air between them, knew that Andre was watching her, could feel how worried he was about her leg, how much he wanted her to do whatever it took to get herself to safety. Even if it meant leaving him behind. She hoped he could feel that leaving wasn't an option for her. They were going to walk out of here together or not at all.

"We want the living-forever spell for everyone in the room," Douglas said. "The one that will make us invulnerable to disease and death."

"You want the immortal flesh spell." Emma raised her eyebrows. "You're sure about that? You want to live forever?"

"We figure ruling Manhattan will be a lot easier if we can't get killed. And when you're kings . . . why not live forever?" Francis crossed his arms and stared at her, as if waiting for further argument.

He'd be waiting a long time. "Fine. No problem. Get whatever blood you've got ready and make a circle big enough for all of you to fit inside."

The immortal flesh spell was one of the easier spells to translate, and did, if the writings were to be believed, make people invulnerable to disease and death. It didn't, however, make them invulnerable to damage. If one of these men were shot or stabbed, the bullet holes and open wounds would never heal. And if someone were to sever their heads from their bodies or, say, blow them to bits in a massive explosion . . . Well, their "immortality" might be a hell of a lot shorter than they were expecting.

She'd help arrange the details herself, *after* she and Andre were safely away from this place.

They're not going to let you walk out of here alive. Once you cast the spell, it's over. They'll shoot you and let Andre die.

"I want Dr. Finch up here with the antivenom," Emma said as she watched Douglas finish up the circle, pouring red liquid from a gallon container out onto the carpet.

The cold, metallic smell of blood flooded the room, making her stomach ache and a primal breed of fear itch along her skin. The smell of blood had always terrified her. She wondered whether some part of her mind remembered the first time she'd smelled that smell, when it had been her own blood flowing out to coat an altar.

"Sorry, can't do that," Francis said, actually putting some effort into sounding "sorry." "We need to make sure we get what we need before you get what you need. That's just the way it works."

"So I'm just supposed to take your good word that you won't kill us both as soon as I give you what you want?" *Or what you think you want, you sacks of shit.*

"My word is good."

"I'll be sure to remember that at your father's funeral."

Anger sparked in Little Francis's eyes before he smiled. "Hey, I promised him I'd take care of things here while he was away. I never promised not to blow up his plane somewhere over Canada." There was something reptilian in his face, something that assured her all her fears were founded.

"I won't work the spell until I see Dr. Finch standing next to Andre's chair with a needle full of real antivenom, not whatever shit you shot me up with earlier today." Emma returned his smile, forcing herself not to look at Andre. If she saw his spark getting worse, she'd lose what was left of her ability to reason, and they'd both be screwed. "So you go work on getting that rounded up, and I'll start working through the spell to make sure I've got the translation correct."

"You're not in a position to make demands," Francis said, all traces of civility vanishing fast.

"Neither are you." Emma looked up from the book she'd been

about to open. "You need to work harder at making me believe you're going to save Andre's life. A lot harder."

Little Francis's lips pressed together until they were nothing but a puckered white line at the bottom of his face. But finally, after a stare-down that lasted less than four or five seconds, he turned and gestured for Anthony. "Tony, go get the doc and the real antivenom. Get them back here in less than five."

The panic coursing through Emma's blood abated the slightest bit, just enough for her to feel how bad her leg hurt beneath her makeshift tourniquet. She cast a quick look down at where her jeans clung to the skin beneath, coated with her own blood. Thankfully, the flow seemed to be slowing. She wasn't going to bleed out on the floor, but she'd have plenty of blood for casting if the immortal flesh spell required demon-marked blood. She'd have to look and see. It wasn't a spell she'd paid particular attention to, and she couldn't remember whether—

Emma's fingers froze and cramped as she flipped open the book and stared down at its pages. They were blank. Every single one. Someone had glued the cover of the grimoire around a blue, lined notebook, one of the small ones like Father Paul had always carried in his front pocket to write down the names of the people he'd promised to pray for. Had it been Ginger? Had she suspected something fishy was going on and taken steps to protect the book she knew could be used as a tool for evil?

"So where do we need to be?" Little Francis asked, closer than he had been a second before.

Emma tilted the book toward her, hiding the blank pages, struggling to keep the panic from her face. "In the circle. Everyone who wants to be transformed by the spell should stand inside the circle."

"Everybody in," Little Francis ordered. "Let's get this shit done and start owning this city."

"Be careful not to smear the lines," Douglas added, scurrying around the edge of the circle. "And leave your boxers and briefs on the outside. We don't—"

"Keep your pants on," Emma said, grateful for the distraction Douglas provided. She slammed the book closed just as Little Francis took a step in her direction. "You don't have to be naked. Nudity isn't mentioned in any of the spells."

"Of course it isn't mentioned." Douglas propped his hands on his hips and shot a glare in her direction. "It's understood that clothing is removed before entering a magic circle. It's like a microwave dinner. Everyone knows you take it out of the cardboard before you put it in the oven."

"You're an idiot," Emma said, mentally scrambling for a plan B. She couldn't tell Francis the book was empty. That would lead him right back to Ginger, the last person who'd laid hands on it. Francis would let Andre die and go after Ginger, knowing that Emma would work the spell to save her friend's life. And Mikey would let Francis have her. Obviously he didn't know that his uncle was dead, or the family business was falling apart.

She had to think. Think!

You don't need to think; you need to cast the spell you know. You don't have any other choice.

The voice inside her head was her own, but the thrill zigzagging through her body was all darkness. Her mark wanted the lives of these men even more than she did. But why? She'd fed the aura-demon hunger more in the past day than she usually did in a month. Why did it want more? Why did it lust to hear the sounds of the demon's lexicon spilling from her lips?

Better question: Did it matter? Andre was going to die if she didn't get rid of these men and get him the antivenom he needed. She couldn't let that happen, even if it meant becoming more of a monster than she was already.

"I have a college degree," Douglas huffed. "You may be the demon girl, but I have dedicated hundreds of hours to study."

"I've never seen anyone take their clothes off before a ritual." Emma fingers grew cold as she mentally tracked her way through the words of the spell she'd once hoped would be her salvation. The irony that—only a few hours ago—she'd discovered a way to feed that would have eliminated the need to work demon spells was not lost on her.

But that was the story of her life: hope followed closely by disappointment, followed up with a healthy dose of horror.

"She's trying to ruin everything, Francis! I swear!" Douglas stomped his bare foot.

You have no idea, little man. Beneath her skin, darkness bubbled and leapt, thrilling to the ancient words streaming through Emma's mind, urging her to speak, to cast, to free the hunger to feed as it never had before.

"We'll keep what we've got on," Francis said, sounding frustrated. "Just get in the circle, Douglas, and bring Andre with you."

"What?" Emma's head snapped up. No. They couldn't. If he was inside the circle, he'd suffer the effects of the spell along with the rest of them.

"I can't lift him and the chair," Douglas whined. "He's heavy."

"Somebody get Andre in the circle," Francis said. "Pete or somebody."

"No. Don't!" Emma struggled to stand despite the agony pulsing in her right knee. "Don't put him in the circle. He doesn't want to be immortal."

"How the fuck would you know?" Francis asked, losing patience with her, as well. "Who doesn't want to live forever?"

"Lots of people. And I know Andre doesn't." She stood, wavering on one leg, desperately searching for something that might sway Francis. "He's Catholic. We talked about it when we were at the church earlier. He—"

"I'm Catholic." Francis laughed and gestured for the large Death Ministry man squatting by Andre's chair to continue. "The good thing about being Catholic is that you can always ask for forgiveness later."

"Please. Don't. He—"

"I don't know how dumb you think I am, Emma, but I'm smarter than I look," Francis said, his face utterly serious, not seeming to understand that he'd just insulted himself. "Whatever you do to us, you do to your new boyfriend. That way we can all be sure we're getting what we asked for."

Emma caught Andre's eye as he was lifted and carried toward the circle. It was almost as if he *knew* that she didn't have the spell book. His sad eyes told her he realized they were both out of options. His skin was growing golder with every passing minute, and she had no spells, nowhere to run, and a bullet above her knee that would ensure she didn't get far even if she tried.

But Andre couldn't know that she did have a spell up her sleeve, a spell that could have saved both of their lives if only she could have convinced Francis to—

Gunshots sounded outside the door, echoing down the hall,

making everyone turn in their direction and draw the weapons stuffed in the backs of their boxer shorts. Francis was still outside the circle, but so were Andre and the guy charged with toting him over to join the rest of the men. Two big men against one wounded woman. Not great odds, but they were better than any other odds she was going to get. It was now or never.

Emma raised her hands and spoke, the guttural words of the demon language flowing from her tongue as if she'd been uttering them all her life. And maybe a part of her had, the part that belonged to the demon realm, that celebrated death and rejoiced in carnage.

As she finished the spell and the darkness came spilling out of her mouth like some biblical plague of locusts, Emma fisted her hands at her sides and fought to hold on to the other part of herself. The human Emma who could feel empathy and love, who had finally lost her heart to a man she would do anything to save.

CHAPTER TWENTY

*A*ny lingering doubts about the existence of demon spells and dark magic faded as Emma spoke words in a language Andre couldn't identify, then opened her mouth, releasing a shimmering stream of . . . flies.

Or something that looked a hell of a lot like flies.

Tiny black, buzzing dots rushed toward the blood circle and the men standing inside it, swarming over their bare skin, covering them until every man looked like a shadow of himself. Shadows that writhed and screamed, colliding with one another in a desperate attempt to run from the biting, stinging specks of black.

But there was nowhere to run. The blood glowed bright red on the floor, creating some kind of invisible fence. Each time one of the men drew too close to the markings, he was repelled back to the center, back into the heart of the swarm.

And then there were more screams—raw and feral—and gunfire and beneath it all the buzzing from the horde.

You're losing your mind. Andre closed his eyes and shook his head, struggling to clear it. Surely he was hallucinating. The Hamma in his bloodstream was making him see things that weren't happening, making him imagine all this. He swallowed against the nausea rolling through his midsection, blinked away the spark-infused sweat rolling into his eyes.

"Holy fucking— Shut it down! Shut it down!" Andre looked up in time to see Francis lunge for Emma, grabbing her by the shoulders and shaking her like a doll. Her head snapped back and forth, her eyes rolling back in her head. "Stop that shit. Now!"

Andre struggled against the rope binding him to the chair, rage banishing the effects of the drugs for a moment as he fought to gain his freedom. He was going to kill Francis for touching Emma, then kill him again for ripping their family apart, then kill him again for murdering his father and poisoning him with Hamma claws, then—

"Fuck this shit." The man who'd been dragging Andre's chair toward the circle bolted for the door, knocking Andre over in the process.

He hit the ground hard, shoulder bruising, breath rushing from his chest, making him even more highly aware of his racing heart. He felt about ten seconds away from a heart attack. He needed that antivenom, but he wasn't a fool. Francis didn't intend for him to live. Whatever Dr. Finch was bringing up here, it was probably another breed of poison. His only chance of survival was to grab Emma and run for the door and hope they could find a cab willing to take them to the nearest ER.

He could do it. If he could only gain his freedom while chaos still ruled.

Shoving away the rotten feeling spreading through his insides, Andre brought his knees to his chest, caught the bottom of the chair with his heels, and shoved. Simultaneously, he lifted his arms as high behind him as he could, silently thanking his trainer for making him stretch after every lifting session.

One try, then two, and finally the chair flipped beneath him, the back digging into his spine for several painful inches before it completed its turn from right side up to upside down. He was still bound to the middle and unable to use his hands, but his feet were free. He could run. Or at least walk. He rolled onto his stomach and scrambled into a standing position, swaying as his guts cramped hard enough to make him moan. The rush of the Hamma was coming faster now. The pellets must have burst in his stomach. He had to hurry; he had to get to Emma before he was too sick to be of any help to her.

He stumbled across the room, dragging the chair behind him. Francis now had the woman he loved by the neck, his thick hands squeezing so tightly that Emma's face had flooded red and her veins stood out in sharp definition. He was strangling her to death. The realization gave Andre the strength to run the last few steps. He hurled himself at Francis headfirst, ramming into his cousin's rib cage hard enough to send a flash of light streaking behind his eyes.

They fell to the ground, and Emma collapsed beside them, coughing as she struggled to breathe. Andre slammed his head into his cousin's, barely noticing the pain as skull knocked against skull. He didn't have the use of his hands; there was no choice but to use his head.

He was rearing back for another attack when a burst of electricity exploded inches from his face. He looked down to see Francis's eyes bulge wide. His cousin had been hit with a stun gun. A gun set to full strength if the bowing of his spine as the pulse surged through his body was any indication. When he fell back to the floor, he was completely motionless but for the twitching of his eyelids. Francis wouldn't be a danger to Emma or anyone else for several hours. It was time to get out of here, time to—

"A little to your left," a male voice said, one Andre recognized but didn't fear. Who was it? If only his reeling head would clear. "She's right by your—"

"I know. I can see her." A woman's voice this time, coming closer. "Check on Andre."

"Andre, are you okay?" The man was so close now that it seemed the words had been shouted directly into his ear.

Andre spun toward the hands busy at his wrists, and the world spun along with him. His vision wavered, and it took several seconds for his eyes to focus in on the face of the man untying him. When he did, his relief was so profound, he could have cried like a goddamn baby.

It was his cousin Jace, one of the few people he had no doubt he could still trust.

Jace finished freeing him from the chair and pulled the gag from his mouth. "Francis gave me an overdose of Hamma." Andre forced the words out, though his tongue felt thick and unwieldy in his mouth. "He said Dr. Finch had some antivenom, but—"

"Fuck, I stunned him on the way in. Let me go see if he had the antivenom in his bag and I can shoot you up myself." Jace slapped Andre on the shoulder before turning to where his wife knelt by her sister on his other side. "Sam, I'm going into the hall. I'll be back in two. Maybe less. Francis is down at about sixty-three degrees, and the rest of them are trapped in the—"

"I can see them, all of them," Sam said, her usually brown eyes glowing an eerie blue. Just like the blue light that came from her sister's hands when she was feeding her demon mark. "Just hurry and get something for Andre."

Andre met Sam's strange eyes and, for the first time, those eyes connected with his, holding his gaze for a tense moment before she turned her attention back to her sister. She could see him. Despite the fact that she'd been blind since she was a child, Sam could really *see* him. If the stories he'd heard were correct, that probably wasn't good news. Sam could see only people who were on the verge of a major transition in their lives.

One of the most common "transitions" was death.

"Emma. Sweetie, can you hear me?" Sam brushed the hair out of Emma's face, but Emma only twitched in response. Her eyes were rolled so far back in her head that only the whites showed. "Emma, talk to me. Emma, what did you do?" Sam raised her voice, struggling to be heard over the men still moaning in pain inside the circle. At least the screams had stopped, but the low, pitiful moans were almost worse. There was more than defeat in those sounds; there was death. "Honey, you have to—"

"She cast a spell," Andre said, the room tilting and the ground waving beneath him when he tried to move closer to Sam and Emma. He swallowed hard, fighting the nausea that threatened to turn him inside out.

"Oh god. What were you thinking?" Sam asked, her fear for her sister obvious in her voice.

"She was . . . trying to save my life. They were going to take me into the circle." Andre willed his racing heart to slow. He had to hold on, had to do whatever he could to help Emma. "She sent those flies . . . they came out of her mouth." He sucked in a deep breath that only made the sickness spreading through his body worse.

Sam sighed and cast sad eyes toward the circle. "Well, they should be coming back soon. Looks like they're almost finished."

It took several seconds for his body to respond to his brain's command, but finally his arms and legs cooperated in helping him turn just enough to see the men who had betrayed him. Or what was left of them. Inside the circle, only two men still moaned and writhed. The rest of them were already still and motionless on the carpet and didn't look like they'd be getting up again.

The flies had abandoned the dead, who lay shriveled and deformed, twisted into shapes human bodies should be incapable of making. For a moment, Andre was certain it was his own wavering vision that made the corpses appear so distorted, but when the room steadied, the horrific view remained the same. Worse, even. Because now he could see the men's faces, see the expressions of terror and agony that spoke of the nightmarish pain they'd endured before they were allowed to die.

Emma had done that to them. She'd killed nearly twenty men in a manner any court in the world would deem torturous, monstrous.

He'd been prepared to kill his cousin seconds ago and threatened to kill Anthony for shooting Emma, but the truth was that Andre had never taken a human life. Ever. He'd never even seen a dead person outside of a funeral home. The rest of the Contis dealt with the disposal of inconvenient corpses. He was the man who worked within the law, who bent it and stretched it and occasionally broke it, but never in a way that would earn him the death penalty.

But Emma . . . she'd committed mass murder.

The reality of that hit home with a vengeance, making the sight before him even more horrible. It wasn't just a murder scene; it was a testimony to the fact that the woman he loved really was two different people.

"Which arm do you want this in?" Jace had returned and was kneeling by his side with a prepped syringe and an alcohol swab.

"Is that . . . the real—" Andre broke off as a wave of bile rose in his throat. Whether it was caused by the Hamma overdose or the slaughter he couldn't seem to tear his eyes away from, however, he couldn't say.

"It's not what he had prepped. I mixed it myself. That's why it took so long." Jace helped him peel off his jacket and roll up the sleeve of his shirt. "I'm ninety percent sure this is the antivenom."

"Only ninety. That's . . . comforting."

"That's going to have to be good enough." Jace swabbed the crook of his arm. The sharp, astringent scent of alcohol cut through the air, helping clear Andre's mind enough for him to force his eyes away from the circle, where the last man had finally stopped moving. "You need this. The sooner the better."

The fear lurking in Jace's usually shuttered features told him he must look as horrible as he felt. He and Jace had always been close, best friends as well as cousins. Seeing Jace in a coma last spring had torn him up inside. Silently, he prayed Jace would be spared the experience of seeing him hooked up to a dozen machines, fighting for his life. Grieving Uncle Francis's passing would be hard enough. The elder Francis had been everything to Jace: an adopted father, a mentor, and a friend. It was going to kill him to know that he was gone, murdered by his own son.

"You ready?" Jace asked.

Andre nodded, watching with strange detachment as the needle pierced his skin and the silver liquid flowed into his vein. Even knowing the pain that would hit in a few seconds as the venom and antivenom waged war on the battlefield of his internal organs couldn't seem to penetrate the fog that had settled around his mind. He couldn't think—or feel—much of anything. He knew only that he was numb and strangely cold and sore all over. He was probably going into shock.

Scratch that. He was *definitely* going into shock.

The buzzing of the flies drew closer, and a black cloud streamed over his head—close enough for him to see that the specks of black weren't flies at all, but tiny drops of black liquid that sparkled as they drifted by. Still, he couldn't seem to summon an appropriate response. He simply turned his head and watched the droplets merge together, becoming a thin stream of oil that flowed down to Emma's mouth and slipped through her parted lips.

By the time the antivenom began to burn through his arms and legs, the blackness had disappeared inside of her, tucked away like a secret. But the dark wasn't a secret anymore. It was a very real, very terrifying reality, one he wasn't sure he knew how to deal with.

He loved Emma, but . . . Could he build a life with a woman who lived with a monster locked away inside her? He didn't know. He only knew that a part of him was almost relieved when his racing heart finally hit the wall. The stillness in his chest was oddly peaceful. Calming. Seductive.

Andre was dimly aware of Jace shouting and guiding him onto

his back on the carpet, but soon his eyes slid closed and the outside world faded away. And then there was only himself, alone, slowly being burned away by the drugs whispering through his system.

Emma came back to herself just as Jace began rescue breathing. On Andre. Andre wasn't breathing. She hadn't saved him. And now the darkness inside her was more formidable than ever. She could feel it surging through her blood, pressing against the inside of her skin, shoving at the boundaries of her flesh in an attempt to make more room for itself.

"No. No, no, no," Emma moaned. It was happening. She was becoming a monster, just like her brother.

"Calm down. You're going to be okay." Sam tucked her hair behind her ears, ran soothing hands in circles on her back.

Sam. Sam and Jace were here. Everything was going to be okay. Emma glanced back at Jace, who was performing chest compressions on his cousin. No. Everything wasn't going to be okay. Inside her, the darkness squirmed into the base of her brain, making clear thought almost impossible. She'd murdered an entire room full of people, and a few feet away, the man she loved was dying. Nothing was okay.

"Andre," she said, grabbing Sam's arm. "It's an overdose. They made him swallow Hamma claws. I have to—"

"Jace already gave him the antivenom. Now, give him space. He knows what he's doing." Sam held her in place with a hand on her arm. "We're going to figure out a way to undo this."

"We can't. Francis killed his father; he—"

"We know."

"How do you—"

"When I talked to Andre this morning, I could tell something was wrong. We booked a flight right away and were deboarding the plane from Seattle when we got a message from the family Francis was supposed to meet in Vancouver. The crash is all over the news. Then we got your message and headed straight here. I'm just sorry we didn't get here sooner. Before . . ." Sam trailed off, but Emma could guess how her sister would have completed the sentence.

Before you turned yourself into a monster. For nothing.

No, it couldn't be for nothing. Andre had to be okay. She'd make him be okay.

"I have to go to him."

"Emma, no, you—"

"Let me go, Sam." Something in her voice must have told Sam that she wouldn't be taking no for an answer. Her sister released her arm with a sigh, and Emma was off, crawling across the carpet to Andre, a part of her surprised to find that her knee no longer hurt. What the darkness had stolen from those men had healed her, a small drop of goodness in the midst of the awful.

"Andre. Andre, can you hear me?" She crouched near his head, running a soft hand through his hair, whispering into the shell of his ear. He was so beautiful, even sweaty and covered in spark. It was impossible to imagine a world without him, without his smile and his smart-ass remarks and his touch.

God, his touch. He might never touch her again. She was a repulsive freak. But that was okay. It would be worth it if Andre lived. He had to live.

"Andre, please. You have to fight this." Panic pulsed inside her chest as Jace moved in to give Andre two strong breaths, then moved back to his chest for more compressions, with no noticeable response from his cousin. Andre wasn't breathing; his heart wasn't beating. It was only a matter of time before he was gone forever.

Tears spilled down Emma's cheeks while the darkness churned and frothed inside her. She could feel the demonic presence pushing at her thoughts, her feelings, her memories, trying to replace her fear with hatred, her sadness with hunger. Connecting to the magic of the spell had given her demon link an incredible surge of power. But it couldn't consume her completely, not while there was still a chance for Andre. She loved him too much to let the darkness take her over. She had to fight back, had to cling to the human part of her and do everything possible to save his life.

"I'm going to try to pull some of the drug out of him and into me," Emma said, threading her fingers into Andre's hair, hooking up to his mind in the same way she had a few hours before.

"Can you do that? Is it safe?" Sam sat beside her, watching as the blue light burst from Emma's hands.

Sam's blue eyes flicked from Emma to Andre, supposedly looking for some sign that Emma's touch was helping or hurting. It was only then that Emma realized her sister was seeing her. Her and Andre. It was a bad sign, but one she struggled to ignore. She had to try to save him, and this was the only thing she could think of that might help.

Besides, it wasn't like things could get any worse.

"I pulled the drug out of two other men. One of them died, but the other one . . . I'm not sure about . . ." Emma trailed off as she focused her attention entirely on the man beneath her fingertips.

Memories flowed in from his mind—Andre catching her sneaking out of the strip club, Andre gagged and bound and watching her crumple to the floor after she was shot—but she pushed past them. She didn't want his memories; she didn't want to feed on him. She wanted to feed on something else....

Emma closed her eyes, ignoring the sweat that had broken out on her upper lip, struggling to find the toxin floating through Andre's body. She pictured the pellets of drugs in her mind's eye, imagining what they must have looked like as they traveled down to Andre's stomach. For the first few seconds, the visualization did nothing, but then, slowly, Emma became aware of a knot in Andre's energy, a place where the flow of life force had slowed and cramped around a foreign invader.

That was it. The Hamma. It had to be. It hadn't all made it into his bloodstream just yet.

Carefully, holding on to the sensation, Emma psychically encouraged the knot to open, to give up the poison locked inside. She coaxed and cajoled, kneading at the place with her mind until finally the cramped energy released with a spasm. Emma pounced on the fistful of Hamma, pulling it toward her, imagining the gold poison seeping into her fingers, flooding her with the venom.

At first, she felt nothing, not even the usual jolt of energy she received from a feeding, but then . . . her heart began to speed . . . and her stomach cramped, balling into that familiar pit of nasty. Faster and faster, until her pulse beat behind her aching eyes and the world spun in great, throbbing circles.

Inside her, the darkness howled, protesting the invasion of the poison, screaming that silent scream only she could hear. It rocketed through her mind, fracturing her thoughts, destroying her focus, biting and scraping and clawing away every psychic wall she'd ever erected. Soon, she was aware of only the pain, a pain so horrible there were no words to describe it. And then, even the pain faded as something within her threw up one last frantic barrier, protecting her from the sensation of her brain being shredded to bits.

She was outside of her body, outside of time, locked away in some secret inner space she hadn't known existed. But even from that padded room deep in her own mind, she was dimly aware of the sound of a man drawing a deep breath and calling out her name.

Andre. He was going to live.

It was her last thought before she collapsed onto the cool, hard floor of her inner prison and fell into a sleep deeper than she'd ever known, so deep she wasn't sure she'd ever wake up.

CHAPTER TWENTY-ONE

*S*he'd risked her life to save his. Willingly, without hesitation. Even if Sam and Jace hadn't been there to tell him what Emma had done, Andre would have known the truth. He would have sworn he'd sensed Emma with him, heard her voice in his ear, felt the soft brush of her hands against his cheek and the sweep of her spirit inside him. She'd brought him back from the brink of death.

The second he'd pulled in his first breath, he'd realized that it didn't matter if she was part monster. She was Emma, the woman he loved. He knew firsthand what it was like to carry a dark thing inside of him that he was ashamed for anyone else to see. But Emma had seen it and fallen for him regardless. She was brave and beautiful and amazing, and there was no way he was going to let what had just happened change the way he felt.

So she'd killed some people. She'd only used her power against Little Francis and his men once it was a matter of survival. She'd also saved a hell of a lot of lives. Now it was time for someone to save hers.

"What are you doing, man?" Jace asked when he scooped Emma into his arms and started for the door. "We shouldn't move her. She needs an ambulance. You both need—"

"No. No doctors," Sam said. "They won't be able to help her."

"But she's full of venom. She needs antivenom, and I used the last of it on—"

"The antivenom poisons her." Andre turned back to Sam and Jace. "It doesn't help. She has to feed in order to get the Hamma out of her system."

"Then let her suck the life out of Francis." Jace motioned to where their cousin still lay motionless on the floor. "You almost died, Andre, and what Emma does takes years off of people's lives. Sometimes it even—"

"I know, Jace. We've found another way for her to feed, a way that doesn't seem to do any damage."

"What? But she—"

"Let them go, Jace. I can't see Andre anymore, and I'd like the same to be true for Emma." Sam's fear for her sister was clear in her voice. "Take care of her, Andre. . . . I'm afraid the Hamma's going to kill her."

"It won't." Andre kicked open the door and headed out into the hall. He had to find someplace private, safe. The family apartments on either side of the hall would be perfect. Sure, the hallway was full of men stunned out of their minds and twitching on the floor, but beggars couldn't be choosers.

He stepped over a lifeless-looking Dr. Finch—half hoping Jace had killed the bastard—and into a room with a queen-sized bed and its own bathroom. Andre locked the door behind them and hurried into the bath, breathing a sigh of relief when he saw the giant tub dominating one corner of the room. Exactly what he was looking for.

Emma's arms were covered with gold dust from the sparking. She was beginning to look like a life-sized Academy Award. He had to get the Hamma residue off her skin. Hopefully that would help her body flush out the toxin. A bath and some food and she'd be fine. She *had* to be fine.

Emma moaned softly and her eyelashes fluttered as he set her down on the toilet seat and reached over to start the water.

"Emma? Are you awake? Can you hear me?" he asked, his heart racing when she moaned again and wrapped her limp arms around his neck.

"Bad . . . so bad." She slumped against his shoulder as if she lacked the strength to hold up her head. Which she probably did. He'd never seen anyone spark so bright. Most people would have died before they processed this much Hamma.

"It's okay. You're going to feel better in a few minutes," Andre promised, willing himself to believe his own words.

He swiftly and efficiently stripped away Emma's clothes—shocked to see her bullet wound had completely healed—and lifted her again, settling her into the bathwater. She slid down, resting her head against the sloped side of the tub, trailing her fingers through the water lapping softly around her thighs.

Andre looked down, momentarily frozen by the sight of the woman he loved completely nude for the first time. *God*, she was so beautiful, pale and smooth and shimmering like some sort of goddess, too gorgeous to be real, too perfect to touch. Her teacup-sized breasts turned up toward the ceiling, pale nipples pulled tight in the air-conditioned room. She was smaller than any woman he'd been with in recent memory, but her tits made him crazy. He was dying to kiss along that achingly soft skin, to take one pink tip in his mouth and then the other, to suck and nibble until she writhed beneath him, begging him to push inside her.

"Yes. Please . . ."

Andre's eyes flew to meet Emma's, shocked to find her watching him with the hint of a smile on her tired face and desire in her honey-colored eyes. He hadn't really expected what they were about to do to be particularly pleasurable for either of them. He'd assumed he'd be too afraid for Emma, and Emma . . . well, he'd assumed she was too far gone to feel much of anything except the desire to live. The fact that she could still want him—that she could reach for him with her trembling arms—blew him away.

His throat clenched tight and his hands shook as he stripped off his shirt and pants and made quick work of the underwear Emma had teased him about earlier in the day. As he eased into the water beside her, pulling her into his arms, he prayed she'd be making fun of him again soon. He wanted to spend the rest of their lives together fighting over stupid things like boxers versus briefs, making love and memories that had nothing to do with death.

The energy she'd pulled from the men in the circle was still at work within her—doing its best to banish the drugs that threatened her survival—but Emma couldn't say for sure whether it was that energy or the sound of Andre's voice that had brought her back from the edge. All she knew was that the second Andre's skin touched hers, she felt stronger, cleaner, closer to the land of the living. His warm hands gripped her hips and moved her through the water, up and over, until she laid on top of him, her back against his chest, her ass nestled close to where he was already thicker, harder.

But not quite hard enough . . .

"Don't be scared of me," she whispered, laying her hands gently on top of his, sighing when he smoothed his palms up her ribs to hover just beneath her breasts.

"I'm not. I love you." His pressed a soft kiss to her throat, his lips lingering to feel her pulse speed beneath her skin.

"Even after . . . what you saw?"

"It doesn't matter." He reached for the soap in the dish. "Now, let's get you cleaned up."

"Are you sure? It doesn't disgust you?" Emma sucked in a breath as Andre's soapy hands ran up and down her arms before moving back to her ribs, teasing closer and closer to where her nipples ached for his touch.

"It scared me at first," he said, his voice strong and steady, even when he captured her nipples in his soapy hands and tugged. Slick skin slipped through his fingers, but he found her sensitive flesh again and again, rolling and plucking and teasing until her head fell back onto his shoulder with a moan. "But you could never disgust me. Ever."

Emma arched, rubbing her bottom against where Andre was harder, hotter, before lifting one leg from the water and watching him soap her up from thigh to toe. "But I—"

"You didn't choose to carry that thing inside you, and you've got nothing to be ashamed of. Killing people who are trying to kill you is self-defense." He finished with one leg and urged her to lift the other. As she shifted and her thighs brushed together, Emma gasped aloud. She was so wet, past ready to have Andre inside her. "That thing is like a cancer. But we're going to send it into remission."

"Yes." Emma's fingers dug into the thick muscles of Andre's arms as he lifted his hips, carrying her completely out of the water, giving him access to the last bit of un-soaped Emma.

His touch was light, a whisper between her legs, teasing in and out of her swollen folds, making her even slicker before he dropped his hips and water rushed over her thighs. Emma moaned in protest, but before she could complete the sound, he'd dropped the soap back in the dish and lifted her again. His strong hands claimed a thigh each and spread her wide, lifting her knees up and out, baring her to him in a way that was almost lewd . . . and entirely arousing.

"You have the most beautiful pussy." His voice was thick and rough, his breath hot against her neck as he brushed his thumbs down her outer lips, pulling them gently apart, baring the slick, pink cleft of her core to his touch. His finger tapped softly against her swollen clit—once, twice—making her breath hitch and things low in her body tighten. "After we're finished here, I'm going to take you into the bed in the next room and taste you. I want to—"

"I want you. Now," Emma said, a shudder running through her entire body as Andre shifted his hips and his cock sprung up between her legs.

He was so hard that little veins stood out along the length of him, turning his shaft nearly purple. The sight of him, so engorged and ready, his thickness nestled against where she was slick and wet, made her hotter than she would have dreamed possible. She'd nearly died today. *Several times.* But with Andre so close—his warm skin pressed to hers, the safety of his body cradling her own—that didn't seem to matter. She wanted him for reasons that had nothing to do with needing to purge the Hamma from her system.

"You want me?" His fingers teased through her swollen flesh again, then moved to circle her clit, drawing a raw sound of need from her throat.

"Yes. Fuck me, please, just—" Emma cried out as Andre reached down and guided his cock inside her. He pushed all the way to the end of her body, filling her in a different way than it had the other times they'd made love. The tip of his cock bumped against a new place, a bundle of nerves that sent a jolt of electricity surging through her. Emma's back arched and her breasts thrust toward the ceiling.

She gasped, and her breath rushed out. "I thought the G-spot was a myth."

"That's okay. I thought aura demons were a myth," Andre whispered into her ear as he pulled back until only the tip of him remained inside her heat. "We've both been mistaken once or twice today."

Something in his voice made her think of the memory she'd seen in his mind, the one of him watching her sneak away from Boudreaux's. She tensed, holding herself away from him when he tried to move. "I'm sorry I lied to you again. I just wanted to try to fix things. I didn't want you to have to hurt anyone, especially your family. I didn't mean to—"

"It's over. Just make sure it never happens again."

"Never. I promise."

"Good." He shoved inside her again, making her call his name. The blue light erupted a few seconds later, bursting from their straining bodies, setting the room on fire. Together, they burned. Andre drove in and out, in and out, while his fingers stayed busy at her clit, flying back and forth with perfect, gentle pressure until the tension inside her could no longer be contained by flesh and blood.

Emma came with a sound—half sob, half cry of victory. The bliss ripped through her body, shredding her to pieces and then putting her back together again, re-forming her as a being full of beauty and pleasure. Within her, the darkness twisted and thrashed, fighting to stay wakeful, watchful, but it was no match for the drugging effects of satisfaction and love. She sensed the dark craving lessen, the way it did after a feeding. She knew the second it lay down and went to sleep, the predator banished for a time by an act of celebration rather than violence.

Her entire body went limp with relief. It was over. It really was. The danger had passed and the rebuilding of their lives could begin. Emma floated on the tide of the aftermath of what Andre did to her, smiling and relaxed, filled with sensations of such pure well-being that even Andre's sudden shout couldn't faze her.

"Shit!" Andre cursed as he reached for the faucet with his foot, shoving the lever into the "off" position. They'd forgotten about the running water, and now it overflowed, streaming down the side of the mammoth tub to pool on the already flooded floor.

"Oops," Emma said, laughing softly despite herself.

So much had happened, so much horror had been packed into the past few hours. But even knowing there were still more than a dozen bodies to be cleaned up and disposed of couldn't banish her grin. She was too happy, too grateful to have been given another chance with Andre, another chance to—

"Shit!" She vaulted into a seated position, splashing more water out of the tub.

"What's wrong? Where—"

"The book." Emma rose to her feet, water streaming down her body, and reached for one of the towels hanging on the wall. "The spell book was empty. The pages were blank."

"Do you think Ginger still has it?" Andre asked, flipping open the drain before grabbing a towel of his own, his swift movement testimony to how seriously he was taking all things aura demon. "Do you think she realized Francis was up to something and gave him a book filled with blank pages on purpose?"

"Maybe. Hopefully. But we need to get in touch with her right away."

"At least Mikey's not involved in this. If she's with him, she's safe. At least . . . safe from normal danger."

"Right. Normal danger. Like we've got any of that going on around here." Emma frowned down at her and Andre's clothes, which floated on the flooded floor. "We're going to need something to wear."

Andre wrapped his towel around his waist and opened the bathroom door. "I've got a few pairs of gym clothes down in the locker room. The pants will be huge on you, but—"

"Andre! Emma! Open the fucking door!" It didn't sound like the first time Jace had asked, but Emma couldn't remember hearing him call out before.

That bathroom door must have been thicker than it looked, or at least pretty damned soundproof, which was good news. The last thing she wanted was for her sister and her husband and half the stunned criminals outside to have heard her screaming Andre's name midorgasm. Once the dust settled, she and Andre were going to find someplace completely private, where they could be with each other purely for pleasure's sake, without supernatural intrigue.

"We're coming. Hold on." Andre was at the door a second later but paused before opening it, making sure Emma was wrapped up in her own towel before flipping the locks.

"What the fuck? Why did you lock the door, and where's . . ." Jace trailed off as his eyes landed on Emma and then just as quickly looked away. "Oh. Okay. So she's better. Good."

"She's better? Let me in." Sam pushed around her husband, her eyes once again a deep brown. "Emma? Are you in here?"

"I'm right here. And I'm fine."

Sam scanned the area slightly to Emma's right with a smile. "I can't see you anymore. Thank god."

"Don't go thanking anyone just yet," Andre said. "That spell book Francis wanted is still out there. The book in Emma's purse was filled with blank pages."

"We think Ginger has it, but we can't be sure," Emma said.

"She and Mikey are holed up together somewhere upstate." Andre began to pace the narrow stretch of carpet between the queen-sized bed and the wall. "Near wherever the kidnappers were ordered to take Ginger."

"Kidnappers?" Sam asked.

"Francis wanted to send all the people loyal to his father on a wild-goose chase. So he had a couple of his new Death Ministry allies kidnap Ginger." Emma's eyes met Andre's, offering silent comfort for the death of the uncle he loved. "He was planning to use Ginger as a bargaining tool to convince me to work a demon spell."

"I say we call Mikey and see if he can get her to cough up the missing pages." Andre crossed to the phone on the wall.

"Are you sure it's a good idea to call Mikey?" Jace asked. "Why is he holding Ginger there if he's not in on this? For all we know, he could be waiting for orders from Francis to torture her until Emma cooperates."

"I don't think so, but listen in and we'll see how he sounds." Andre punched in a few numbers and hit the speaker button, filling the room with tinny ringing. "My gut tells me Mikey's trying to help. He said Ginger was really shaken up. He was afraid she'd have some kind of panic attack if he brought her back to the—"

"Hello? Who is this?" The man who answered wasn't Mikey. Even Emma, who'd spoken with Andre's other cousin only a few times, knew that much.

But the voice was still familiar, comforting.

"Who's this?" Andre asked, on the defensive. "Where's Michael Conti?"

The man on the other end of the line took a breath and cleared his throat. Even before he spoke again, the sounds were enough for Emma to make a positive ID. "Mr. Conti gave me his phone and asked me to answer calls from New York City. My name is Father Paul Whitaker. I'm a friend of Emma Quinn's. I was told she was—"

"Father Paul. I'm here. It's me. Emma," she said, tears pricking at the backs of her eyes. It was so good to hear his voice, so strange, but somehow not as surprising as it should have been. After all, how many times today had she wished she could talk to him—four or five at the very least? Father Paul had told her once that wishes were like prayers, which was why it was so important to be careful what you wished for.

"Emma, I had a feeling we'd speak soon. You've been in my prayers. I've missed you."

"I've missed you, too." She wanted to say she was sorry, but her lips wouldn't form the words. Not here, not now. She wanted them to be alone; she wanted to look into his eyes and know that he understood just how much she regretted going against his advice.

"It's good to hear your voice, but sadly . . . there's been some trouble." Father Paul cleared his throat again, and Emma would have sworn she could feel the pain in that small sound. "There's a woman here. Ginger Spatz?"

"Yes, she's my roommate," Emma said, shocked to hear Ginger's name. How had Ginger and Mikey ended up at Father Paul's?

"She said she was a friend of yours. . . ."

"What's wrong? What happened?" Emma clutched at the towel wrapped around her chest.

"I think she may have read one of the grimoire's spells aloud," he said, his fear clear in his voice. "There's no other explanation for how she came to be here. She's nearly insensible, but Michael says she insisted on breaking through the gate and driving onto our private property. She said she was going to the place where it begins. I think she meant the caves."

"Caves?" Andre asked. "Sorry, but I—"

"The caves where our parents first summoned the aura demons aren't far from where Emma grew up. Her caretaker bought the land to keep demon worshippers away," Sam said. "But why would Ginger want to go to the caves, Father?"

"If she read the grimoire aloud . . . she could have invited a demonic possession." Father Paul's grim words sent a shiver through the room. "She could be acting under the aura demons' compulsion. I've given her a sedative, and she's resting in the guest room now. Michael is watching her sleep, but I—"

"We'll have people up there to help as soon as we can," Jace said.

"Thank you," Father Paul said. "I'll be waiting, and Emma . . . I . . . I should have destroyed the book the day I found it."

"No, I shouldn't have stolen it. I'm sorry." Emma forced back the tears in her eyes.

"See you soon." Father Paul hung up, and the wall phone shut off with a loud beep that echoed through the silent room.

Jace was the first to break the silence. "Much as I hate to say it, I think I'm the smart choice to stay here and clean up the mess. I have a few freelance hunter friends I can call." He turned to Andre. "If you're feeling up to it, you—"

"I'm up to it. I'll drive Sam and Emma upstate." Andre squeezed her hand. "Just let us run downstairs and grab some clothes."

"I'll meet you in the garage in ten minutes," Sam said. "It's going to be fine. We'll get Ginger and help her through this, and everything will be fine."

Emma held on to Sam's comforting words as she and Andre hurried out into the hall, stepping over half a dozen bodies to get to the elevator.

"Your sister's an amazing shot. Especially for someone who can't see."

"She probably could see those guys," Emma said as they stepped into the elevator and pushed the first-floor button. "I'm imagining they're getting ready to transition to a pretty miserable time in their lives. Will Jace and his friends let them live?"

"I don't know, and I don't really care." Andre pulled her close. "This isn't your fault, you know."

"Then whose fault is it?" The door dinged open, and she moved out into the deserted hall, bound for the gymnasium. Andre stopped her with a hand on her elbow. She turned, giving in to the urge to lean into him, to wrap her arms around his waist and lay her cheek on his bare chest. He felt so good, even now, even knowing another mess was waiting for them in the New York countryside.

"It's just . . . what happened. And we'll deal with it. Me and you."

"So we're me and you?" she asked, knowing they were wasting time but unable to help herself. "Officially?"

"As official as we can get until I get a ring on your finger."

Emma tilted her head back, searching his face. "A ring? Like a wedding ring? You aren't serious."

"I am. I'm old." He shrugged and grinned that dimple-popping grin that made him look about fifteen. "Old guys like to get married. Especially old guys who have finally kicked a decade of addiction."

"You think . . . you really think—"

"I don't *think*. I know." The grin faded, replaced by a look that made Emma's breath catch. "I don't want anyone but you. If you don't like that, then you should have fallen in love with someone younger."

Emma smiled, her heart beating so fast it felt like the Hamma had hold of her again. But it wasn't drugs. It was just Andre . . . and the amazing way he made her feel. "Yeah. I guess I should have. Too late now."

"Guess so," he said, taking her hand and leading her down the hall.

"But we're not having babies until I'm at least thirty."

"I don't know. We didn't use a condom a couple of times. . . ."

"The timing's off. No way it could have happened."

"Good." Andre winked over his shoulder. "I want to do everything with you, but kids are going to have to wait. I need at least half a dozen years of fucking you without worrying about little eyes and ears."

Emma followed him into the men's locker room, too full to know what to say. She knew only that she loved this man, that the thought of sharing her life with him made her happy even in the midst of tragedy, hopeful in times of crisis. He was everything she'd never dared hope for and more.

He stopped in front of a locker and spun the combination, pulling out clothes and shoes. She took the sweatpants and T-shirt he offered, standing on tiptoe to press a soft kiss to his cheek. "I love you."

"Love you, too." His hand brushed her cheek, touching her like she was something to be treasured, someone worthy of love and goodness. For the first time in her life, Emma believed he might be right, and she was going to prove it by cleaning up the rest of the mess she'd made. With Andre's help.

"You ready?" Andre asked a few minutes later, once they were both dressed.

"I am." And she was. Ready for anything, so long as she had this man by her side.

EPILOGUE

Two weeks later

*I*t was a beautiful night, cool and fresh and filled with fireflies and magic. There was nothing better than evening in upstate New York in the summertime. Sitting in the porch rocker, sipping a bottle of Finger Lakes Chardonnay with the man she loved by her side, watching Sam and Jace walk hand in hand through the fields in front of Father Paul's house in the setting sun—it was almost possible for Emma to forget this had ever been a place of sadness for her.

It helped, of course, that her demon mark was under control, fed by love instead of violence, and as dormant as it had ever been. It was also nice that the few kids presently in Father Paul's care— twelve-year-old twin girls and a five-year-old boy—weren't particularly depressing cases. The girls suffered pain associated with their demon marks, but only when they were apart for too long, and the boy—an energy vampire much like herself—had, amazingly, learned to feed on plants. His hunger resulted in dead trees sprinkled throughout the forest behind the house, but the group home needed wood for the stove anyway.

Andre and Jace had already felled some of the trees for the aging Father Paul, putting up enough firewood to last the coming winter and beyond. And Father Paul . . . he'd been as amazing as ever. He'd welcomed her back without any anger or resentment, bringing home that "Prodigal Son" Bible lesson he was so fond of in a decidedly personal way. Once Sam and Jace had joined them there—Jace deciding it would be wise for the remaining, loyal Conti bounty members to lie low until the police finished their investigation of the arson at the Conti offices and the "disappearances" of half the Conti staff—the time upstate had felt almost like a vacation.

Suddenly, the front door slammed open and an angry Ginger in a borrowed blue dress stormed out the door and down the porch steps. A second later, Michael Conti slammed after her. "Ginger, wait. I'm . . . I'm sorry!"

Almost like a vacation, if that vacation involved purging one of your best friends of a minor aura demon possession with disgusting things like saltwater cleanses, mud baths, and a strict vegetarian diet that had Emma jonesing for a big hunk of meat.

"Just leave me alone. I want to go for a walk. By myself!" Ginger called over her shoulder, freezing when she saw Emma and Andre on the porch. "Oh . . . sorry, guys. I . . ." Her blue eyes glazed for a moment before sharpening once more. "I just need to take a walk. Will you tell Big Brother over there that it's okay if I take a walk?"

"It's okay if she takes a walk, Mikey," Emma said.

"But it'll be dark soon, and she always gets lost in the woods," he said, driving a frustrated hand through his dark curls. His hair was even wavier than Andre's. "I'm only trying to—"

"Then I'll walk in the field! Just give me some room." Ginger was much stronger and saner than she'd been when they arrived, but Michael was still extremely protective.

"Fine! But if you pass out, don't expect me to come carry you back to the house."

"Fine!" Ginger yelled.

"Fine!" Mikey yelled back before spinning on his heel and storming back into the house. Ginger stared after him for a second, regret in her big blue eyes, before she turned back to Emma. "I'll be back in twenty minutes. Save me a glass of that, will you?"

"Sure." Emma watched Ginger turn and head into the gently waving grass. Beside her, Andre laughed beneath his breath. "What's so funny?" Emma asked, turning back to him, marveling again at how handsome he looked in jeans and a slightly wrinkled white button-up with rolled-up sleeves.

He was beautiful, perfect, and he was hers. Tonight he'd sleep in her bed, make love to her until she was sure she'd never come down from the high of being with him. And then they'd fall asleep tangled up in each other. They'd wake up just as tangled, and the first thing he'd do was smile, a grin so bright and full of hope that she knew he felt the same way she did: that his life had become a beautiful dream and he didn't ever, *ever* want to wake up.

"I think they've got a thing for each other," Andre said, nodding toward Ginger. "Her and Mikey."

Emma cocked her head, skeptical. "Really? They seem . . . mutually annoyed."

"First sign of infatuation."

"Really?" Emma smiled around the edge of her glass as she took another sip of liquid deliciousness. Andre was right; wine was way better than beer.

"Pretty soon he'll be telling her that her nails are filthy," he said, nearly making Emma snort her drink through her nose. "And she'll be telling him he's a vain asshole with an eyebrow-waxing obsession. Next thing you know . . . they'll be engaged."

"Is that how it works?" she asked, laughing as he brought their joined hands to his lips and pressed a kiss to each of her not-quite-as-filthy nails.

"Yes." Andre squeezed her hand, a promise that his kisses would continue at length as soon as they were alone. "Just wait and see."

Emma turned back to the field. Ginger had caught up with Sam and Jace. The three of them stood at the far edge of the property, where the hill sloped down and the valley opened up in a view Emma wished her sister could see. Still, Sam didn't seem to need anything else to make her happy—even sight. She had Jace, and she had a secret of her own, one she hadn't told anyone but Emma. Emma had promised she wouldn't tell anyone, but surely "anyone" didn't include her future husband.

"I have secret knowledge, too, you know." Emma leaned in to whisper her next words near Andre's ear. "Sam thinks she's knocked up."

"Knocked up?"

"Pregnant." Emma rolled her eyes.

"I know what it means," he said with a laugh, "but you don't call it 'knocked up' when the man and woman are married."

"Sure you do. It sounds sexier that way." Emma leaned back in her chair, smiling. It felt like all she did was smile these days. But it was hard not to. She'd never been so happy, couldn't believe this was her life and she was going to spend the rest of it with the best friend she'd ever had. A best friend who was also an amazing lover and maybe, one day, would be the father of her own children. The thought made her smile grow even wider. "When I'm pregnant I'm going to tell everyone that my old man knocked me up."

He snorted. "Sounds like I beat you."

"Does not. It's nice."

"You're crazy."

"I'm awesome," she said, pleased when he laughed even louder and pulled her into his lap. "You're just too old-fashioned."

"If I were that old-fashioned, you'd be sleeping alone, little girl." He nuzzled his face into her neck, kissing her bare skin, making her shiver.

"If Father Paul catches you sneaking into my room, I still might be, old man." She turned and kissed him, licking the buttery sweetness of the wine from his lips until he moaned.

"I love you," he whispered against her mouth.

"I love you, too. Want to go for a walk in the woods?"

"But everyone else is walking in the field," he said, pulling back to gaze up into her eyes.

"Exactly." She winked, and he smiled, and in minutes they were racing each other to the trees, eager to continue conquering their demons together.

Don't miss the first book in
Anna J. Evans's Demon Bound series!

SHADOW MARKED

Available now

*S*amantha Quinn wasn't afraid of the dark.

Even when she was walking the edge of the ruins, where the demonic infestation had transformed New York City's Greenwich Village into a maze of rubble inhabited by bloodthirsty predators, the darkness could be an unexpected ally.

The scary things got cocky in the shadows. Careless. They made noise—claws on the concrete, rough skin scraping along crumbling brick, eager breath rasping through thickly scaled lips—things even sighted people could hear if they were really listening.

To a woman who'd been legally blind since the age of six, the sounds of an approaching demon were like gunshots—impossible not to notice, and easy to avoid if you had practice ducking and covering. Which she did. A girl couldn't grow up on the south end of the island without learning how to run and hide.

Or when to pay attention to the feeling that something bad was going to happen.

"I'll be there in ten, fifteen minutes, tops."

"Wonderful! We can't wait to—"

"Gotta hang up. Bye." Sam tapped the bud clipped to her ear, ending the phone call without waiting for Mrs. Choe to say her good-byes.

Ellen and her husband, Chang-su, had lived in the neighborhood for forty years and had raised four children in the wake of the infestation twenty years before—when demons emerging from caves beneath the Atlantic Ocean had found the densely populated, burrowlike habitats they sought in the cities of New York and Boston. The Choes knew there were times when safety dictated the rude termination of a phone call. But they wouldn't be worried. Demons were easy to avoid if you stuck to the main streets and made a run for it on the rare occasions when the creatures prowled too near to the edge of the ruins.

The descendants of the ancient dinosaurs—monsters that had escaped from caves near the earth's core during a series of massive worldwide earthquakes near the end of the past century—weren't particularly quick. They had to rely on their prey being careless and letting them get close enough to employ the demons' various deadly natural weapons. Sam wouldn't let them get close. She had these streets memorized, and her ability to distinguish areas of light and dark kept her from running into any large obstacles. Sure, she had her share of spills, but she felt confident she could take care of herself, even on the city streets.

It's just dumb luck, Sam. Someday you'll fall at the wrong time and something will get you.

Ah, Stephen. Brother, friend, voice of doom. Why was it always *his* voice that got going in her head at night, when she was trying to pull off the "brave New Yorker" thing?

Because I'm right. You know I'm right. You should move back in with me so you'll have someone looking out for you, so you won't—

Sam did her best to banish her brother's voice, focusing on where she was going, not where she'd been, increasing her speed until her sandals made tiny scraping noises against the concrete as they chased the white cane tapping ahead. She was on her own now. She had her own place, her own life, and she didn't need anyone taking care of her, no matter what her brother thought.

The Choes hadn't been surprised to hear she'd finally gotten her own apartment. But then, they'd never treated her like an invalid or an oddity. To them, she was just another girl from the neighborhood, and the only florist they wanted to handle their daughter's wedding. Sam was gradually making a name for herself above the demon barricade, but Hand Picked was already the hottest thing going below Fourteenth Street. Arranging flowers based solely on smell and texture created some fairly fantastic-looking combinations.

Obviously Sam had never seen any of her own arrangements, aside from the occasional silhouette when the sun shone brightly through her shop window, but she took her clients' word for it that they were stunning. Old friends or not, the Choes wouldn't hire less than the best for their daughter. They'd finally gotten Sin Moon hooked up with a nice Korean boy who owned a house in the suburbs, far from the dangerous community where they'd been trapped when property values plummeted in the wake of the infestation. They meant to stage a wedding celebration worthy of such an event. *And* they wanted to approve every last detail months in advance.

Hence the centerpiece Sam was presently cradling with her left arm. She'd promised to bring the sample arrangement over as soon as she finished cleaning up the shop for the day, no matter what the hour.

But as the pungent smell of fresh demon waste mingled with the scents of lavender and wild roses, she began to doubt the wisdom of journeying out alone after seven o'clock. Demonic attacks had been on the rise in recent months. Attacks always increased in the spring, when the warmer temperatures brought certain breeds out of their winter hibernation, but this year it was worse than usual.

Somewhere, deep in the ruins, a young girl screamed, startling

Sam and nearly making her drop the flowers she'd worked on all afternoon.

"Damn it." She stumbled to the side, regaining her grip on the basket, but clocking her shoulder on something big, hard, and foul-smelling in the process.

A Dumpster, but one that wasn't used much. The stink wasn't fresh, but more the lingering sourness of ancient vegetables mixed with rotted meat and coffee grounds. Gross, but it was probably the best hiding place she was going to find around here.

After using her cane to check the area behind the Dumpster—grateful for once for the smaller demons that had all but eliminated the city's rat problem south of the barricade—Sam set the center-piece on the ground and turned back to the ruins. She'd never ven-tured inside by herself and had dared take the shortcut between her apartment and her brother's bar only when accompanied by half a dozen of his biggest, burliest friends, but for some reason she *had* to follow to its source the cold, slippery energy oozing across her skin.

The scream hadn't come again, but the smell was stronger than ever, as was the certainty that something horrible was happening. A woman had screamed in her dream and there had been blood, so much blood. She'd felt it as if she were in the woman's skin. It had oozed down her face, hot and wet, slipping between her lips before she could think to shut her mouth.

She'd had her share of portentous dreams, but never anything so violent. She was positive that if she didn't find the woman who'd screamed before whatever hunted her did, that blood would be spilled and an innocent person would die. For once, she had a chance to do something to prevent the awful thing she'd seen from happening. There was no way she could live with herself if she didn't at least try.

Still, the rational part of her mind argued that she should call for one of the many demon-control patrols always a scream away in this part of Manhattan. It was their job to keep the streets safe, to make sure the thousands of tourists who came to New York to see the demonic urban habitat didn't get themselves killed trying to get a picture of some of the more fantastic species.

New York City and Boston were the only two infested cities on the East Coast, and Boston's habitat wasn't nearly as visitor-friendly. The Beantown officials had hesitated to blast closed the subway tunnels and allowed the demons to infest a larger portion of the city. So New York pulled the majority of the tourists from Canada and the United States, of which there were thousands every week.

Even decades after the initial emergence, people were still fascinated by the dangerous, extraordinary-looking creatures. And as long as they stayed in their tour bus, demons weren't usually a threat—at least, no more so than lions observed from a jeep trundling through the African savanna. The barriers erected in the collapsed subway tunnels and the Fourteenth Street barricade kept the demons contained, and the demon-control patrols took down the rare beast that dared to leave the burrowlike habitat they had created during the destruction of the initial infestation. Demon control also dealt with the homeless and the drunks, and looked into the reports of concerned citizens.

They would take a report, get a police task force down here within a half hour, and—

The scream came again, higher and even more terrified. "And they'll be too late," Sam said, setting a swift pace toward the sound before she could second-guess herself. She tripped twice on the uneven pavement before she reached the first bend in the path, and the smell actually seemed to be growing fainter as she walked, but she didn't think of turning back.

She was the only one who could save this woman. Hell, she might be the only one who could even *hear* her. Whether it was simply that her ears functioned better than an average person's because she was missing one of her other senses, or something more paranormal in nature, Sam had always heard things other people missed.

Like the sound of something breathing nearby. Something big. *Really* big.

Heart thudding in her throat, Sam edged closer to the crumbling buildings on her right, moving into the darkest shadows, where most people would never think to look. Her gut told her that, whatever she'd heard, it wasn't human, but getting out of the middle of the path couldn't hurt.

There were human predators here as well. Several of the most violent city gangs called the ruins home. With crime in New York at an all-time high, everything below Fourteenth Street was low-priority to the metro police once typical tourist hours were over. They assumed the freaks who chose to live next door to demon nests deserved what they got, including a bunch of thugs for neighbors.

No one seemed to remember that the prices the government had offered people for their homes in the wake of the infestation hadn't been enough to pay for the moving trucks out of Manhattan. A lot of the families had been stuck where they were, figuring a home next to demons was better than no home at all.

And, in the beginning, they'd all expected the government to *do* something about the infested wreckage.

But demons were as ancient as cockroaches and just as hard to get rid of. Then there was the matter of demon tourism. In a global economy ravaged by the recession of the early part of the century, anything that brought money into the city was considered a good thing. Eventually, government officials had stopped trying to eradicate the demon habitat, settling for a half-assed kind of population control accomplished largely by freelance bounty hunters who flocked to the city to hunt amid the ruins.

Bounty hunters who were often just as dangerous as the creatures they hunted.

Whoever or whatever was watching her, its breath slowly getting swift and shallow with excitement, it wasn't a good thing. It was a bad thing. A *very* bad thing, and that very bad thing was ready to pounce upon the prey it had spotted in the shadows. It was simply waiting for the right moment, enjoying the fear it could feel rolling from its victim.

Sam tasted the mocha she'd made just before leaving the shop and swallowed hard. Now wasn't the time to lose control of her stomach. She could do that later, bent over the cool bowl in her cozy apartment, worshiping the porcelain god the way she had on her eighteenth birthday, when her brother had finally allowed her to order anything she wanted from his bar.

God, Stephen was going to go crazy when he found out she'd been wandering around here by herself, acting like some drunk tourist who wanted to dance with the devil in the pale moonlight. He'd warned her a thousand times not to go within fifty feet of the ruins. He was going to kill her for getting killed like this.

The thought was almost enough to make Sam laugh, even though the giant, breathing thing was so close she could taste it. Fire and sulfur and the hint of some exotic fruit, mixed with the unmistakable smell of demon waste. It was definitely a demon, but not the one she'd smelled before. The scent from her dream was gone, vanished along with the sound of the woman's screams.

Whoever she'd heard, the woman was probably already dead. And now, because she was a stupid blind girl who thought she could play the hero, she was going to die, too.

"But I'm going to hurt you first," she whispered to the thing in front of her as she thumbed open the secret compartment on her cane, flicking the switch that turned the red-tipped end deadly.

Switchblades were illegal in the city, so she assumed switchcanes weren't something the police would approve of—especially when the woman wielding the knife couldn't see where she was aiming her deadly weapon—but abiding by the letter of the law wasn't a priority for most Southies. Sam wasn't any different. Being blind didn't automatically mean she was a law-abiding citizen or helpless or sweet.

Or willing to wait for someone else to make the first move.

"Come and get me already," she yelled, lifting her cane and lunging forward, aiming a few inches below where it seemed the breath was coming from.

An outraged squeal echoed off the bricks, but there wasn't time to celebrate her hit. Seconds later, her cane was ripped from her hands and the smell of fruit got even stronger as something whizzed by her face. *Shit!* She'd heard of demons that shot poison quills into their prey to immobilize them before they began to feed. They were alleged to be relatively small for demons, but size didn't matter when you were passed out cold on the ground and the thing coming for you had sharp teeth and claws.

Sam ducked and felt the air stir above her head. So far, she'd been lucky, but she could avoid a hit for only so long. She had to put some distance between her and the demon before it was too late.

Whirling around with her hands held out in front of her, Sam started to run, praying she remembered the obstacles she'd encountered on the way in well enough to avoid them. Without her cane, she had no way of "seeing" the ground in front of her before she stepped, no way of—

She cursed as she tripped over something round and hard and fell to the ground, the whizzing needles of the demon that hunted her pinging against the concrete near her scraped hands. On instinct, Sam curled into a fetal position, her body still trying to protect itself though her mind knew this was it. She was down, and the thing behind her was coming, and this time there would be no escape.

All of sudden she was six years old again, bound and tied and waiting for the invisible demons the cult had summoned to take what her parents had invited them to take, to steal what they needed to steal. But this time, it wouldn't just be her eyes. This time, it would be her life.